HANS ANDERSEN'S
FAIRY TALES

HANS ANDERSEN'S FAIRY TALES

Translated by
VALDEMAR PAULSEN

BARNES
&NOBLE
BOOKS
NEW YORK

Originally published in 1916.

This edition published by Barnes & Noble, Inc.,
by arrangement with Checkerboard Press, Inc.

1995 Barnes & Noble Books

ISBN 1-56619-768-6

Printed and bound in the United States of America

M 9 8 7 6 5 4 3 2 1

THE CONTENTS

ANDERSEN'S FAIRY TALES

OLÉ LUKÖIÉ

No one in the whole world knows so many stories as Olé Luköié! He certainly can tell stories!

Along in the evening when little children are sitting properly at the table or on their little chairs, Olé Luköié arrives. He comes up the stairs noiselessly, for he walks in his stocking feet. He opens the door very softly and—whisk! he sprays sweet milk in the children's eyes. Just a very little, but enough so that they cannot keep their eyes open and thus get a glimpse of him. Then he tiptoes up behind them and blows softly on the back of their necks; and their heads become oh, so heavy!

But it does not hurt, oh, no! for Olé Luköié is fond of the children and means to do them good. He just wants them to be quiet, and knows that they are best of all when they have been put to bed. They must be quiet so that he can tell them his stories.

Now when the children are asleep, Olé Luköié seats himself on the bed. He is nicely dressed. His coat is of silk, but it is impossible to tell what color it is, for it shines green, red, and blue, just as he happens to turn. Under each arm he holds an umbrella, and one of them has pictures on it. This one he places over the good children and then they dream the pleasantest stories all night long. The other umbrella has nothing at all on it, and this one he places over the naughty children, who then sleep stupidly, and, when they awake in the morning, have not dreamed the least bit.

Now we shall hear how Olé Luköié, every evening for one whole week, came to a little boy whose name was Hjalmar, and what he told him! There are no less than seven stories, for there are seven days in a week.

MONDAY

"Look here!" said Olé Luköié the first evening, after he had got Hjalmar to bed. "Now I am going to decorate your room!" and immediately all the flowers in the flower pots became great trees, their branches extending out under the ceiling and along the walls so that the whole room looked like the most beautiful arbor. All the branches were full of flowers, and every flower was prettier than a rose, and smelled very sweet. If anyone tried to eat a flower, it tasted sweeter than jam. There were fruits, gleaming like gold, and there were cakes, bursting with raisins. It was all very, very beautiful. But just then came a terrible wailing from the table drawer where Hjalmar's school books lay.

"Now what is that!" said Olé Luköié, going over to the table and opening the drawer. It was the slate, which had a terrible cramp, for a wrong number had got into the example in arithmetic, and it was about to fall to pieces. The slate pencil hopped and jumped at the end of the string with which it was tied, just as if it had been a little dog. It wanted to help the example but it could not!

Then from Hjalmar's copybook, too, came a wailing that was really awful to listen to! Down the side of every page stood all the large letters, each with a small one by its side, a whole row up and down. It was the copy, and beside it stood some letters that thought they looked like it—letters Hjalmar had written. But they lay almost as if they had stumbled and fallen over the pencil line on which they should have been standing.

"Look, this is the position you ought to take!" said the Copy. "See, slanting this way, with a brisk, even swing!"

"Oh, we should like to," said Hjalmar's letters, "but we cannot, we are too poorly!"

"Then you must take a pill!" said Olé Luköié.

"Oh, no!" they cried, and immediately stood up so straight and strong that it was a pleasure to look at them.

"There, no story telling for us to-night!" said Olé Luköié. "Now I will have to exercise them! One, two! One, two!" and forthwith he put the letters through their exercises. They stood up straight and firm and as healthy as any copy could stand. But when Olé Luköié went away, and Hjalmar looked at them in the morning, they were just as weak and miserable as ever.

TUESDAY

As soon as Hjalmar was in bed, Olé Luköié sprayed all the pieces of furniture in the room with his little magic atomizer, and immediately they all began to talk. Each talked about himself, with the exception of the cuspidor, which stood silent and inwardly vexed that they could be so vain as to talk only of themselves and think only of themselves, without the slightest thought for him who stood so modestly in the corner and let himself be spit upon.

Over the dresser hung a large painting in a gilded frame. It was a landscape, in which were tall old trees, flowers growing in the grass, a large body of water, and a river which flowed around behind the forest, past many castles, and far out into the stormy ocean.

Olé Luköié touched the painting with his magic atomizer and immediately the birds in the trees began to sing, the branches swayed, and the clouds moved along swiftly. One could see their shadows glide over the landscape.

Olé Luköié now lifted little Hjalmar up to the frame, and the boy put his feet into the picture, right into the high grass; and there he stood! The sun shone down on him through the branches of the trees. He ran to the water and seated himself in a little boat which lay there. It was painted red and white, the sails gleamed like silver, and six swans, each with a golden circlet around its neck and a shining blue star on its head, drew the boat past the green forests, where the trees told about robbers and witches, and the flowers whispered about the lovely little elves and what the butterflies had told them.

The most wonderful fish, with scales like silver and gold, swam after the boat. Sometimes they made a leap, falling back with a splash into the water. Birds, red and blue, small and large, flew along behind the boat in two long rows! The gnats danced and the beetles said "Boom! boom!" They all wanted to follow Hjalmar, and each one had a story to tell.

That certainly was a pleasure trip! Sometimes the forest was very thick and dark; sometimes it was like the most glorious garden, full of sunshine and flowers.

There were great palaces of glass and of marble, and on
the balconies stood princesses. These were all little
girls that Hjalmar knew very well; he had often played
with them. They held out their hands, each offering
the loveliest sugar heart that any cake woman could
sell, and Hjalmar grasped one end of each heart as he
sailed by. The princess kept tight hold of her end of
the heart and so each of them got a piece, she the smaller
and Hjalmar much the larger. At each palace, little
princes stood sentry. They shouldered golden swords,
and by their orders raisins and tin soldiers were showered
down. They certainly were real princes!

Now Hjalmar sailed through forests, now through
great reception rooms, or through the center of a town.
He passed through the town where his nurse lived, she
who had carried him in her arms when he was a very
little boy, and had been so fond of him. She nodded
and beckoned to him, and sang the pretty little verse
she had made up herself and sent to Hjalmar.

> I 've loved thee, and kissed thee, Hjalmar, dear boy;
> I 've watched thee waking and sleeping;
> May the good Lord guard thee in sorrow, in joy,
> And have thee in His keeping.

All the birds sang with her, the flowers danced on their
stems, and the old trees nodded just as if Olé Luköié
were telling stories to them, too.

WEDNESDAY

My, how the rain poured down outside! Hjalmar
could hear it in his sleep! and when Olé Luköié opened
a window the water stood even with the sill. A whole
sea of water billowed outside the window, and the

most splendid ship imaginable lay close by the house.

"Do you want to go sailing with me, little Hjalmar?" said Olé Luköié. "You can visit foreign lands to-night and be back again by morning!"

And in a moment there stood Hjalmar, dressed in his Sunday clothes, right in the middle of the gallant ship. The weather immediately became fine, and the ship sailed away through the streets, steered around the church, and then everything was one great wild ocean. Olé Luköié and the little boy sailed on until the land was no longer to be seen. They saw a flock of storks that also came from home and were traveling toward the warm countries. The storks flew in a row, one behind the other, and they had already traveled far, very far. One of them was so tired that his wings could hardly carry him any longer. He was the very last in the row and soon he was left a long way behind. At last he sank, with outspread wings, lower and lower. He made a few more strokes, but it was of no use. Now he touched the rigging of the ship with his feet, now he slid down the sail and—bump! there he stood on the deck.

The cabin boy took him and put him in the hen house with the chickens, ducks, and turkeys. The poor stork stood there among them quite disheartened.

"Just look at that!" said all the chickens.

The turkey cock puffed himself up as much as he could and asked who the stranger was. The ducks walked backward and nudged each other. "Qua-ack! qua-ack!" said they.

Then the stork told about warm Africa, about the pyramids, and about the ostrich which ran like a wild horse over the desert. But the ducks did not understand what he said and so they nudged one another.

"Shall we all agree that he is stupid?"

"Of course he is stupid!" said the turkey cock; and then he gobbled loudly. But the stork now remained silent and thought of his Africa.

"Those are a couple of fine thin legs you have!" said the turkey. "How much a yard?"

"Quack! quack! qua-ack!" snickered all the ducks; but the stork pretended not to hear.

"You might just as well laugh, too," said the turkey cock, "for that was very wittily said! Or was it, perhaps, too low for you? Alas, alas, he has no sense of humor! But let us continue to be interesting among ourselves."

Then he gobbled, the hens clucked, and the ducks quacked, "Gick! gack! gick! gack!" It was surprising how amusing it was to them.

But Hjalmar walked over to the hen house, opened the door, and called to the stork, which stepped out on the deck. It was now quite rested and seemed to nod to Hjalmar as if to thank him. Then it spread its wings and flew away to the warm lands, while the chickens clucked, the ducks quacked, and the turkey cock's whole head grew fiery red.

"To-morrow we shall make soup of you," said Hjalmar, and just then he awoke and found himself lying in his little bed. It had certainly been a wonderful journey Olé Luköié had permitted him to take that night!

THURSDAY

"What do you think!" said Olé Luköié. "Now don't be frightened! Look, here is a little mouse!"

And he held out his hand toward Hjalmar, with the pretty, tiny creature in it. "It has come to invite you to a wedding. There are two little mice who want to enter the marriage state to-night. They live under your mother's pantry floor, and that is said to be a lovely place!"

"But how can I get through the little mouse hole in the floor?" asked Hjalmar.

"Leave that to me!" said Olé Luköié. "I will make you small without any trouble!" Then he touched him with the magic atomizer and he immediately became smaller and smaller, until at last he was not so big as a finger. "Now you can borrow the Tin Soldier's clothes. I think they will fit, and it looks smart to be in uniform when in company."

"Of course!" said Hjalmar, and the next moment there he was, dressed like the most spick and span of tin soldiers.

"Will you please be seated in your mother's thimble?" asked the little mouse. "Then I shall have the honor of drawing you!"

"Will the young lady really take the trouble!" said Hjalmar; and so away they rode to the mouse wedding. First they entered a long passage under the floor, which was barely high enough for them to ride through in the thimble. The whole passageway was illuminated with rotten wood.

"Is there not a delicious odor here?" asked the mouse that was pulling Hjalmar along. "The whole passage has been greased with bacon rinds! Nothing could be more delightful!"

Now they entered the room where the wedding was

to take place. Here, to the right, stood all the little lady mice, whispering and giggling just as if they were making fun of each other. To the left stood all the gentlemen mice stroking their whiskers with their forepaws. But in the middle of the floor were seen the bridal couple, standing in a hollow cheese rind and kissing each other constantly, right before everybody, for, you see, they were engaged and were now to be married.

More and more guests kept coming, so many that they were about to tread each other to death. Besides, the bridal couple had stationed themselves in the middle of the doorway, so that one could neither get in nor out. The whole room, like the passageway, had been greased with bacon rinds, and that was the entire banquet. For dessert, however, a pea was shown about, in which a little mouse of the family had bitten the name of the happy pair, that is, the first letter of the name. This was something quite above the ordinary.

At the close of the evening the mice all said it was a lovely wedding and that the conversation had been most entertaining.

Then Hjalmar drove home again. He certainly had been in grand company. But then, you see, he had also been obliged to make himself very small, and to put on a tin soldier's uniform.

FRIDAY

"It is unbelievable how many older people there are who would like to get hold of me!" said Olé Luköié, "especially those who have done something wrong. 'Good little Olé,' they say to me, 'we cannot close our

eyes and so we lie all night long and see our evil deeds,
sitting like ugly goblins on the edge of the bed and throwing hot water over us.   Won't you please come and drive
them away so we can get a good night's sleep?' and then
they draw a deep sigh.   'We would really be glad to
pay for it.   Good night, Olé!   You will find the money
on the window sill!'

"But I never do it for money," added Olé Luköié.

"What shall we do to-night?" asked Hjalmar.

"Well, I do not know whether you care to go to a
wedding again to-night.   It is a different kind of a
wedding from yesterday's.   Your sister's largest doll,
the one that looks like a man and is called Herman, is
to be married to the doll Bertha.   Besides it is the dolls'
birthday and so they will receive many, many presents."

"Yes, I know all about that!" replied Hjalmar.
"Whenever the dolls need new clothes, my sister always
lets them celebrate a birthday or a wedding!   That
has already happened at least a hundred times!"

"Yes, but to-night is the hundred and first wedding,
and when one hundred and one has struck, all is over!
That is why this one will be so splendid.   Just look
there!"

Hjalmar looked toward the table.   There stood the
little cardboard house with lights in the windows, and
all the tin soldiers presenting arms outside.   The bridal
couple sat on the floor, leaning against the table leg.
They were quite thoughtful, and perhaps with good
reason.   However, Olé Luköié, dressed in grandmother's
black skirt, read the marriage service.   When the cere-
mony was over, all the pieces of furniture in the room
struck up the following beautiful song, written by the

pencil. It was sung to a melody somewhat like the soldiers' tattoo:

> Let the song swell like the rushing wind,
> In honor of those who this day are joined
> Although they stand here so stiff and blind,
> Because they have both a leathery rind.
> Hurrah! Hurrah! though they're deaf and blind,
> Let the song swell like the rushing wind.

After the song, the pair received the presents, but they had declined to accept eatables of any kind for they intended to live on love.

"Shall we go to the country, or shall we travel abroad?" asked the bridegroom.

The swallow, who was a great traveler, and the old hen, who had hatched out five broods of chicks, were consulted. The swallow told about the lovely warm lands where the grapes hung in great heavy bunches, where the air is so mild and the mountains glow with colors unknown here!

"But our kale does not grow there!" said the hen. "I stayed in the country one summer with all my chicks. There was a sand hole near by in which we could walk about and scratch, and we also had entry to a garden in which kale grew! Oh, how green it was! I cannot imagine anything more beautiful!"

"But one stalk of kale looks just like every other," said the swallow. "And then the weather is often bad!"

"Yes, but one is used to that!" said the hen.

"But it gets cold and it freezes in this country!"

"That makes the kale better!" said the hen. "Besides, it gets very warm here, too! Did we not have a summer, four years ago, which lasted five weeks? It was so hot one could hardly breathe! Then we have not all the wild and poisonous creatures that infest those warm countries of yours, and we are free from robbers. He is a good-for-nothing who does not consider our country the most beautiful—he certainly does not deserve to be here!" The hen was so agitated that she wept. "I have traveled, too. I rode in a coop about twelve miles, and I must say there is no pleasure at all in traveling!"

"Yes, the hen is a sensible woman!" said the doll Bertha. "I do not care to travel among the mountains, for there is nothing but ups and downs, ups and downs. No, no, we will move out to the sandpit, and walk about in the cabbage garden."

And so it was settled.

SATURDAY

"Am I to hear some stories now?" asked little Hjalmar, as soon as Olé Luköié had got him to bed.

"This evening we have no time for that," replied Olé Luköié, as he spread his finest umbrella over him. "Just look at these Chinamen!"

The whole umbrella looked like a great Chinese bowl with blue trees and pointed bridges on which stood little Chinamen nodding their heads.

"We must have the whole world prettily polished up for to-morrow," said Olé, "for to-morrow is a holiday; to-morrow is Sunday. I must go to the church steeple to see that the little church sprites polish the bells, to make them sound sweetly, and I must go out into the field to see if the breezes are blowing the dust from the grass and leaves; and, the most important work of all, I must have all the stars down to polish them! I take them in my apron. But first each one must be numbered, and the holes in which they are set up there must be numbered, that they may be put back in the right places again; otherwise they would not sit tight, and we should have too many shooting stars, as one after the other came tumbling down."

"Now look here, Mr. Olé Luköié," said an old portrait which hung upon the wall of the bedroom where Hjalmar slept, "I am Hjalmar's great-grandfather! I thank you for telling the boy stories, but you must not confuse his ideas. The stars couldn't be taken down and polished! The stars are world-orbs, just like our own earth, and that is the good thing about them!"

"I thank you, old great-grandfather," said Olé Luköié, "I thank you! You are the head of the family; you are the ancestral head. But I am older than you! I am an ancient heathen; the Romans and Greeks called me the Dream God! I have been in the noblest houses, and am admitted there still! I know how to act when in company with big or little! Now tell your own story!" And away went Olé Luköié, taking his umbrella with him.

"Well, well! One may not even give one's opinion nowadays!" said the old portrait.

And then Hjalmar awoke.

SUNDAY

"Good evening!" said Olé Luköié. Hjalmar nodded, and then ran and turned his great-grandfather's portrait to the wall, that it might not join the conversation as it had yesterday.

"Now you must tell me stories—about the 'five

green peas that lived in one pod,' about the 'cock's foot that paid court to the hen's foot,' and about the 'darning-needle who put on such airs that she thought herself a sewing needle!' "

"But one can get too much of a good thing!" said Olé Luköié. "You know that I prefer showing you things! I will show you my own brother. His name, like mine, is Olé Luköié, but he never comes to anyone more than once. When he does come he takes people upon his horse, and tells them stories. He knows but two. One of these is so exceedingly beautiful that no one in the world can even imagine it, and the other so dreadful and awful that it cannot be described!"

Then Olé Luköié lifted Hjalmar up to the window, and said, "There you see my brother, the other Olé Luköié. They also call him Death! See, he does not seem so terrible as they make him appear in the picture-books, where he is nothing but bones and joints! That is silver embroidery on his cloak; that is a splendid hussar's uniform! A mantle of black velvet flies behind him over the horse! See how he gallops along!"

And Hjalmar saw how that other Olé Luköié rode along, taking young people as well as old upon his horse. Some he placed in front of him, and some behind. But first he always asked, "What is the condition of your report book?"

"Fine," they all replied.

"Yes, but let me see it myself," he said.

Then each one had to show him the book. Those who had "good" and "very good" and "excellent" written in their books were placed in front of him on the horse, and the lovely story was told to them; but those who had "middling" or "tolerably well," had to sit up behind and hear the very terrible story. They trembled and wept and wanted to jump off the horse, but this they could not do, for they had all, as it were, grown fast to it.

"But Death is a most splendid Olé Luköié!" said Hjalmar. "I am not afraid of him!"

"Nor need you be," replied Olé Luköié, "but see that you have good marks in your report book!"

"Now, that is certainly instructive!" muttered the great-grandfather's portrait. "It does do some good to give one's opinion, anyhow." And thereupon he was quite content.

There, now you have heard the story of Olé Luköié! This evening he can tell you some more himself!

THUMBELINA

There was once a woman who wished very much for a little tiny child. But she did not know where she could get one, and so she went to an old witch.

"I would so love to have a little child!" she said to the witch. "Will you please tell me where I can get one?"

"O yes, that can easily be managed," said the witch. "Here is a barleycorn; but it is not at all the kind that grows in the farmer's field, or is fed to the chickens. Plant it in a flowerpot, and see what happens!"

"Thank you," said the woman, and she gave the witch twelve bright shillings.

Then she went home and planted the barleycorn, and immediately up sprang a great, beautiful flower which looked exactly like a tulip; but the petals were tightly closed, as though the flower were still a bud.

"That is a lovely flower," said the woman; and she kissed its beautiful red and yellow cup. Just as she kissed it the flower opened with a loud pop! It was a real tulip, as one could see; but in the middle of the flower upon the green stamens sat a tiny little maiden, wonderfully delicate and beautiful. She was not over half a thumb's length in height, and so she was called Thumbelina.

She was given a beautifully polished walnut-shell for a cradle, with blue violet-leaves for mattresses, and a rose-leaf for a coverlet. There she slept at night; but in the daytime she played about on the table, where the woman had set a plate with a wreath of flowers all around it, their stalks standing in water. On the water in this plate floated a great tulip-leaf, and on this the little maiden could sail from one side of the plate to the other. She had two white horse hairs with which to row, and a very pretty sight it all made, indeed! She could sing also, and so delicately and sweetly that nothing like it had ever before been heard in this world.

One night, as she lay in her pretty bed, an old Toad came hopping in through the window, where a pane had been broken out. The Toad was very ugly, big, and damp, and it hopped right down on the table where Thumbelina lay sleeping under the red rose-leaf.

"That would be a lovely wife for my son!" said the Toad, and without more ado she seized the walnut-shell in which Thumbelina slept, and hopped away with it through the broken window-pane down into the garden.

There flowed a great, broad brook; the ground at the edge of the water was swampy and soft, and here lived the Toad and her son. Ugh! he was ugly and repulsive; he looked just like his mother.

"Croak! croak! brek-ke-ke-kex!" That was all he could say when he saw the pretty little maiden in the walnut-shell.

"Don't talk so loud, or she will wake up!" said the old Toad. "She could run away from us yet, for she is as light as a bit of swan's-down! We must put her out in the brook on one of the broad water-lily leaves. It will seem just like an island to her, she is so small and light. Then she cannot run away while we are getting the parlor in order under the soft mud, where you two are to keep house together."

Out in the brook grew many water-lilies. Their broad green leaves looked as if they were floating on top of the water. The leaf farthest out in the brook was the largest. So the old Toad swam out and on it laid the walnut-shell with Thumbelina still asleep.

Early in the morning the poor little maid awoke, and when she saw where she was she began to cry bitterly, for there was water on all sides of the great green leaf, and she could not get to land.

The old Toad sat in the marsh, decking out her room with marsh grasses and yellow weeds — it was to be made very pretty for the new daughter-in-law; then she swam out, with her ugly son, to the leaf where Thumbelina stood. They had come to fetch her pretty bed, which was to be placed in the bridal chamber before she herself entered it. The old Toad bowed low in the water before her and said:

"This is my son; he is to be your husband, and you shall live splendidly together down in the mud."

"Croak! croak! brek-ke-ke-kex!" was all the son could say.

Then they took the dainty little bed and swam away with it, leaving Thumbelina all alone on the great leaf. She wept, for she did not want to live with the nasty Toad or have her ugly son for a husband. The little fishes swimming in the water below had seen the Toad and heard what she had said; so they put their heads out of the water, for they wanted to get a look at the little girl. When they saw how wonderfully pretty she was, they felt very sorry that she should have to go down to live with the ugly Toad. No, that must never be! They crowded round the green stalk which held the leaf on which the little maiden stood, and gnawed it off with their teeth. Away floated the leaf, far down the stream, with Thumbelina—far away, where the Toad could not get her.

Thumbelina sailed on and on; the little birds that sat in the bushes saw her, and sang, "What a lovely little maiden!" Farther and farther floated the leaf, and thus out of the country traveled Thumbelina.

A beautiful little white Butterfly kept fluttering round her, and at last alighted on the leaf, for it liked Thumbelina very much; she, too, was pleased and happy, for now the Toad could not get her, and everything was so beautiful about her as she floated along. The sun shone upon the water, which glistened like the brightest gold. Then she took her girdle and bound one end of it round the Butterfly, fastening the other end of the ribbon to the leaf. The leaf now glided onward much faster, and Thumbelina, too, for she was standing on the leaf, you know.

Just then a big Beetle came flying along; he saw her and immediately clasped his claw round her slender waist, and flew with her up into a tree. The green leaf went floating away down the brook, and the Butterfly with it, for you know he was fastened to the leaf, and could not get loose.

My! how frightened poor little Thumbelina was when the Beetle carried her off into the tree! But she was most sorry for the beautiful white Butterfly that she had bound to the leaf; if he could not free himself, he would have to starve to death. The Beetle, however, did not trouble himself at all about that. He seated himself with her on the biggest green leaf of the tree, gave her the honey of flowers to eat, and declared that she was very pretty, though she did not in the least resemble a Beetle. Later, all the other Beetles who lived in the tree came to pay a visit. They looked at Thumbelina, and all the young lady Beetles shrugged their shoulders.

"Why," they said, "she has only two legs! What a wretched appearance!"

"She has no feelers!" they cried.

"Her waist is quite slender — fie! she looks just like a human being — how ugly she is!" said all the lady Beetles.

And yet Thumbelina was so very, very pretty. That, too, was the opinion of the Beetle who had found and seized her. But when all the others declared she was ugly, he, too, believed it at last, and would not have her at all—she might go where she pleased.

They flew down from the tree with her, and set her upon a daisy, and she wept because she was so ugly that the Beetles would not have her. And yet she was the loveliest little being one could imagine, and as fine and delicate as a rose-leaf.

All the summer through poor Thumbelina lived quite alone in the great wood. She wove herself a bed out of blades of grass, and hung it under a large burdock leaf, which protected her from the rain; she gathered the honey from the flowers for food, and drank of the dew which every morning lay on the leaves.

Thus summer and autumn passed. But now came winter, the cold, long winter. All the birds that had sung for her so sweetly flew away; trees and flowers lost their leaves; the great leaf under which she had lived shriveled up, and nothing remained of it but a withered stalk. She was dreadfully cold, for her clothes were torn and she herself was so frail and delicate. Poor little Thumbelina! She would surely freeze to death.

Now it began to snow, and every snowflake that fell upon her was like a whole shovelful thrown upon one of us, for we are tall, and she was only an inch long. Then she wrapped herself in a withered leaf, but it would not warm her and she shivered with the cold.

Close to the wood where the Beetle had left her lay a great cornfield; but the corn had long since been cut and only the naked dry stubble stood up out of the frozen ground. To her it seemed just like wandering through a great forest; and, oh! how she trembled with cold. Then she came to the door of the Field Mouse, a little hole under the stubble. There, warm and comfortable, the Field Mouse lived, with a whole roomful of corn, a glorious kitchen, and a pantry. Poor Thumbelina stood at the door just like a poor beggar girl, and asked for a tiny piece of barleycorn, for she had not had the smallest morsel to eat for two whole days.

"You poor little creature," said the Field Mouse— for after all she was a good old Field Mouse—"come into my warm room and dine with me."

She was much pleased with Thumbelina.

"If you like," she said, "you may stay with me through the winter, but you must keep my room clean and neat, and tell me stories, for of them I am very fond."

So Thumbelina did as the kind old Field Mouse bade her, and lived very comfortably and well.

"I am expecting a visit very soon," said the Field Mouse one day. "My neighbor is in the habit of coming to see me once a week. He is even better off than I am,

has great rooms, and wears a beautiful black velvety
fur coat. If you could only get him for a husband you
would be well off. But he cannot see. You must tell
him the prettiest stories you know."

Thumbelina, however, did not care about this; she
thought nothing of the neighbor, for he was a Mole.
He came and paid his visits in his black velvet coat.
The Field Mouse told how rich and how learned he was,
and how his house was more than twenty times larger
than hers; he possessed great learning, but did not like
the sun and beautiful flowers, for he had never seen them.

Thumbelina had to sing, and she sang both "Ladybird, ladybird, fly away home," and "When the parson
goes a-field." The Mole fell in love with her, because
of her beautiful voice; but he said nothing, so sedate
was he.

A short time before, the Mole had dug a long passage
in the ground from his own house to theirs, and Thumbelina and the Field Mouse received permission to walk
here whenever they pleased. But he begged them not
to be afraid of the dead bird that lay in the passage. It
was a real bird with wings and beak. It certainly must
have died only a short time before, and was now buried
just where the Mole had made his tunnel.

The Mole took a bit of decayed wood in his mouth,
for, you see, it glimmers like fire in the dark, and walked
ahead, lighting them through the long, dark passage.
When they came to where the dead bird lay, the Mole
thrust his nose against the ceiling and made a great
hole through which the daylight could shine. In the
middle of the floor lay a dead Swallow, his beautiful
wings pressed close against his sides, and his head and

feet drawn in under his feathers; the poor bird had certainly died of cold. Thumbelina was so very sorry for him! She was very fond of all the little birds; they had sung and twittered so prettily for her all through the summer. But the Mole gave it a push with his short legs, and said, "Now he does n't squeak any more. It must be miserable to be born a little bird. I'm thankful that can happen to none of my children; such a bird has nothing but his 'twee-tweet,' and has to starve in the winter!"

"Yes, as a clever man you may well say that," observed the Field Mouse. "Of what use is all this 'twee-tweet' to a bird when the winter comes? He must starve and freeze. But they say that's very aristocratic!"

Thumbelina said nothing; but when the two others turned their backs to the bird, she bent down, put aside the feathers which covered its head, and kissed the closed eyes.

"Perhaps it was he who sang so prettily to me last summer," she thought. "How much pleasure he gave me, the dear, beautiful bird!"

The Mole now closed up the hole through which the daylight shone, and accompanied the ladies home. But during the night Thumbelina could not sleep; so she got out of bed and wove a large, beautiful carpet out of hay. This she carried down and spread over the dead bird, and laid soft cotton, which she had found in the Field Mouse's room, around him, so that he might lie soft and warm in the cold ground.

"Farewell, you pretty little bird!" said she. "Farewell! and thanks to you for your beautiful song last summer when all the trees were green and the sun shone warm upon us.'' Then she laid her head on the bird's breast.

As she did so she was frightened, for it seemed as if something was knocking inside there. It was the bird's heart. He was not dead; he was only numb with the cold. Now he had been warmed, and had come to life again.

In autumn all the swallows fly away to the warm countries; but if one happens to be belated, it gets so cold that it drops down as if dead, lies where it falls, and is covered by the cold snow.

Thumbelina trembled exceedingly, so startled was she; for the bird was large, very large compared with her, who was only an inch in height. But she took courage, laid the cotton closer round the poor Swallow, and brought a leaf that she had used as her own coverlet, and laid it over the bird's head.

The next night she crept out to him again, and now he was alive, but quite weak; he could only open his eyes for a moment and look at Thumbelina, as she stood before him with a bit of decayed wood in her hand, for she had no lantern.

"I thank you, pretty little child," said the sick Swallow; "I have been warmed. Soon my strength will return, and I shall be able to fly about again in the warm sunshine."

"Oh!" she said, "it is so cold outside. It is snowing and freezing. Stay in your warm bed, and I will nurse you."

Then she brought water in the petal of a flower; and the Swallow drank, and told her how he had torn one of his wings in a thorn-bush and so had not been able to fly so fast as the other swallows, that were flying away, far away, to the warm countries. At last he had fallen to the ground. He could remember nothing more, and did not in the least know how he had come where she had found him.

The Swallow remained there all winter, and Thumbelina was good to him and loved him very much. Neither the Field Mouse nor the Mole got to know a thing about him, for they did not like the poor Swallow. As soon as spring came, and the sun warmed down into the earth, the Swallow said good-by to Thumbelina. She had opened the hole which the Mole had made in the ceiling, and the sun shone brightly in upon them. The Swallow asked if Thumbelina did not want to go with him; she could sit on his back, and they would fly far away into the greenwood. But Thumbelina knew that the old Field Mouse would be grieved if she left her thus.

"No, I cannot!" said Thumbelina.

"Farewell then, farewell, you dear, sweet girl!" said the bird as he flew out into the sunshine. Thumbelina stood looking after him and the tears came into her eyes, for she was very fond of the poor Swallow.

"Twee-tweet! twee-tweet!" sang he, and flew away into the green forest.

Thumbelina was very sad. She was not permitted to get out into the warm sunshine. The corn which was sown in the field over the house of the Field Mouse grew high into the air. It was like a great thick forest for the poor little girl who, you know, was only an inch in height.

"You must get your wedding outfit made this summer, Thumbelina," said the Field Mouse. You see, their neighbor, the tiresome Mole in the fur coat, had courted her. "You must have woolen and linen clothes both! You must lack nothing when you become the Mole's wife!"

Thumbelina had to turn the spindle, and the Mole hired four spiders to spin and weave for her day and night. Every evening he paid her a visit; and was constantly saying that when the summer was over, the sun would not shine nearly so hot; now it burned the earth as hard as a stone. Yes, when the summer was over, then he would wed Thumbelina. But she was not at all happy, for she did not like the tiresome Mole in the black fur coat. Every morning when the sun rose, and every evening when it set, she crept out to the door; and when the wind blew the tops of the corn stalks apart, so that she could see the blue sky, she thought how bright and beautiful it was out there, and wished heartily she could see her dear Swallow again. But he would never come back, she thought. He was doubtless flying far away in the fair green forest.

When autumn came Thumbelina had her whole wedding outfit ready.

"In four weeks you are to be married," said the Field Mouse to her. But Thumbelina wept, and declared she would not have the tiresome Mole.

"Nonsense!" said the Field Mouse. "Don't be obstinate, or I will bite you with my white teeth. Why, it is a lovely man you are getting. The queen herself has nothing like his black velvet furs; and his kitchen and cellar are full. Be thankful for your good fortune."

Now came the day the wedding was to take place. The Mole had already come to fetch Thumbelina; she was to live with him, deep under the earth, and never come out into the warm sunshine. He did not like the sunshine, you know. The poor child was very sorrowful; she was now to say good-by to the glorious sun, which, after all, she had been allowed by the Field Mouse to look at from the threshold of the door.

"Farewell, thou bright sun!" she said, stretching out her arms toward it, and walking out a little way from the house of the Field Mouse. The corn had now been reaped, and only the dry stubble remained in the fields. "Farewell!" she repeated, and flung her arms round a little red flower which bloomed there. "Greet the little Swallow from me, if you see him again."

"Twee-tweet! twee-tweet!" a voice suddenly sounded over her head. She looked up and there was the little Swallow just flying by. He was very happy to see Thumbelina. Then she told him how unwilling she was to have the ugly Mole for her husband, and that she would have to live deep under the earth, where the sun never shone. And she could not keep from weeping as she told it.

"The cold weather is coming," said the Swallow, "and I am going to fly away to the warm countries. Will you come with me? You can sit on my back! Just tie yourself fast with your girdle, and then we shall fly away from the ugly Mole and his dark room, far away, over the mountains to the warm countries, where the sun shines brighter than it does here; where it is always summer and lovely flowers always bloom. Do fly with me, dear little Thumbelina, you who saved my life when I lay frozen in the dark underground passage.''

"Yes, I will go with you!" said Thumbelina. She seated herself on the bird's back, with her feet on his outspread wings, and tied her girdle fast to one of his strongest feathers. Then the Swallow flew high in the air, over forests and over seas, high up over the great mountains where the snow always lies; and Thumbelina felt cold in the bleak air. But then she crept under the bird's warm feathers, and only stuck out her little head to admire all the wonders below her.

Then they arrived in the warm countries. There the sun shone far brighter than in the cold North; the sky seemed twice as high; and in the ditches and on the hedges grew the most beautiful blue and green grapes. In the woods hung lemons and oranges; and the air was fragrant with myrtle and balsams. On the roads the loveliest children ran about, playing with great bright-colored butterflies. But the Swallow flew still farther, and it became more and more beautiful. Under some of the most majestic green trees by the blue sea stood an ancient palace of dazzling white marble. Vines clustered around the lofty pillars; at the very top were many swallows' nests, and in one of these lived the Swallow who carried Thumbelina.

"Here is my house," said the Swallow; "now select for yourself one of the pretty flowers which grow down yonder, and I will set you down on it. There you shall have everything just as you wish."

"That is lovely!" she cried, and clapped her little hands.

A great marble pillar was lying on the ground broken

into three pieces; between these pieces grew the most beautiful large white flowers. The Swallow flew down with Thumbelina and set her on one of the broad petals. But what was the little maid's surprise! There in the midst of the flower sat a little man, as white and transparent as if he had been made of glass. He wore the most beautiful of golden crowns on his head, and the loveliest wings on his shoulders; and he was no bigger than Thumbelina. He was the angel of the flower. In each of the flowers dwelt such a little man or woman, but this one was king over them all.

"My! how beautiful he is!" whispered Thumbelina to the Swallow.

The little Prince was very much frightened at sight of the Swallow, for it was quite a giant beside him, who was so small. But when he saw Thumbelina, he was very glad. She was the very prettiest maiden he had ever seen, and so he took his golden crown from his head and placed it on hers, asked her name, and if she would be his wife; then she should be Queen of all the flowers. Now this was truly a different kind of man from the son of the Toad, and the Mole with the black velvet fur. So she said "Yes" to the charming Prince. And out of every flower came a lady or gentleman, so dainty that they were a delight to behold. Each one brought Thumbelina a present; and the best gift of all was a pair of beautiful wings which had belonged to a great white fly. These were fastened to Thumbelina's back, and now she also could fly from flower to flower. Then there was great rejoicing, and the little Swallow sat up above in his nest and sang for them, as well as he could. Yet in his heart he was sad, for he was so fond, so fond of Thumbelina, and would have liked never to part from her.

"You should not be called Thumbelina," said the Flower Angel to her; "that is an ugly name, and you are so beautiful. We will call you Maia."

"Good-by, good-by," said the little Swallow as he set out on his return to the northern lands. There in Denmark above the window of the room where lives the man who knows how to tell stories, he had a little nest. To this man the Swallow sang "twee-tweet, twee-tweet!" and that is how we got the whole story.

THE SNAIL AND THE ROSEBUSH

Around a garden was a hedge of hazel bushes, and beyond that were broad fields and meadows with cows and sheep. But in the middle of the garden stood a Rosebush in bloom, and under it lay a Snail, who thought he had a great deal within him, since he had himself.

"Wait till my time comes," he said; "I shall accomplish something more than to yield roses, or to bear hazel nuts, or to give milk as the cows and sheep do."

"I expect a great deal from you," said the Rosebush. "May I ask, when it will appear?"

"I shall take my time about it," said the Snail. "But you are always in such great haste! And that never arouses curiosity or suspense as to what to expect."

The following year the Snail lay in about the same spot in the sunshine under the Rosebush, which put forth its buds and unfolded its flowers, always fresh, always new. And the Snail crept half out of its shell, stretched out its feelers, and then drew them back again.

"Everything looks just as it did last year. There has been no progress anywhere. The Rosebush keeps to its roses, and beyond that it will never get!"

The summer passed, the autumn passed, and the Rosebush yielded roses and buds steadily until the first snow fell. The weather became cold and raw; the Rosebush bent down toward the ground, and the Snail crept into the earth. Then a new year commenced; the roses bloomed anew, and the Snail came forth.

"You are an old Rosebush now," it said. "It is about time you were withering away. You have given the world all that was in you. Whether that has been of any importance or not, is a question I have no time to think about. But one thing is plainly evident, you have not done the least for your own development; otherwise something very different would have come of you. Can you say anything in your own defense? You will soon be nothing more than a bare stick! Can you understand what I am saying?"

"You terrify me," said the Rosebush. "I had never thought of that."

"No; it seems that you have never been much given to thinking! Have you never discovered or explained to yourself why you blossomed, and in what way the blossoming came about? Just so, and not in some other way?"

"No!" said the Rosebush. "I bloomed in gladness, for I could not do otherwise, the sun was so warm and the air so refreshing. I drank of the clear dew, and of the heavy rain; I breathed, I lived! From the ground a strength rose up within me, from above a strength came down to me. I felt a happiness, always new, always great, and therefore I always had to put forth buds and flowers. That was my life. I could not do otherwise!"

"You have led a very easy life," said the Snail.

"Yes, you are right. Everything was given to me," said the Rosebush; "but still more was given to you! You are one of those deep, meditative natures, one of the highly gifted that will astonish the world."

"I have no such design at all," said the Snail. "The world is nothing to me! I have enough to do with myself, and I have enough in myself."

"But should not all of us here on earth give to others the best that is in us, bring what we can? Yes, it is true, I have given only roses! But you? You, who received so much, what have you given to the world? What will you give to it?"

"What have I given? What will I give? I spit upon it! It is worthless! It is nothing to me! Bear your roses; beyond that you cannot go! Let the hazel bush bear nuts! Let the cows and sheep give milk! They have each of them their public; I have mine within myself. I am going into myself, and there I shall stay. The world is nothing to me!" And forthwith the Snail went into his house, and closed it up.

"How sad it is!" said the Rosebush. "However much I might desire it, I cannot creep into myself. I must always spring forth, spring forth into roses. The petals fall, and the wind carries them away! But I saw one of my roses laid in the housewife's psalm book; one of my roses found a place on the breast of a young and beautiful girl, and another was kissed in joy by the lips of a child. It did so much good; it was a true blessing. That is my memory, my life!"

And the Rosebush blossomed on in innocence, and the Snail idled away in his house; the world was nothing to him.

And years rolled by.

The Snail was dust in the dust; the Rosebush was earth in the earth. The rose of remembrance in the psalm book had fallen to dust—but in the garden bloomed new rosebushes, in the garden grew other snails. They crept into their houses, spat contemptuously—the world was nothing to them.

Shall we read the story again from the beginning? It will never be different.

THE STEADFAST TIN SOLDIER

There were once five-and-twenty tin soldiers; they were brothers, for they had all been cast from an old tin spoon. They shouldered their muskets and looked straight before them; and their uniforms were splendid in red and blue. The first thing they heard in the world, when the lid was taken off the box in which they lay, were the words "Tin Soldiers!" shouted by a little boy, as he clapped his hands in glee. The soldiers had been given to him on his birthday, and now he joyfully set them out on the table. Each soldier was exactly like every other, except one, and he had but one leg. He had been cast last of all, and there had not been enough tin to finish him, but he stood as firm on his one leg as the others on their two; and he is the very one that became remarkable.

On the table on which the soldiers had been placed stood many other playthings, but the toy that attracted most attention was a delightful castle of cardboard. Through the little windows one could look straight into the rooms. Before the castle stood a number of little trees, round a little looking-glass which was to represent a lake. Wax swans swam on this lake and were mirrored in it. All this was very pretty; but the prettiest of all was a little lady who stood in the open doorway of the castle. She, too, was cut out of paper, but she had a dress of the clearest gauze, and a little narrow blue ribbon, that looked like a scarf, over her shoulders; and in the middle of this ribbon was a shining tinsel rose as large as her whole face. The little lady stretched out both her arms, for she was a dancer; and she lifted one leg so high that the Tin Soldier could not see it at all, and thought that, like himself, she had but one.

"That would be just the wife for me!" thought he; "but she is very grand. She lives in a castle, while I have only a box, and there are five-and-twenty of us about that. It is no place for her! But still I must try and make her acquaintance!"

Then he lay down at full length behind a snuff-box which stood on the table; there he could easily watch the dainty little lady, who continued to stand on one leg without losing her balance.

Along in the evening all the other tin soldiers were put into their box, and the people in the house went to bed. Now the toys began to play at "visiting," and at "war," and at "having dances." The tin soldiers rattled in their box, for they wanted to join the fun; but they could not lift the lid. The nutcracker threw somersaults, and the pencil amused itself on the slate; there was so much noise that the canary awoke, and began to take part in the conversation, and that in verse. The only two who did not stir from their places were the Tin Soldier and the Dancing Lady; she stood straight up on the points of her toes, and stretched out both her arms; he was equally steady on his one leg; and he never turned his eyes away from her a single moment.

The clock struck twelve — and, pop! the lid flew off the snuff-box. There was no snuff in it, Oh, no! but there was a little black Goblin. It was a Jack-in-the-box, you see.

"Tin Soldier!" said the Goblin. "Keep your eyes to yourself, will you!"

But the Tin Soldier pretended not to hear him.

"Just you wait till to-morrow!" said the Goblin.

When morning came and the children were out of bed, the Tin Soldier was placed in the window; and whether it was the Goblin or a draft that did it, all at once the window flew open, and the Soldier fell head over heels down from the third story. That was a terrible fall! His leg stuck straight up in the air, and thus he remained standing, with helmet downward and his bayonet between the paving-stones.

The servant-girl and the little boy came down directly to look for him, but though they almost trod upon him, they could not see him. If the Soldier had shouted, "Here I am!" they would surely have found him; but he did not think it fitting that a soldier dressed in full uniform as he was should cry out loudly.

It now began to rain; the drops fell faster and faster, and soon it was streaming down. When the shower was over, two street boys came by.

"Look!" said one of them. "there lies a tin soldier. He must have a boat ride."

So they made a boat out of a newspaper, put the Tin Soldier in the middle of it, and away he sailed down the gutter. The two boys ran along beside him and clapped their hands. Goodness preserve us! how the waves rose in that gutter, and what a current! You see it had been a very heavy shower. The paper boat rocked up and down, and sometimes spun round so quickly that the Tin Soldier trembled; but he didn't move, and never changed countenance; he looked straight before him, holding his musket.

All at once the boat went into a long drain, and it became as dark as it had been in his box.

"Where am I going now?" he thought. "Yes, yes, it is all the Goblin's fault! Ah! If the little lady were only sitting here in the boat with me, it might be twice as dark for all I should care."

Just then a great Water Rat, which lived in the drain, came up to the boat.

"Have you a passport?" asked the Rat. "Out with your passport!"

But the Tin Soldier kept silence, and held his musket tighter than ever.

The boat rushed on, and the Rat after it. My! how he gnashed his teeth, and shouted to the straws and bits of wood:

"Stop him! Stop him! He hasn't paid toll—he hasn't shown his passport!"

But the current ran faster and faster. The Tin Soldier could already see the bright daylight where the drain ended; but he heard a terrible roaring noise that was indeed enough to frighten the bravest of men. Just think, where the tunnel ended, the drain dropped into a great canal; and for him that was as dangerous as for us to be carried down a great waterfall.

He was already so near it that he could not stop. The boat rushed out, the poor Tin Soldier stiffening himself as much as he could, and no one could say that he had as much as blinked. The boat whirled round three or four times, and was full of water to the very edge. It would surely sink. The Tin Soldier stood up to his neck in water, the boat sank deeper and deeper, the paper grew more and more limp. Then the water closed over the Soldier's head. He thought of the pretty little Dancer, and that he would never see her again; and in the Soldier's ears rang the song:

> Farewell, farewell, thou warrior brave,
> For thou must die this day!

Then the paper boat went to pieces, and the Tin Soldier fell through; but at that moment he was swallowed up by a great fish.

Oh, how dark it was! It was worse even than in the drain; and it was very narrow, too. But the Tin Soldier remained calm, and lay at full length, gripping his musket.

The fish rushed about, making the most fearful movements, and then became quite still. After a long time something suddenly flashed through it like a gleam of lightning. It was now quite light, and a voice exclaimed loudly, "The Tin Soldier!"

The fish had been caught, carried to market, and sold. It had been taken into the kitchen, where the cook had cut it open with a large knife. She seized the Soldier round the body with two fingers, and carried him into the living room. All were anxious to see the remarkable man that had traveled about inside of a fish; but the Tin Soldier was not at all proud. They placed him on the table, and there — what curious things may happen in this world! The Tin Soldier was in the very room in which he had been before! He saw the same children, and the same toys stood on the table; there was the pretty castle with the graceful little Dancer. She was still balancing herself on one leg, and held the other high in the air. She, too, remained steadfast. That moved the Tin Soldier; he was very near weeping tin tears, but that would not have been proper. He looked at her and she looked at him, but they said nothing.

Just then one of the little boys took the Tin Soldier and flung him into the stove. He gave no reason at all for doing this. It must have been the fault of the Goblin in the snuff-box.

The Tin Soldier stood there in the bright glow, and felt a heat that was terrible; but whether this heat proceeded from the real fire or from the love within him he did not know. His colors had vanished; but whether that had happened on the journey or had been caused by grief, no one could say. He looked at the little lady, she looked at him, and he felt that he was melting; but he still stood firm, shouldering his musket. Then suddenly the door flew open, a draft of air caught the Dancer, and she flew like a sylph right into the stove to the Tin Soldier; she flashed up in a flame, and was gone. Then the Tin Soldier melted into a lump; and next day, when the servant-maid took out the ashes, she found him in the shape of a little tin heart. But of the Dancer nothing remained except the tinsel rose, and that was burned as black as a coal.

THE WILD SWANS

Far away, there where the swallows fly in winter, lived a king who had eleven sons and one daughter, Elise. The eleven brothers, the princes, went to school wearing stars on their breasts and swords at their sides. They wrote on golden slates with diamond pencils, and could recite just as well by heart as they could read from the book. Anyone hearing them knew immediately that they were princes. Their sister Elise sat upon a little footstool made of looking-glass, and she had a picture book which had cost half the kingdom to buy.

Oh, these children were very, very happy! But thus it was not always to be.

Their father, who was king over all the land, married a wicked queen who was not at all kind to the poor children; they felt that on the very first day. There were great festivities at the castle, and the children played at visiting and having company. But instead of letting them have all the cakes and baked apples they could eat, as they were used to having, the queen gave them only some sand in a teacup, telling them they could make believe that it was something to eat.

The following week she sent little Elise into the country to live with some peasant people, and it did not take her long to make the king believe so many bad things of the boys that he cared no more about them.

"You shall fly out into the world and look after yourselves," said the wicked queen; "fly away as great voiceless birds!"

But she could not make things as bad for them as

she would have liked, for they turned into eleven beautiful wild swans. With strange cries they flew out of the palace window, away over the park and the forest.

It was still very early in the morning when they reached the peasants' cottage where their sister Elise lay asleep. They hovered over the roof, turning and twisting their long necks, and flapping their wings; but no one heard or saw them, and they had to fly on. They soared up toward the clouds and far out into the wide world. They flew away over a great dark forest, which stretched to the shore of the sea.

Poor little Elise stood in the peasants' room, playing with a green leaf, for she had no other toys. She made a little hole in the leaf and looked through it at the sun, and it seemed to her as if she saw her brothers' bright eyes. And every time the warm sunbeams shone upon her cheek, it reminded her of their kisses.

The days went by, one just like the other. When the wind blew through the hedges outside the house, it whispered to the roses, "Who could be more beautiful than you?" The roses shook their heads and answered, "Elise!" And when the old woman sat in the doorway of a Sunday reading in her psalm-book, the wind turned the pages and said to the book, "Who could be more devout than you?" "Elise!" answered the book. And both the roses and the book of psalms spoke the exact truth.

When she was fifteen Elise had to go back home, but when the queen saw how pretty she was, she was filled with anger and hatred toward her. She would willingly have turned her into a wild swan, too, like her brothers, but she did not dare do it at once, for the king wanted to see his daughter.

In the early morning the queen always went to her bath, which was built of marble and adorned with soft cushions and beautiful carpets.

There she took three toads, kissed them, and said to the first, "Sit upon Elise's head when she comes to bathe, that she may become stupid and sluggish like you." "Sit on her forehead," she said to the second, "that she may become homely like you, so that her father won't know her!" "Rest near her heart," she whispered to the third. "Let an evil spirit come over her, that will make her suffer." Then she put the toads into the clear water, which immediately took on a tinge of green. She called Elise, undressed her, and made her go into the bath. As she dipped under, one of the toads got into her hair, another on her forehead, and the third on her breast, but Elise seemed not to notice them at all. When she stood up three scarlet poppies floated on the water; had the creatures not been made poisonous from having been kissed by the sorceress, they would have been changed into crimson roses. None the less, flowers they became from merely having rested a moment on the good girl's head and near her heart. She was too pure and innocent for the enchantment to have any power over her.

When the wicked queen saw this, she rubbed walnut juice on Elise's skin, so that she became quite brown. Then she smeared her face with some evil-smelling ointment, and tangled up her beautiful hair; it would have been quite impossible to recognize the pretty Elise.

When her father saw her he was quite horrified and said that she could not be his daughter. Nobody would have anything to say to her, except the watch dog, and the swallows, but they were poor animals whose opinion went for nothing.

Poor Elise wept, and thought of her eleven brothers, who were all far away. She crept sadly out of the palace and wandered all day over fields and marshes, into the great forest. She did not know in the least where she was going but she felt very sad, and longed for her brothers. No doubt, they too, like herself, had been driven out into the world; and she made up her mind to seek and find them.

She had been in the wood only a short while when night fell. She had quite lost her way; so she said her evening prayer, lay down on the soft moss, and leaned her head against a little stump. It was very still and the air was mild, and round about in the grass and on the moss, hundreds of glow-worms shone like green fire. When she touched one of the branches above her gently, the glowing insects fell down to her like a shower of stars. All night long she dreamed about her brothers. Again they were children playing together; they wrote upon golden slates with diamond pencils and looked at the wonderful picture book that had cost half a kingdom. But they no longer wrote just lines and circles on their slates as they used to do; no, they wrote down all their bravest deeds, and everything that they had seen and experienced. In the picture book everything was alive— the birds sang, and the people walked out of the book and spoke to Elise and her brothers. But when she turned the page, they immediately skipped back into their places so that there should be no confusion among the pictures.

When she woke the sun was already high. It is true she could not see it, for the lofty forest trees spread their branches thick and close, but beyond, the sun-beams played like a shimmering veil of gold. A fragrance of grass and growing things was in the air, and the birds were almost ready to perch upon her shoulders. She could hear the splashing of water, for near by were many bubbling springs, which all flowed out into a pool with the loveliest sandy bottom. It was surrounded with thick bushes, but at one place the deer had made an opening, and there Elise passed through to the water's edge. It was so clear, that had not the branches moved in the breeze, she would have believed they were painted on the bottom, so plainly was every leaf reflected, those through which the sun shone as well as those in the shadow.

When she saw her own face in the water she was quite frightened, so brown and ugly was it; but when she wet her little hand and rubbed her eyes and forehead, her skin gleamed white again. Then she took off all her clothes and went into the fresh, clear water. A lovelier royal child than she could not have been found in all the world.

When she had dressed again, and braided her long hair, she went to one of the sparkling springs and drank out of the hollow of her hand. Then she wandered far-ther into the forest, though whither she did not know. She thought of her brothers, and she thought of a merci-ful God who would not forsake her. He had made the wild apples to grow to feed the hungry. He showed her one of these trees, the branches of which were bending low beneath their weight of fruit. Here she made her midday meal. Then she placed supports under the heavy branches and walked on into the thickest part of the forest. It was so quiet that she heard her own footsteps; she heard every little withered leaf which bent under her feet. Not a bird was to be seen, not a ray of sunlight could make its way through the close, leafy branches. The tall trunks stood so near together that when she looked straight before her it seemed as if fences of heavy beams surrounded her on every side. Here was a solitude such as she had never known before.

That night was very, very dark; not a single little glow-worm sparkled in the moss, and very sadly Elise lay down to sleep. Then it seemed to her as if the branches above her parted and our Lord looked down upon her with His loving eyes, and little angels peeped out from above His head and under His arms.

When she woke in the morning she was not sure whether she had dreamed this, or whether it had really happened.

She began to walk, and after having gone a few steps met an old woman with a basketful of berries, some of which she gave the girl. Elise asked if she had seen eleven princes ride through the wood.

"No," said the old woman, "but yesterday I saw eleven wild swans, with golden crowns on their heads, swimming down the stream not far away."

She led Elise a little farther on, to a slope, at the foot of which flowed a winding stream. The trees on either bank stretched their leafy branches over the stream toward one another, and wherever, from their natural growth, they could not reach one another, they had torn their roots loose from the ground, and leaned out over the water with closely interlacing branches.

Elise said good-by to the old woman, and walked

along by the river till it flowed out on the great open shore of the sea.

The beautiful sea lay before the maiden; but not a single sail was to be seen on it, not a single boat. How was she ever to get any farther? She looked at the numberless little pebbles on the beach; they had all been worn smooth and round by the waves. Glass, iron, stone, whatever had been washed up, had been given its form by the water, which yet was much softer than her fine little hand.

"It keeps on rolling tirelessly, and everything rough and hard it finally makes smooth and round. I will be just as untiring! Thank you for your lesson, you clear, rolling waves! Some time, so my heart tells me, you will bear me to my beloved brothers!"

With the seaweed washed up on the shore lay eleven white swans' feathers; she picked them up and tied them together. Drops of water lay on them, but whether these were dew or tears no one could have told. It was very lonely there by the shore. But the little maid did not feel it, for the sea presented endless changes — more in the course of a few hours than an inland fresh-water lake could show in a whole year. If a big black cloud came up, it seemed as if the sea wanted to say, "I, too, can look black"; and then the wind blew and the waves showed their white crests. But if the clouds shone red, and the wind slept, then the sea looked like a rose-leaf. Now it was green, now white, but no matter how still it lay, there was always a gentle motion at the shore, where the water rose and fell gently like the breast of a sleeping child.

When the sun was about to sink, Elise saw eleven

wild swans, with golden crowns on their heads, flying toward the shore. Swaying they flew, one behind the other. The line looked like a long white ribbon. Then Elise climbed up the bank and hid behind a bush; the swans settled close by her and flapped their great white wings.

As soon as the sun sank beneath the water, the swans' feathers suddenly disappeared, and there stood eleven handsome princes, Elise's brothers. She gave a loud cry, for though they had altered greatly, she knew it was they — she felt that it must be they and no others; and into their arms she sprang, calling them by name. They were too happy for words when they recognized their little sister who had grown so tall and beautiful. They laughed and cried, and soon had told each other about how cruel their stepmother had been toward them all.

"We brothers," said the eldest, "fly about like wild swans, as long as the sun is above the horizon. When it goes down we regain our human forms. So at sundown we must always be careful to have a place to alight, for should we happen to be flying up among the clouds when the sun goes down, we should fall, in our human forms, to the depths below. We do not live here; there is another land, just as beautiful as this, beyond the sea; but the way to it is very long and we have to cross the mighty ocean to reach it. There is no island on our way where we can spend the night; only one solitary little cliff juts up out of the water, midway. It is but just large enough for us to rest upon, side by side, and if there is a heavy sea the water dashes over us; yet we thank God for it. There we stay over night in our human forms, and without it we could never visit our beloved Fatherland, for our flight takes two of the longest days in the year. But once a year may we visit the home of our fathers, and we dare stay here for only eleven days. We fly about over the great forest, whence we can catch a glimpse of the palace where we were born and where our father lives, and beyond it the high tower of the church where our mother lies buried. Here we feel as if the trees and bushes were related to us; here the wild horses gallop over the moors, as we used to see them in our childhood. Here the charcoal burners sing the old songs we used to dance to when we were children. This is our Fatherland and hither we are drawn, and here we have found you, you dear little sister! We may stay here two days longer, and then we must fly away across the ocean, to a lovely country, indeed, but not our Fatherland! How can we ever take you with us? We have neither ship nor boat!"

"How can I save you?" said their sister, and they went on talking to each other, nearly the whole night through, sleeping for a few hours only.

Elise was awakened in the morning by the rustling of the swans' wings above her; her brothers were again transformed, and flew round in great circles, till she lost sight of them in the distance. But one of them, the youngest, stayed behind. The swan laid his head in her lap, and she stroked its white wings. All day they remained together. Toward evening the others returned, and as soon as the sun went down there they stood in their natural forms.

"To-morrow we must fly away, and dare not come back for a whole year, but we cannot leave you like this!

Have you the courage to go with us? My arm is strong enough to carry you through the forest, and surely all our wings together ought to be strong enough to bear you across the ocean."

"Yes, yes, take me with you!" said Elise.

They spent the whole evening weaving a kind of net out of the elastic bark of the willow and the tough rushes; they made it large and strong. Elise lay down upon it, and when the sun rose and the brothers turned to swans again, they took hold of the net with their bills and flew high up toward the clouds with their precious sister, who was still fast asleep. The sunbeams fell right in her face, so one of the swans flew over her head that his broad wings might shield her.

They were far from land when Elise woke; she thought she must still be dreaming, it seemed so strange to be carried through the air high over the ocean. By her side lay a branch of lovely ripe berries, and a number of sweet-tasting nuts, which her youngest brother had gathered for her, and she smiled at him gratefully. She knew it was he who flew above her, shading her from the sun.

They were up so high that the first ship they saw looked like a white sea-gull floating on the water. A great cloud came up behind them like a mountain, and Elise saw her own shadow on it, and that of the eleven swans flying there like giants in size. It was a grander picture than she had ever seen before, but as the sun rose higher, and the cloud fell farther behind, the swaying shadow picture disappeared.

They flew on and on all day like an arrow whizzing through the air, but they went more slowly than usual, for now they had their sister to carry. Bad weather came, and night was drawing on. With terror in her heart, Elise saw the sun sinking, and still the solitary rock was nowhere to be seen. The swans seemed to be taking stronger strokes than ever; alas! she was the cause of their not being able to travel faster; as soon as the sun went down they would become men, fall head-long into the sea, and drown. She prayed to God from her inmost heart, but still she could not see the rock. The black clouds drew nearer and nearer, and strong gusts of wind foretold a storm. The clouds looked like a great, threatening, leaden wave rushing ever forward, while the lightning flashed ceaselessly.

The sun was now right at the edge of the sea. Elise's heart quaked. Then the swans shot downward so sud-denly that she thought she was falling; then they hovered again. Half of the sun was below the horizon, and now for the first time she saw the little rock below her. It looked no bigger than the head of a seal sticking out of the water. The sun sank quickly, now it was no bigger than a star; then her foot touched solid earth, and the sun went out like the last spark in a bit of burning paper; she saw her brothers stand arm in arm around her, and there was only just room enough for them and her. The waves beat against the rock, and dashed over them like a shower of drenching rain. The heavens gleamed with one continuous flame, and peal on peal rolled the thun-der. But sister and brothers held each other's hands and sang a psalm which gave them courage and comfort.

At dawn the air was clear and still. As soon as the sun rose, the swans flew off with Elise, away from the island. The sea still ran high, and, when they were flying in the air, the white foam on the dark green ocean looked like millions of swans floating on the water.

When the sun rose higher, Elise saw before her, half floating in the air, a mountain country with great masses of shining ice on the heights. And in the midst lay a palace that seemed miles in length, with steep colonnades and porticoes built one above the other. Below swayed forests of palm trees and gorgeous blossoms as big as mill wheels. She asked if it was the land to which she was going, but the swans shook their heads, because what she saw was a mirage, the beautiful and ever-changing palace of Fata Morgana. No mortal dared enter there. Elise gazed at it, and, as she gazed, palace, forests, and mountains fell away, and in their place stood twenty proud churches, all alike, with high towers and pointed windows. She seemed to hear the notes of the organ, but it was the ocean she heard. Now she was close to the churches, and lo! they had changed to a great fleet sailing away below her; she looked down and it was only sea fog moving along over the waters. Yes, endless transformations kept passing before her gaze until the real land to which she was bound rose before her, with its beautiful blue mountains covered with forests of cedar, and its cities and palaces. Long before the sun went down, she sat among the hills in front of a large cave covered with soft green creepers, which looked like embroidered carpets and tapestry.

"Now we shall see what you will dream here to-night," said the youngest brother, as he showed her the cave chamber where she was to sleep.

"Would that I might dream how to save you," she said, and this thought filled her mind completely. She

prayed earnestly to God for His help, and even in her
sleep she continued her prayer. Then it seemed to her
that she was flying high in the air to Fata Morgana's
cloud castle, and that the fairy came to meet her. She
was wonderfully charming and brilliant, and yet she
resembled closely the woman who gave her the berries
in the wood and told her about the swans with the golden
crowns.

"Your brothers can be saved," she said, "but have
you courage and endurance? The sea is indeed softer
than your little hands, and yet it wears away the hardest
stones, but it does not feel the pain your fingers would
feel. It has no heart, and does not suffer the sorrow and
anguish you must endure. Do you see this stinging-
nettle I hold in my hand? Many of its kind grow round
the cave where you sleep; only those and the ones which
grow on the graves in the churchyards may be used.
Remember it well! You must pluck them, though they
burn and blister your hands. Crush the nettles with
your feet and you will have flax, and of this you must
weave eleven coats of mail, with long sleeves. Throw
these over the eleven wild swans and the charm is broken!
But remember that from the moment you begin this
work until it is finished, even though years pass meanwhile, you must not speak. The first word you say will
go like a death-dealing dagger straight to your brothers'
hearts. Their lives hang on your tongue. Mark well
all I have told you!"

At the same moment she touched the girl's hand
with the nettle; it felt like burning fire and Elise woke.
It was bright daylight, and close to where she had slept
lay a nettle like that she had seen in her dream. She

fell upon her knees with thanks to God and left the cave
to begin her work.

She seized the odious nettles with her delicate fingers,
and they burned her like fire; great blisters rose on her
hands and arms, but she suffered gladly could she thus
deliver her beloved brothers. With her bare feet she
crushed every nettle, and twisted the green flax.

The brothers came back at sunset, and they were
very much alarmed at finding Elise so silent; they
thought it was some new witchcraft exercised by their
evil stepmother. But when they saw her hands, they
understood what she was doing for their sakes; the
youngest brother wept, and wherever his tears fell, she
felt no more pain, and the burning blisters disappeared.

She spent the whole night at her work, for she could
not rest till she had delivered her dear brothers. All
the following day while the swans were away she sat
solitary, but never had the time flown so quickly. One
coat of mail was finished and now she began the next.
Then a hunting-horn sounded among the mountains;
she was much frightened, the sound came nearer, and
she heard dogs barking. In terror she rushed into the
cave, tied the flax she had collected and woven into a
bundle, and seated herself upon it.

At that moment a big dog bounded forward from
the thicket, and another and another. They barked
loudly, ran back and then forward again. In a few
minutes all the huntsmen were standing outside the
cave, and the handsomest of them was the king of the
country. He stepped up to Elise, and never had he
seen a more beautiful girl.

"How came you here, you beautiful child?" he asked.

Elise shook her head, for she dared not speak; the salvation and the lives of her brothers depended upon it. She hid her hands under her apron, so that the king should not see what she had to suffer.

"Come with me!" he said. "You cannot stay here! If you are as good as you are beautiful, I will dress you in silks and velvets and put a golden crown upon your head, and you shall live with me and have your home in my richest palace!" Then he lifted her up on his horse; she wept and wrung her hands, but the king said, "I only wish your happiness; some day you will thank me for what I am doing!" Then he dashed away among the mountains, holding her before him on his horse, and all the huntsmen followed.

As the sun went down, the magnificent royal city with churches and domes lay before them, and the king led her into the palace, where great fountains played in lofty marble halls, and where walls and ceilings glowed with paintings; but she had no eyes for all that, but only wept and sorrowed; passively she allowed the women to dress her in royal robes, to braid pearls into her hair, and to draw gloves over the blistered fingers.

She was so dazzling in her loveliness as she stood there in all her pretty clothes that the courtiers bowed still lower before her, and the king wooed her for his bride, though the archbishop shook his head, and whispered that he feared the beautiful wood maiden must be a witch, who dazzled their eyes and charmed the king's heart.

But the king did not listen; he ordered the music to play, the richest food to be brought, and the loveliest girls to dance before her. She was led through fragrant

gardens into gorgeous apartments, but not a smile came
to her lips, or shone forth in her eyes; sorrow sat there
like an eternal heritage. Then the king opened the
door of a little chamber close by the room where she was
to sleep. It was adorned with costly green carpets, and
looked exactly like the cave where she had lived. On
the floor lay the bundle of flax she had spun from the
nettles, and from the ceiling hung the shirt of mail that
had been finished. One of the huntsmen had brought
all these things away as curiosities.

"Here you may dream that you are back in your
former home!" said the king. "Here is the work upon
which you were engaged; now, in the midst of your
splendor, it will amuse you to recall those times."

When Elise saw all these things so dear to her heart,
a smile for the first time played upon her lips, and the
blood came back to her cheeks. She thought of the
deliverance of her brothers, and she kissed the king's
hand; he pressed her to his heart, and ordered that all
the church bells ring the marriage peals. The lovely,
voiceless girl from the woods was to be queen of the land.

The archbishop whispered evil words into the ear of
the king, but they did not reach his heart. The wedding
was to take place, and the archbishop himself had to
put the crown upon the bride's head. In his evil ill will
he pressed the narrow circlet tightly down upon her
forehead so that it hurt her. But a heavier circlet lay
about her heart, her grief for her brothers, and she did
not feel the physical pain. Her lips were sealed, for a
single word from her would cost her brothers their lives,
but her eyes were full of great love for the good and handsome king who did everything he could to make her

happy. Every day she grew more and more attached to him, and longed to confide in him, to tell him her sufferings; but dumb she must remain, and in silence complete her task. So at night she stole away from his side into the little chamber which was made to resemble the cave, and here she knitted, finishing one shirt after another. When she came to the seventh, she had no more flax; she knew that the nettles she was to use grew in the churchyard. But she had to pluck them herself. How was she to get there?

"Oh, what is the pain of my fingers compared with the anguish of my heart?" she thought. "I must venture it, and the good God will not desert me!" With as much terror in her heart as if she were doing an evil deed, she stole down, one moonlight night, into the garden, and between the long rows of trees out into the silent streets to the churchyard. There she saw, sitting on one of the largest gravestones, a group of hideous ghouls, who took off their tattered garments, as if they were about to bathe. Then they dug down into the freshly-made graves with their long, skinny fingers, took out the bodies, and devoured them. Elise had to pass close by them, and they fixed their evil eyes upon her; but she said a prayer as she passed, picked the stinging nettles, and hurried back to the palace with them.

Only one person had seen her, and that was the archbishop, who was up while others slept. Surely, now his opinion that all was not as it should be with the queen was justified; she was a witch, and so she had charmed the king and all the people.

He told the king in the confessional what he had seen and what he feared, and when those hard words passed his lips, the sculptured saints shook their heads as if to say: "It is not so; Elise is innocent." But the archbishop explained it differently, and said that they were bearing witness against her, and that they shook their heads at her sin. Two great tears rolled down the king's cheeks, and he went home with doubt in his heart. He pretended to sleep at night, but no quiet sleep came to his eyes. He perceived how Elise got up every night and went to her little private room. Day by day his face grew darker. Elise saw it but could not imagine the cause of it. It alarmed her, and what was she not already suffering in her heart for the sake of her brothers! Her salt tears ran down upon the royal velvet and purple, where they lay like sparkling diamonds; and all who saw the rich splendor wished to be queen.

She had, however, almost reached the end of her labors; only one shirt of mail was wanting. But again she had no more flax and not a single nettle. Once more, for the last time, she must go to the churchyard to pluck a few handfuls. She thought with dread of the solitary walk and the horrible ghouls; but her will was as strong as her trust in God.

Elise went, but the king and the archbishop followed her. They saw her disappear within the grated gateway of the churchyard, and when they approached they saw the ghouls sitting on the gravestone as Elise had seen them; and the king turned away, for he thought among them her whose head that very evening had rested on his breast.

"The people must judge her," he said. And the people judged that she should be burned in the glowing flames!

She was led away from her beautiful royal apartments to a dark, damp dungeon, where the wind whistled through the grated windows. Instead of velvet and silk they gave her the bundle of nettles she had gathered; on that she could lay her head. The hard, burning shirts of mail she had knitted were to be her covering. But they could have given her nothing more precious. She set to work again and prayed to God. Outside her prison the street boys sang derisive songs about her, and not a soul comforted her with a kind word.

Toward evening she heard the rustle of swans' wings close to the bars of her window. It was her youngest brother, who had at last found her. He sobbed aloud with joy although he knew that the coming night might be her last; but then, too, her work was now almost done and her brothers were there.

The archbishop came to spend the last hour with her as he had promised the king. But she shook her head at him, and by looks and gestures begged him to leave her. That night she had to finish her work, or else all would be wasted — all — pain, tears, and sleepless nights. The archbishop went away with bitter words against her, but poor Elise knew that she was innocent, and she went on with her work.

The little mice ran about the floor bringing nettles to her feet, so as to give what help they could, and a thrush sat at the grating of the window, where he sang all night as merrily as he could to keep up her courage.

Dawn was just breaking and the sun would not rise for another hour, when the eleven brothers stood at the gate of the palace and asked to be taken to the king. This could not be done, was the answer, for it was still night; the king was asleep and no one dared wake him. They entreated, they threatened, the watch came, and even the king himself stepped out and asked what it meant; but just then the sun rose, and no more brothers were to be seen, only eleven wild swans flying away over the palace.

The whole populace streamed out of the town gates to see the witch burned. A miserable horse drew the cart in which Elise was seated. They had put upon her a garment of coarse sackcloth, and all her wonderful long hair hung loose about her beautiful head. Her cheeks were deathly pale, and her lips moved softly, while her fingers unceasingly twisted the green flax. Even on the way to her death she did not abandon her unfinished work. Ten shirts lay completed at her feet and she was knitting the eleventh.

The populace scoffed at her. "See how the witch mutters. No psalm-book has she in her hands; no, there she sits with her loathsome sorcery. Tear it away from her, into a thousand pieces!"

The crowd pressed around her to destroy her work, but just then eleven white swans came flying and perched on the cart around her and flapped their great wings. The crowd gave way before them in terror.

"It is a sign from Heaven! She must be innocent!" they whispered but they dared not say it aloud.

The executioners seized her by the hand, but she hastily threw the eleven shirts over the swans, and there stood eleven handsome princes; but the youngest had a swan's wing in place of an arm, for one sleeve was wanting to his shirt of mail; she had not had time to finish it.

"Now I may speak! I am innocent!"

The people who saw what had happened bowed down before her as if she had been a saint, but she sank lifeless in her brothers' arms; so great had been the strain, the terror, and the suffering she had endured.

"Yes, innocent she is, indeed," said the eldest brother, and he told them all that had happened.

While he spoke a wonderful fragrance, as of millions of roses, spread around. Every faggot around the stake had taken root and shot out branches, and a great, high hedge of red roses had grown up. At the very top was one pure white flower, shining like a star. This the king broke off and placed on Elise's breast, and she woke with joy and peace in her heart.

All the church bells began to ring of their own accord, singing birds flocked around them, and such a bridal procession passed back to the palace as no king had ever seen before!

THE UGLY DUCKLING

Everything was so lovely out in the country! It was summer. The cornfields were yellow, and the oats were green; the hay had been put up in stacks in the green meadows, and there the stork went about on his long, thin, red legs, talking Egyptian, for that was the language he had learned from his mother. All around the fields and meadows were great forests, and in the midst of the forests lay deep lakes. Yes, it certainly was glorious out there in the country.

In the midst of the sunshine lay an old farm surrounded by deep canals, and from the wall down to the water grew great burdocks, so high that little children could stand upright under the tallest of them. It was just as wild as in the thickest wood, and here sat a Duck upon her nest; she must hatch out her little Ducklings, you see. But she was now almost tired out because it took such a long time and visitors were so few and far between. The other Ducks liked better to swim about in the canal than to run up and sit down under a burdock to quack with her.

At last one eggshell after another cracked open. "Peep! peep!" In all the eggs were little creatures that stuck out their heads.

"Quack, quack!" said the Duck; and out the little ones tumbled as fast as they could, looking all about them under the green leaves; and the mother let them look as much as they pleased, for green is good for the eyes.

"What a big world it is!" said all the young ones, for

they certainly had much more room now than when they lay in the eggs.

"Do you think this is the whole world?" said the mother. "It extends far beyond the other side of the garden, right into the parson's field! But there I have never been. You are all here, are you not?"—and thereupon she stood up. "No, not all; the largest egg is still there! How long is this to last? I am really tired of it." And then she sat down again.

"Well, how are you getting along?" asked an old Duck who had come to pay her a visit.

"It takes such a long time with one of the eggs," said the setting Duck. "It will not hatch. But just take a look at the others; they are the prettiest ducks I have ever seen. They all look like their father; the wretch, he never comes to see me."

"Let me see the egg that will not hatch," said the old visitor. "Depend upon it, it is a turkey egg. I was fooled that way once, and had my trouble and anxiety with the young ones, for, you see, they are afraid of the water. I could not get them out. I quacked and scolded, but it was no use. Let me see the egg. Yes, that's a turkey egg! You just let it lie where it is and go teach the other children how to swim."

"I think I will sit on it a little while longer," said the Duck. "I've sat so long now that I may as well sit a few days more."

"Just as you please," said the old Duck; and then she went away.

At last the egg broke. "Peep! peep!" said the little one, and tumbled out. It was very large and very ugly. The Duck looked at it.

"That is a terribly large Duckling," said she; "none of the others looks like that; can it really be a turkey chick? Well, we shall soon find out. Into the water he must go, if I have to push him into it."

The next day the weather was fine; the sun shone on all the green burdock leaves, and the Mother Duck with all her little ones came down to the water's edge. Splash! into the water she jumped. "Quack! quack!" she called, and then one Duckling after another tumbled out. The water closed over their heads, but they came up in an instant, and swam capitally; their legs worked of themselves, and there they were, all in the canal, the ugly, gray Duckling with them.

"No, it's not a turkey," said the mother; "see how well it uses its legs, and how upright it holds itself. It is my own child! On the whole it's very pretty, when one takes a good look at it! Quack! quack!—come with me. I'll take you into the world, and introduce you in the poultry yard; but always keep close to me, so that no one treads on you; and look out for the cat!"

So they went to the poultry yard. There was a terrible commotion, for two families were quarreling about an eel's head, and in the end the cat got it.

"See, that is the way of the world!" said the Mother Duck; and she whetted her bill, for she, too, wanted the eel's head. "Use your legs!" she said. "See that you bustle about, and bow your heads before the old Duck yonder. She is the most distinguished of all here; she is of Spanish blood — that's why she is so fat; and do you see, she has a red rag round her leg; that's something particularly fine, and the greatest distincton a Duck can receive; it signifies a wish not to lose her, and

that she may be recognized by man and beast. Shake
yourselves—keep your legs apart! A well-bred Duck
keeps its legs apart as much as possible, just like father
and mother, so! Now bend your necks and say 'Quack!'"

And they did so; but the other Ducks round about
looked at them, and said quite loudly:

"Just look at that! Now we're to have all that
crowd, too; as if there were not enough of us already!
And—fie! how that Duckling yonder looks; we won't
stand that!" And one Duck flew up immediately, and
bit it in the neck.

"Let him alone," said the mother; "he does no harm
to anyone."

"Yes, but he's too large and peculiar," said the Duck
that did the biting; "and therefore he must be licked."

"Those are pretty children the mother has there,"
said the old Duck with the rag around her leg. "They're
all pretty but that one; that was a failure. I wish she
could alter it."

"That cannot be done, your Highness," replied the
Mother Duck. "He is not pretty, but he has a really
good disposition, and swims as well as any other; I may
even say, better. I think he will grow prettier, and
in time become smaller; he has lain too long in the egg,
and therefore is not properly shaped." And then she
smoothed the feathers on its neck and patted it here
and there. "Moreover, he is a drake," she said, "and
therefore it doesn't make so much difference. I think
he will be very strong; he will make his way all right."

"The other Ducklings are lovely," said the old Duck.
"Make yourselves at home; and if you find an eel's
head, you may bring it to me."

And so they made themselves at home. But the poor Duckling that had been hatched out last and looked so ugly, was bitten and pushed and jeered at, and as much by the chickens as by the ducks.

"He is too big!" they all said.

The turkey cock, who had been born with spurs, and therefore thought himself an emperor, blew himself up like a ship in full sail, and bore straight down upon it; then he gobbled, and grew very red in the face. The poor Duckling did not know whether to stand or sit, and became very miserable, because it was so ugly and was scoffed at by the whole yard.

Thus the first day passed; and thereafter things became worse and worse. The poor Duckling was chased about by every one; even its brothers and sisters were quite unkind to it, and said, "If only the cat would catch you, you ugly creature!" And the mother said, "Would that you were far away!" And the ducks bit it, and the chickens pecked it, and the girl who had to feed the poultry kicked at it with her foot.

Then it ran away, flying over the hedge fence, and making the little birds in the bushes fly up in fear.

"That is because I am so ugly!" thought the Duckling. It shut its eyes, but kept running on. Thus it came to the great moor where the wild ducks lived. Here it lay all night, weary and downcast. In the morning the wild ducks flew up, and looked at their new companion.

"Pray, who are you?" they asked; and the Duckling turned in every direction and bowed as well as it could. "You are remarkably ugly!" said the wild ducks. "But we are quite indifferent to that, so long as you do not marry into our family."

Poor thing! It certainly did not think of marrying, and only hoped to be allowed to lie among the reeds and drink some of the swamp water.

There it remained two whole days; then came thither two wild geese, or, properly speaking, two wild ganders. It had not been long since each had come out of the egg, and that is why they were so saucy.

"Listen, comrade," said one of them, "you are rather ugly, but I like you. Will you go with us and become a bird of passage? Near here, on another moor, are a few sweet, lovely, wild geese, all unmarried, and all able to say 'Honk!' You have a chance of making your fortune, ugly as you are!"

"Piff! paff!" resounded at that moment through the air, and both ganders fell dead in the swamp; the water became blood red. "Piff! paff!" sounded again, and whole flocks of wild geese rose from the reeds. Then there was another report. A great hunt was on. The hunters were lying in wait all round the moor, and some were even sitting in the branches of the trees which spread far over the reeds. The blue smoke rose like clouds among the thick trees, and was wafted far away across the water; the hunting dogs came — splash, splash! — into the swamp, and the rushes and the reeds bent down on every side. The poor Duckling was in great fright! It turned its head to put it under its wing, but at that moment a great big dog stood close beside it! His tongue hung far out of his mouth and his eyes gleamed wickedly; he thrust out his head toward the Duckling, showed his sharp teeth, and — splash, splash! — on he went without seizing it.

"Oh, heaven be thanked!" sighed the frightened

Duckling. "I am so ugly that even the dog does not care to bite me!"

And so it lay quite still while the shots whizzed through the reeds as the guns banged away. Not until late in the day was silence restored; but the poor Duckling did not dare rise; it waited several hours more before it looked about, and then it hurried away from the moor as fast as it could. It ran over field and meadow; the wind was so strong that it was difficult to make any headway.

Toward evening the Duckling came to the miserable little hut of a peasant. This hut was so dilapidated that it seemed undecided on which side to fall and therefore had remained standing. The wind whistled round the Duckling in such a way that the poor creature was obliged to sit down in order to withstand it; the tempest grew worse and worse. Then the Duckling noticed that one of the hinges of the door had given way, and the door hung at such a slant that it could slip through the gap into the room; and this it did.

Here lived an old woman with her Cat and her Hen. The Tom Cat, whom she called Sonnie, could arch his back and purr; he could even give out sparks, but this was when one stroked his fur the wrong way. The Hen had unusually short legs, and therefore she was called Chickabiddy-Shortshanks. She laid good eggs, and the woman loved her as if she had been a child.

In the morning the strange Duckling was at once noticed, and the Tom Cat began to purr and the Hen to cluck.

"What is the trouble?" said the woman, looking all round. She could not see very well, and so she thought the Duckling was a fat duck that had strayed. "This is a rare prize," she said. "Now I shall have duck eggs. I hope it is not a drake. That I must find out."

And so the Duckling was admitted on trial for three weeks, but no eggs came. The Tom Cat was master of the house while the Hen was the lady, and they always said, "We and the rest of the world!" for they thought they were half the world, and by far the better half. The Duckling thought one might have a different opinion, but that the Hen would not allow.

"Can you lay eggs?" she asked.

"No."

"Then have the goodness to hold your tongue."

And the Tom Cat said, "Can you curve your back, and purr, and give out sparks?"

"No."

"Then you cannot have any opinion of your own when sensible people are speaking."

So the Duckling sat in a corner and felt very blue; then it thought of the fresh air and the sunshine, and was seized with such a strange longing to float on the water that it could not help telling the Hen of it.

"What are you thinking of?" cried the Hen. "You have nothing to do, and that's why you have such fancies. Purr or lay eggs, and such notions will pass away."

"But it is so charming to swim on the water," said the Duckling, "so refreshing to let it close above one's head, and to dive down to the bottom."

"Yes, that must be a pleasure, truly," said the Hen. "You must have gone crazy! Ask the Cat about it— he's the cleverest person I know—ask him if he likes to swim on the water, or to dive; I won't speak about myself. Ask your mistress, the old woman; no one in the world is wiser than she. Do you think she has any desire to swim, and to let the water close over her head?"

"You don't understand me," said the Duckling.

"We don't understand you! Then pray who is to understand you? You surely don't pretend to be more clever than the Cat and the old woman—I won't say anything as to myself. Don't be conceited, child, and be grateful for all the kindness you have received. Did you not get into a warm room, and have you not fallen in with company from which you may learn something? But you are a chatterer, and it is not pleasant to associate with you. Believe me, I speak for your good. I tell you disagreeable things, and by that one may always know one's true friends. Now set yourself to learn to lay eggs, or to purr and give out sparks!"

"I think I will go out into the wide world," said the Duckling.

"Yes, do go," replied the Hen.

And then the Duckling went. It swam on the water, and dived, but it was slighted by every creature because of its ugliness.

Now came the autumn. The leaves in the forest turned yellow and brown; the wind caught them so that they danced about, and the sky looked very cold. The clouds hung low, heavy with hail and snowflakes, and on the fence sat the raven, cawing, "Ou! ou!" because of the cold; yes, it was enough to make one shiver just to think about it. The poor little Duckling certainly had a hard time of it.

One evening—the sun was just setting in all his

beauty—a great flock of handsome birds came out of the bushes; they were dazzlingly white, with long, flexible necks; they were swans. They uttered a very peculiar cry, spread out their great, glorious wings, and flew away from that cold region to warmer lands, to fair open waters. They mounted so high, so very high! and the ugly little Duckling had such a strange feeling as it watched them. It turned round and round in the water like a wheel, stretched out its neck toward them, and uttered such a strange, loud cry that it frightened itself. Oh! it could not forget those beautiful, happy birds! When it could see them no longer, it dived down to the very bottom, and when it came up again, it was quite beside itself. It did not know the name of those birds, nor whither they were flying; but it loved them as it had never loved any one before. It was not at all envious of them. How could it think of wishing to possess such loveliness! It would have been glad if the ducks had only endured its company—the poor ugly creature!

And the winter grew cold, very cold! The Duckling was forced to swim about in the water to prevent the surface from freezing entirely; but every night the hole in which it swam about became smaller and smaller. It froze so hard that the ice sheet resounded with sharp cracking noises. The Duckling was obliged to use its legs continually to prevent the hole from closing. At last it became exhausted and lay quite still, and thus froze fast in the ice.

Early in the morning a peasant came by. When he saw what had happened, he broke the ice-crust with his wooden shoe, and carried the Duckling home to his wife. There it revived. The children wanted to play with it; but the Duckling thought they wanted to hurt it and in its terror flew into the milk-pan, so that the milk splashed out into the room. The woman screamed and threw up her hands, at which the Duckling flew down into the butter-tub, and then into the flour-barrel and out again. My, how it did look then! The woman screamed, and struck at it with the fire-tongs, and the children, laughing and shouting, tumbled over one another in their efforts to catch the Duckling. Happily the door stood open, and the poor creature rushed out among the bushes in the newly-fallen snow; there it lay as in a faint, quite exhausted.

But it would be too sorrowful a tale to tell all the misery and want which the Duckling had to endure that winter. It was lying out on the moor among the reeds when the sun began to warm again and the larks to sing.

Beautiful spring had come. Then one day the Duckling lifted its wings; they beat the air more strongly than before, and bore it swiftly away. Before it well knew how it all happened, it found itself in a great garden, where the apple trees were in bloom and the fragrant lilacs bent their long green branches down to the winding streams. Oh, how beautiful it was; such gladness of spring! From the thicket came three glorious white swans; they ruffled their feathers and swam lightly on the water. The Duckling knew the splendid creatures, and a peculiar sadness oppressed him.

"I will go up to them, to the royal birds, and they will kill me, because I, who am so ugly, dare approach them. But that is of no consequence! Better to be killed by them than to be pinched by the ducks, pecked by the chickens, kicked about by the girl who takes care of the poultry-yard, and to suffer in winter!" It flew into the water and swam toward the beautiful swans; they saw it, and came sailing down upon it with rustling feathers. "Kill me!" said the poor creature, and bent its head down upon the water, expecting nothing but death. But what did it see in the clear water? It beheld its own image—and, lo! it was no longer a clumsy, dark-gray bird, ugly and repulsive to look at— it was itself a swan!

It matters nothing to be born in a duck-yard, if one has only lain in a swan's egg.

The Duckling felt quite glad because of all the misery and misfortune it had suffered, for now it could rightly value its happiness and all the splendor that surrounded it. And the great swans swam round it and stroked it with their bills.

Into the garden came little children, who threw bread and corn into the water. The youngest cried, "There is a new one!" and the other children shouted joyously, "Yes, a new one has arrived!" They clapped their hands and danced about, then ran to their father and mother. Bread and cake were thrown into the water, and all said, "The new one is the most beautiful of all! so young and handsome!" and the old swans bowed their heads before it.

Then it felt quite bashful, and hid its head under its wing, for it did not know what to think. It was very happy, and yet not at all proud, for a good heart is never proud or conceited. It thought how it had been perse- cuted and despised; and now it heard them saying that it was the most beautiful of all beautiful birds. Even

the lilac bush bent its branches straight down into the
water before it; and the sun shone warm and mild.   Then
it shook its feathers, lifted its slender neck, and cried
joyously from the depths of its heart:

"I never dreamed of such happiness when I was still
the Ugly Duckling!"

A REAL PRINCESS

There was once a prince, who wanted a princess; but he would have nothing but a *real* princess. So he traveled all over the world to find such a princess. But no matter where he went there was always something wrong. There were plenty of princesses, but that they were *real* princesses he could never be perfectly sure. There was always something or other that was not quite right. So at last he returned home, very downhearted, because he would have liked so much to have had a real princess.

One evening it was very stormy. The lightning flashed and the thunder crashed, while the rain poured down. It was really terrible weather! Then a knocking was heard at the outer gate of the castle and the old king went out to open it.

It was a princess who stood outside. But gracious, how she looked from the rain and the storm! The water streamed out of her hair and her clothes, it ran in at the toes of her shoes and out at the heels, and then she declared that she was a real princess.

"Well, we shall soon find out!" thought the old queen. Without saying a word, she went into the bedchamber, took all the bedclothes off the bed, and placed a single green pea on the bottom of the bed. Then she took twenty mattresses and piled them one on top of the other over the pea, and then piled twenty feather beds on top of the mattresses.

There the princess was to sleep that night.

In the morning they asked her how she had slept.

"Oh, wretchedly!" said the princess. "I have hardly

closed my eyes all night long! Heaven knows what was in that bed! I have been lying on some hard thing, so that my whole body is black and blue with bruises! It is really terrible!"

Then they saw at once that she was a real princess, for she had felt the pea through twenty mattresses and twenty feather beds. None but a real princess could have so tender a skin and be so easily bruised.

So the prince took her to be his wife, for now he knew he had found a real princess. The pea was placed in the museum of art, where it may still be seen if no one has carried it away.

There, now I have told you a real story!

THE TINDER-BOX

A soldier came marching along the highway—left, right! left right! He had his knapsack on his back and his sword at his side, for he had been in the wars, and was now making his way home. As he marched along he met an old witch on the road. She was very hideous, her under lip hanging way down to her breast. "Good evening, soldier," she said. "What a fine sword you have, and what a big knapsack! You certainly are a real soldier. For that you shall have all the money you could wish for."

"Thank you, old witch!" said the soldier.

"Do you see that great tree?" said the witch, pointing to the tree that stood beside them. "It is hollow. You must climb to the top. There you'll see a hole, where you can slip through and get deep down into the tree. I'll tie a rope round your waist, so I can pull you up again when you call me."

"But what am I to do down in the tree?" asked the soldier.

"Get money," replied the witch. "Listen to me. When you reach the bottom of the tree, you will find yourself in a great passageway; it is brightly lighted, for more than a hundred lamps are burning there. Then you will see three doors; you can open them, for the keys are in the locks. If you enter the first chamber you'll see a great chest in the middle of the floor. On this chest sits a dog, and he has a pair of eyes as big as tea-cups. But don't let that bother you! I'll give you my blue-checked apron, which you must spread out on the floor; then go quickly, seize the dog, and set him on my apron; then open the chest and take as many shillings as you like. They are all of copper. Now if you would rather have silver, you must go into the next room. There sits a dog with a pair of eyes as big as mill-wheels. But do not mind that! Set him on my apron, and take all you want of the money. If you want gold, you can have that, too — in fact, as much as you can carry — by going into the third chamber. But the dog that sits on the money chest there has two eyes, each as big as the Round Tower.[1] He is quite a dog, you may be sure. But don't let that bother you in the least, just set him on my apron and he won't hurt you; then you may take as much gold out of the chest as you like."

"That's not so bad," said the soldier. "But what am I to give you, old witch? For there must be something you want out of it, I fancy."

"No," replied the witch, "not a single shilling will I take. All I want you to bring me is an old tinder-box my grandmother forgot when she was down there last."

"Well, then, tie the rope around my waist," cried the soldier.

"Here it is," said the witch, "and here's my blue-checked apron."

Then the soldier climbed the tree and let himself down into the hole, and there he stood, as the witch had said, in the great hall where the many lamps were burning.

He opened the first door. Ugh! There, staring straight at him, sat the dog with eyes as big as tea-cups.

"You're a fine fellow!" exclaimed the soldier as he

[1] The round tower of Trinity Church in Copenhagen, 111 feet high, and unique in Europe. It has a winding stairway up which Peter the Great is said to have driven in a coach and four.

placed him on the witch's apron.   Then he took as many
copper shillings as his pockets would hold, locked the
chest, put the dog on it again, and went into the second
chamber.

Whew!   There sat the dog with eyes as big as mill-
wheels.

"Don't stare so hard at me," said the soldier; "you
might strain your eyes!"   Then he set the dog on the
witch's apron.   But when he saw the silver money in
the chest, he threw away all the copper money he had
taken, and filled his pockets and his knapsack with silver
only.   Then he went into the third chamber.   Oh, but
that was truly too fearful to look at!   The dog there
really had eyes as big as the Round Tower, and they
turned round and round in his head like wheels.

"Good evening!" said the soldier, touching his cap,
for he had never before seen such a dog.   But when he
had looked at him a little while, he thought, "Well,
here goes," so he set the dog on the apron and opened
the chest.   My! what a quantity of gold was there!
He could buy the whole city with it, the cake woman's
entire stock of sweets, and all the tin soldiers, whips,
and rocking-horses in the whole world.   What a quantity
of money!   The soldier threw away all the silver coins
with which he had filled his pockets and his knapsack,
and replaced them with gold; he filled even his boots
and his cap, so that he could scarcely walk.   Now,
indeed, he had plenty of money.   He put the dog back
on the chest, slammed the door, and then called up
through the tree, "Now pull me up, old witch."

"Are you bringing the tinder-box?" asked the witch.

"That's so!" exclaimed the soldier.   "I forgot it

completely." And back he went and found it.

The witch then drew him up, and there he stood on the highroad with pockets, boots, knapsack, and cap full of gold.

"What do you want with the tinder-box?" asked the soldier.

"That's nothing to you," replied the witch. "You have your money — now give me the tinder-box."

"Nonsense!" said the soldier. "Tell me directly what you want with it, or I'll draw my sword and cut off your head."

"No!" cried the witch.

So the soldier struck off her head and there she lay. Then he tied up all his money in her apron, took it on his back like a sack, put the tinder-box in his pocket, and went straight off to the city.

That certainly was a splendid town! The soldier put up at the very best inn, asked for the finest rooms, and ordered his favorite dishes, for now with all his money he was very rich. The servant who had to clean his boots thought them a remarkably old pair for such a rich gentleman, but you see he had not yet bought any new ones. The next day he procured proper boots and handsome clothes. Thus our soldier had become a fine gentleman; and the people told him of all the noted sights of their city, about the King, and about the beauty of the King's daughter.

"How can one get to see her?" asked the soldier.

"She is not to be seen at all," said they; "she lives in a great copper castle with many towers, surrounded by high walls. No one but the King may go in and out, for it has been told in her fortune that the Princess will marry a common soldier, and the King intends to prevent that."

"I'd like to get a look at her," thought the soldier, though that, he knew, was entirely out of the question. He lived a merry life, went to the theater, drove in the King's garden, and gave much money to the poor; and that was very nice of him. He remembered how hard it had once been when he had not a single penny. Now he was rich and had fine clothes. He won many friends, who all said he was a rare fellow and a true gentleman; and that pleased the soldier very much.

But, as he spent money every day and never earned any, he had at last only two pennies left and was obliged to move out of the fine rooms in which he had lived, to a little tiny garret way up under the roof. He had to clean his own boots, and mend them with a darning needle, and none of his former friends came to see him, for there were so many stairs to climb.

One dark evening he could not even buy a candle. Then it occurred to him that there was a little piece of candle in the tinder-box that he had taken out of the hollow tree into which the witch had helped him. He brought out the tinder-box and found the candle-end. But as soon as he struck fire and the sparks flew from the flint, the door burst open, and the dog with eyes as big as tea-cups, the dog he had seen under the tree, stood before him.

"What are my lord's commands?" said the dog.

"What's that!" exclaimed the soldier. "This is certainly a wonderful tinder-box, if I can get everything I want with it! Bring me some money," said he to the dog. Whisk! the dog was gone; and whisk! he was back again, with a great bag full of copper shillings in his mouth.

Now the soldier knew what a valuable tinder-box it was. If he struck once, the dog that sat on the chest of copper money would come; if he struck twice, the dog that watched the silver came; and if he struck three times, then appeared the dog that guarded the gold. Now the soldier moved back into the fine rooms, and appeared again in handsome clothes. Immediately all his friends knew him and thought very much of him, indeed.

"It is a very strange thing that one cannot get to see the Princess," he thought one day. "Everybody says that she is very beautiful; but what good is that if she has to sit locked up in that great copper castle with the many towers? Can I not manage to see her somehow? Where is my tinder-box?" He struck fire, and whisk! there was the dog with eyes as big as tea-cups.

"I admit that it is rather late at night," said the soldier, "but I should very much like to see the Princess for just a moment."

The dog was out of the door in a flash and, before the soldier had time to think, he saw it returning with the Princess. She was seated on the dog's back, and she was so lovely that any one could see she was a real Princess. The soldier could not refrain from kissing her, for, you see, he was a thorough soldier.

The dog ran back again with the Princess, but when morning came, and the King and Queen were drinking tea, the Princess told them she had had such a strange dream during the night, about a dog and a soldier; that she had ridden upon the dog, and that the soldier had kissed her.

"That is a fine state of affairs!" said the Queen.

So one of the old Court ladies was ordered to watch

by the Princess' bed the next night, to see if this was really a dream, or what it could be.

The soldier felt a great longing to see the lovely Princess again; so the dog came during the night, took her away, and ran as fast as he could. But the old lady put on water-boots, and ran just as fast after him. When she saw that they entered a great house, she thought, "Now I know where it is"; and with a piece of chalk she made a large cross on the door. Then she went home and to bed, and the dog returned with the Princess, also. But when he saw that there was a cross drawn on the door where the soldier lived, he, too, took a piece of chalk and marked all the doors in the town with crosses. That was a clever thing to do, for now the Court lady could not find the right door, since there were crosses on them all.

Early in the morning the King and the Queen, the old Court lady, and all the officers went out to see where the Princess had been.

"Here it is!" said the King, when he saw the first door with a cross upon it.

"No, my dear husband, it is here!" said the Queen, who saw another door which also showed a cross.

"But there is one, and there is one!" they all cried; wherever they looked were crosses on the doors. Then they knew that it would do no good to seek farther.

But the Queen was an exceedingly clever woman, who could do more than ride in a coach. She took her great gold scissors, cut a large piece of silk into pieces, and made a lovely little bag; this bag she filled with fine buckwheat grains, and tied it on the Princess' back; when that was done, she cut a little hole in the bag, so that the grains would run out all along the way wherever the Princess might be carried.

In the night the dog came again, took the Princess on his back, and ran with her to the soldier, who loved her very much, and would so gladly have been a prince, that he might have her for his wife.

The dog did not notice how the grain ran out in a stream from the castle to the windows of the soldier's house, where he ran up the wall with the Princess. In the morning the King and Queen saw well enough where their daughter had been, and they arrested the soldier and put him in prison.

There he sat. Oh, how dark and disagreeable it was! "To-morrow you are to be hanged," they told him. That was not an amusing thing to hear, and, worst of all, he had left his tinder-box at the inn. In the morning, between the iron bars of the little window he saw the people hurrying out of the town to see him hanged. He heard the drums beat and saw the soldiers marching. Everybody was running, and among them a shoemaker's boy, wearing his leather apron and slippers. He went at such a gallop that one of his slippers flew off, and struck right against the wall where the soldier sat looking through the bars.

"Halloo, boy! you need n't be in such a hurry," cried the soldier. "Nothing will happen until I arrive. Look here, if you will run to the place where I used to live, and bring me my tinder-box, you shall have four shillings; but you must put your best leg foremost."

The shoemaker's boy wanted the four shillings, so away he went after the tinder-box, brought it to the soldier and—well, now just listen!

Outside the town a great gallows had been erected, and around it stood the soldiers and many hundred thousand people. The King and Queen sat on a splendid throne, opposite the Judges and the whole Council. The soldier already stood on the platform; but as they were about to put the rope round his neck, he said that always, before a poor sinner suffered his punishment, any innocent request of his was granted. He wanted very much to smoke a pipe of tobacco, as it would be the last pipe he would smoke in this world.

The King would not say "No" to this, so the soldier took his tinder-box and struck fire. One — two — three! and there stood all the dogs — the one with eyes as big as tea-cups, the one with eyes like mill-wheels, and the one whose eyes were as big as the Round Tower.

"Now help me, so I won't have to be hanged," said the soldier. And the dogs fell upon the Judges and all the Council, seized one by the leg and another by the nose, and tossed them many feet into the air, so they fell down and were broken all to pieces.

"I will not!" cried the King; but the biggest dog took both him and the Queen and threw them after the others. Then the soldiers were afraid, and all the people cried, "Little soldier, you shall be our King, and marry the beautiful Princess!"

So they put the soldier into the King's coach, and all three dogs danced ahead of it shouting "Hurrah!" The boys whistled through their fingers, and the soldiers presented arms. The Princess came out of the copper castle and became Queen, and she liked that very much. The wedding festivities lasted a week, and the three dogs sat at the table, too, and made big eyes.

THE SHEPHERDESS AND THE
CHIMNEY SWEEP

Have you ever seen a very old wooden cupboard, quite black with age and decorated with carved flourishes and foliage? Just such a cupboard once stood in a living room. It was inherited from great-great-grandmother, and was carved from top to bottom with roses and tulips. There were some of the queerest flourishes imaginable, and among them stuck out little stags' heads with many antlers. But carved right in the center of the cupboard stood a whole man. He certainly was a comical sight. And laugh he did, though it could hardly be called a laugh. It was, rather, a very broad grin.

This man had goat's legs, little horns on his forehead, and a long beard. The children in the room always called him the Billy-Goat-Legs-Major-and-Lieutenant-General-War-Commander Sergeant. That was a hard name to say and there are not many who get that title.

But then, too, the fact that he had been carved out, you see, was quite a distinction. So there he was.

He was always looking over at the table under the mirror, for there stood a lovely little porcelain Shepherdess. Her shoes were gilded, and her dress prettily fastened up with a red rose. And she had a golden hat and a shepherd's crook. She really was very lovely! Close by her stood a little Chimney Sweep, also made of porcelain, but as black as coal. He was just as clean and neat as anybody else, for it was only make-believe that he was a chimney sweep. The porcelain worker could just as well have made a prince out of him, for that was all the same!

There he stood with his ladder, very prettily, and with a face as white and red as any girl's; and that was really a fault for he might well have been just a little bit sooty. He stood quite close to the Shepherdess. They had both been placed where they stood, and since they had been put so, they naturally had become engaged. They were suited to each other, they were young, they were made of the same kind of porcelain, and both were equally fragile.

Close by them stood still another figure that was three times as large as they. It was an old Chinaman, who could nod his head. He, too, was porcelain, and he maintained that he was grandfather to the little Shepherdess. But that, of course, he could not prove. He insisted that he had authority over her, and for that reason he had nodded to the Billy-Goat-Legs-Major-and-Lieutenant-General-War-Commander-Sergeant, who was courting the little Shepherdess.

"In him you will find a husband," said the old Chinaman, "a husband that I almost believe is of mahogany. He can make you Mrs. Billy-Goat-Legs-Major-and-Lieutenant-General-War-Commander-Sergeant. He has the whole cupboard full of silverware, besides what he keeps in secret places!"

"I will not go into that dark cupboard!" said the little Shepherdess. "I have heard it said that he has eleven porcelain wives in there!"

"Then you can be the twelfth!" said the Chinaman. "To-night as soon as a snapping and cracking is heard in the old cupboard, you shall be married as sure as I am a Chinaman!" and then he nodded his head and fell asleep.

But the little Shepherdess wept and looked at her heart's best beloved, the porcelain Chimney Sweep.

"I think I will ask you," she said, "to take me with you out into the wide world, for here we cannot stay!"

"I want to do everything that you want to do!" said the little Chimney Sweep. "Let us go immediately. I know I can support you with my profession!"

"If we were only safely down off the table!" she said. "I shall not be happy until we are out in the wide world!"

He comforted her and showed her how she should put her little foot on the projecting points and the gilded foliage carved on the table leg. He also used his ladder to help her, and there they were, down on the floor. But when they looked over at the old cupboard there was such a commotion! All the carved stags stuck their heads farther out, raising their antlers and turning their necks. The Billy-Goat-Legs-Major-and-Lieutenant-General-War-Commander-Sergeant jumped high in the air, and shouted to the old Chinaman, "They are running away! They are running away!"

That made them a little frightened and they sprang up quickly into the drawer of the window seat.

There lay three or four decks of playing cards, which were not complete, and a little doll-theater, which had been raised up as well as was possible in the drawer. A play was being acted, and all the queens, diamonds and hearts, clubs and spades, sat in the first row fanning themselves. Behind them stood all the jacks, each with a head both above and below, just as playing cards have. The play was about a couple who could not have each other, and the Shepherdess wept because it was so like her own story.

"I cannot bear to look at this!" she said. "I have to get out of the drawer!" But when they got down on the floor again they saw that the Chinaman was awake and was rocking back and forth with his whole body. You see, down below he was all one solid lump!

"Here comes the old Chinaman!" screamed the Shepherdess, and then she fell right down on her fine porcelain knee, she was so unhappy.

"I have an idea!" said the Chimney Sweep. "Shall we crawl down into that big vase standing in the corner? There we could lie on roses and lavender and throw salt in his eyes when he comes."

"That is not enough!" she answered. "Besides, I know that the Chinaman and the vase have been engaged, and there is always a little kindly feeling left when people have been in such relations with each other! No, there is nothing left to do but to go out into the wide world!"

"Have you really the courage to go with me out into the wide world?" asked the Chimney Sweep. "Have you considered how great it is, and that we can never come back here again!"

"That I have!" she said.

The Chimney Sweep looked straight into her eyes, and then he said, "My way lies through the chimney! Have you really the courage to crawl with me through the stove, through the fire box, and through the stove pipe? Then we get out into the chimney and there I know how to get along. We climb so high that they cannot reach us, and farthest up is a hole that leads out to the wide world!"

Then he led her over to the door of the stove.

"It looks black!" she said, but still she went with

him, through the fire box and through the stove pipe, where it was as dark as the blackest night.

"Now we are in the chimney!" he said, "and look! look there! up yonder shines the most beautiful star!"

It was really one of the stars of the sky which was shining down on them as if to show them the way. Up they went. They crept and they crawled; it seemed a fearful distance, up, up, so very far. But he lifted and helped her, supporting her and showing her the best places to put her little porcelain feet. And then at last they reached the very edge of the chimney top. There they seated themselves, for they were really very tired, and well they might be.

The sky with all its stars was above them and all the roofs of the city lay below. They could look far around them out into the wide world. The poor Shepherdess had never imagined it to be like that. She laid her little head against the Chimney Sweep and wept so that the gold cracked off her girdle.

"This is too much!" she said. "I cannot bear it! The world is much too large! If I were only back on the little table below the mirror! I shall never be happy until I am back there again! I have followed you out into the wide world and now you ought to take me home again if you care anything at all for me!"

The Chimney Sweep talked sensibly to her; spoke about the old Chinaman and about the Billy-Goat-Legs-Major - and - Lieutenant - General - War - Commander - Ser-geant. But she sobbed so dreadfully and kissed her little Chimney Sweep so tenderly, that he could not do other-wise than she wished, although it was foolish.

Then, with much difficulty, they crawled down the

chimney again and crept through the stove pipe and the fire box — it was not at all pleasant — and there they were in the dark stove. They listened from behind the door to find out how matters stood in the room. It was very quiet. They peeped out — alas, there in the middle of the floor lay the old Chinaman. He had fallen off the table when he started after them, and there he lay, broken into three pieces. His back had come off in one piece, and his head had rolled away into a corner. The Billy - Goat - Legs - Major - and - Lieutenant - General - War-Commander-Sergeant stood where he always had, in deep meditation.

"It is terrible!" said the little Shepherdess. "Old grandfather is broken to pieces, and it is our fault! I can never survive it!" and she wrung her tiny hands.

"He can still be mended!" said the Chimney Sweep. "He can be mended very easily and well! Calm yourself! When they glue up his back and put a good rivet in the back of his head he will be as good as new again and be able to say many disagreeable things to us!"

"Do you think so?" she cried. Then they crept up again on to the table where they had stood before.

"See how far we got!" said the Chimney Sweep. "We might have saved ourselves all that trouble!"

"If only we had old grandfather riveted!" said the Shepherdess. "Can it be so very expensive?"

And he really did get mended. The family had him glued up the back, a good rivet was placed in his neck, and then he was as good as new. But nod he could not.

"You have become quite haughty since you fell and broke to pieces!" said the Billy-Goat-Legs-Major-and-Lieutenant-General-War-Commander-Sergeant. "It does not appear to me to be anything to make so awfully much out of! Am I to have her or am I not to have her?"

Then the Chimney Sweep and the little Shepherdess looked in such a distressed manner at the old Chinaman! They were afraid that he would nod, but that you know he could not do. And, besides, he found it unpleasant to tell a stranger that he had a rivet in the back of his neck. So the young porcelain people remained together and blessed grandfather's rivet and loved one another till they broke.

LITTLE IDA'S FLOWERS

"My poor flowers are quite dead!" said little Ida. "They were so pretty last night, and now all the leaves hang faded and withered! Why do they do that?" she asked the Student, who was sitting on the sofa. She liked the Student very much, for he could tell her the most wonderful stories and cut such comical figures out of paper — hearts, in the center of which were little ladies who danced, flowers, and great castles, the doors of which could open and shut. He was a jolly Student indeed! "Why do the flowers look so bad to-day?" she asked again, and showed him a bunch of flowers that was quite withered.

"Do you know what is the matter with those flowers?" said the Student. "They were at a ball last night, and that is why they hang their heads so!"

"But the flowers cannot dance!" said little Ida.

"Yes, indeed, they can," said the Student. "When it is dark, and we others are asleep, they jump merrily about. They have a ball almost every night!"

"May any children go to that ball?"

"Oh, yes," said the Student, "the tiny daisies and the lilies of the valley!"

"Where do the most beautiful flowers go to dance?" asked little Ida.

"You have often been outside the town gate near the great castle, have you not, there where the king lives during the summer, and where the beautiful garden is with its many flowers? And you have seen the swans which swim toward you when you give them bread crumbs? You may be quite sure that out there some very wonderful balls take place."

"I was out in that garden yesterday with my mother," said Ida. "But there were no leaves on the trees, and there was not a single flower left! Where are they? Last summer I saw so many!"

"They are inside the castle," said the Student. "You must know that as soon as the king and all the court ladies and gentlemen move to the city, the flowers immediately run up out of the garden and into the castle, and there they have such merry times! You just ought to see! The two most beautiful roses seat themselves on the throne. They are the king and queen. All the red cockscombs range themselves on each side, and bow. They are the chamberlains. Then all the most beautiful flowers come in, and the ball begins. The blue violets make believe they are naval cadets, and dance with the hyacinths and crocuses, which they call young ladies! The tulips and the large yellow lilies are elderly ladies, who watch over the younger set and take care that they conduct themselves properly!"

"But," asked little Ida, "does not any one punish the flowers for dancing in the king's castle?"

"No one really knows anything about it!" said the Student. "Sometimes, of course, the old steward of the castle, who has to keep watch there, comes in during the night. He carries a great bunch of keys with him, but as soon as the flowers hear the rattling of the keys they all become very quiet, hiding behind the long curtains and putting their heads out to peep around. 'It smells like flowers here!' says the old steward of the castle. But he cannot see a single one of them."

"That is fine!" said little Ida, clapping her hands. "But should not I be able to see the flowers, either?"

"Oh, yes," said the Student, "when you go out there again just be sure to remember to look through the window, and you will certainly see them. That is what I did to-day. A long yellow Easter lily lay on the sofa stretching herself. She was one of the court ladies!"

"Can the flowers in the botanical gardens also go out there? Are they able to travel that long distance?"

"Of course they can!" said the Student. "They can fly, if they want to! Have you not seen the beautiful butterflies, some red, some yellow, and some white, that look so much like flowers? That is what they once were; but they leaped from their stalks high in the air, and beat with their leaves as though they were little wings—and away they flew! And because they behaved themselves nicely, they were given permission to fly about in the daytime, too; they did not have to go home again and sit quiet on their stalks. And thus the leaves at last became real wings. That you have seen for yourself! It might be, however, that the flowers in the botanical gardens have never been out at the king's castle, or do not even know that there is such merriment there during the night. So now I am going to tell you something that will astonish the Professor of Botany next door very much. You know him, of course. When you go into his garden you must tell one of the flowers that a grand ball takes place at the castle. Then it will tell the news to all the others, and away they will fly. When the Professor goes to walk in his garden, there will not be a single flower, and he will not be able to understand where they are."

"But how can the flower tell it to the others? The flowers cannot talk!"

"No, of course they can't," answered the Student, "but they can make signs. Have you not seen how the flowers nod when the wind blows a little, and move all their green leaves? That is just as plain as if they talked!"

"Can the Professor understand the sign language?" asked Ida.

"Certainly he can! One morning he went down into his garden and saw a great stinging nettle make signs with its leaves to a pretty red carnation. 'You are so beautiful,' it said, 'and I love you very much!' But the Professor does not like such things, and struck the leaves off the nettle, for you see they are its fingers. But the thorny leaves stung him, and since that time he never dares touch a nettle."

"That is very amusing!" said little Ida, laughing.

"What nonsense to put in a child's head!" said the tiresome Councilor, who had come to pay a visit and was sitting on the sofa. He did not like the Student, and always grumbled when he saw him cutting out the queer, comical figures. Sometimes it was a man hanging on a gibbet and holding a heart in his hand, for he was a heart stealer; sometimes an old witch riding on a broomstick and carrying her husband on her nose. Such things the Councilor could not bear to see, and he would always say, as he did now, "What nonsense to put in a child's head! Nothing but stupid fancies!"

But to little Ida the things the Student told her about her flowers were very amusing, and she thought about them a great deal. The flowers hung their heads because they were tired after dancing all night; they surely were

ill. Then she carried them over to all her other toys,
which were placed on a pretty little table. The table
drawer, too, was full of beautiful things. In the doll's
bed her doll Sophy lay sleeping, but little Ida said to
her: "You will have to get up, Sophy, and be content
with a bed in the drawer to-night. The poor flowers are
sick, and they must sleep in your bed. Perhaps that
will make them well!" Then she picked up the doll;
but it looked very cross and did not say a single word.
Sophy was angry because she could not have her
own bed.

Then Ida placed the flowers in the doll's bed, pulled
the little coverlet over them, and told them to be nice
and quiet. She would make them some tea, so that they
might get well again and be able to get up in the morning.
Then she pulled the curtains close around the little bed,
to keep the sun from shining into their eyes.

All that evening she could not keep from thinking of
what the Student had told her, and when she was ready
for bed herself, she first had to look behind the curtains
of the windows where her mother's prettiest flowers
stood. There were both hyacinths and tulips, and she
whispered to them very softly: "I know where you are
going to-night; you are going to the ball!" The flowers
pretended not to understand, and did not stir a leaf.
But it was not necessary, for little Ida knew what she
knew.

After she had got in bed, she lay a long time thinking
how nice it would be to see the beautiful flowers dancing
out there in the king's castle.

"I wonder if my flowers really have been there?"
But then she fell asleep. Later in the night she woke

up. She had been dreaming about the flowers, and about the Student whom the Councilor always scolded because he told her so much nonsense, as he called it. It was very quiet in the bedroom where Ida was lying; the night lamp was burning on the table, and her father and mother were asleep.

"I wonder if my flowers are still lying in Sophy's bed?" she thought to herself. "Oh, how I should love to know!" She raised herself up a little and looked toward the door, which stood ajar. There in the other room lay the flowers and all her playthings. She listened, and then she seemed to hear some one playing the piano in the sitting room, but very softly and more beautifully than she had ever heard it played before.

"Now all the flowers must be dancing!" she said. "How I should like to see them!" But she did not dare get up, for then she would waken her father and mother. "Oh, if they would only come in here!" she thought. But the flowers did not come, and the music kept on playing sweetly. Then at last she could not resist the temptation—the music was too beautiful. She crept out of her little bed and, going softly over to the door, she peeped into the sitting room. My, but that was a curious sight!

There was no lamp burning in that room, but everything was quite light. The moon shone in through the window halfway across the room. It was almost as light as day. All the hyacinths and tulips stood in two long rows on the floor. On the windowsill all the flower pots stood empty. Down on the floor the flowers danced gracefully around one another, made figures, and held each other by the long green leaves when they whirled

around. At the piano sat a large yellow lily which little
Ida was sure she had seen that summer, for she remembered that the Student had said: "How like Miss Lina
that lily is!" But everybody had laughed at him then.
Now it seemed to Ida, too, that the long yellow flower
resembled the young lady. It had the same manner of
playing. Sometimes it bent its long yellow face to one
side, sometimes to the other, and nodded in tune to the
beautiful music. No one noticed little Ida. She saw
a large blue crocus jump up on top of the table, where
the playthings lay, and walk over to the doll's bed. It
drew the curtains aside. There lay the sick flowers,
but they got up at once and nodded to the others on the
floor to tell them that they too wished to dance. The
old chimney sweep, whose lower lip was broken off, stood
up and bowed to the pretty flowers. They did not look
at all ill. They jumped down to the others, and enjoyed
themselves very much.

Then it sounded as if something fell off the table, and
when Ida looked she saw that it was the little carnival
whip that had jumped down. It thought that it, too,
was one of the flowers. It was really very pretty, and
at one end was a little wax doll with a broad hat on its
head just like the one the Councilor wore. The whip
hopped in among the flowers and stamped very hard,
for it danced a mazurka, a dance which the other flowers
could not manage, because they were so light and were
unable to stamp.

The wax doll on the whip handle suddenly grew large
and tall, spun around over the paper flowers on the rod,
and shouted loudly: "What nonsense to put in a child's
head! Nothing but stupid fancies!" As he said this,

the wax doll looked just like the Councilor, with his
broad hat. It was just as yellow and cross-looking as
the Councilor. But the paper flowers beat against his
thin legs, and then he shrank together again and became
a very little wax doll. It was a very amusing sight, and
little Ida could not keep from laughing. The whip kept
on dancing, and the Councilor had to dance too. There
was no help for it, whether he made himself large and
tall, or remained the little yellow wax doll with the large
black hat. Then the other flowers, especially those
that had slept in Ida's doll bed, pleaded for him, and
succeeded in getting the whip to stop dancing. At
that moment a loud knocking sounded from the table
drawer where Ida's doll Sophy lay with many other toys.
The chimney-sweep doll ran to the edge of the table,
lay down flat on his stomach, and succeeded in opening
the drawer a little way. Sophy rose, and looked around
in surprise.

"There seems to be a ball here to-night!" she said.
"Why has no one told me about it?"

"Will you dance with me?" said the chimney sweep.

"Well, you would be a fine fellow to dance with,
would n't you!" she said, turning her back on him.
Then she sat down on the edge of the drawer and thought
that one of the flowers would surely come and ask her
to dance. But no one came. Then she coughed,
hem-a-hem, *hem*, *hem!* but still not a single one came
near. The chimney-sweep doll danced by himself, and
not so badly, after all.

When it appeared that none of the flowers saw Sophy,
she let herself drop from the drawer to the floor, with
a loud thump. All the flowers came running to her,

and asked whether she had hurt herself. They were
all very nice to her, especially the flowers who had slept
in her bed. But she was not hurt, and all Ida's flowers
thanked Sophy for the soft and comfortable bed, and
acted very lovingly toward her. They took her into the
middle of the room, where the moon was shining brightly,
and danced with her while all the other flowers formed
a circle around them. Now Sophy was content! And
she told them that they might keep her bed. She did
not in the least mind sleeping in the drawer.

"We thank you very much," said the flowers, "but
we cannot live long enough to do so! To-morrow we
shall be quite dead. But tell little Ida to bury us in the
garden where the canary lies. Then we shall grow up
again next summer, and become still more beautiful!"

"No, no, you must not die!" said Sophy, kissing the
flowers. At that moment the hall door opened and a
host of beautiful flowers came dancing in. Ida could not
understand where they had all come from. They surely
must be the flowers from the king's castle! First of all
walked two beautiful roses, with little gold crowns on
their heads; they were the king and queen. Then came
the prettiest of stocks and carnations, bowing to all sides.
They had brought music with them. Large poppies and
peonies blew on pea pods until they were all red in the
face. The bluebells and the little white snowdrops
tinkled like sleigh bells. That was grand music! Then
many other flowers came, and they all danced, the blue
violets and the red primroses, the daisies and the lilies
of the valley. And all the flowers kissed one another.
It was a very pretty sight.

At last the flowers bade one another good night, and

little Ida tiptoed back to bed, where she dreamed about all she had seen.

When she got up next morning she hurried to the little table to see if the flowers were still there. She drew the curtains of the little bed aside and — yes, there lay all her flowers; but they were very withered, much more so than the day before. Sophy lay in the drawer, where she had put her; she looked very sleepy.

"Do you remember what you were to tell me?" said little Ida. But Sophy looked very stupid, and said not a single word.

"You are not good," said Ida; "and they all danced with you, too!" Then she took a little paper box on which beautiful birds were painted, opened it, and placed the dead flowers inside. "This shall be your pretty coffin," she said. "Later, when my cousins come over, they shall help bury you in the garden, so that you may grow up next summer and become more beautiful!"

The cousins were merry boys, named Jonas and Adolph. Their father had given them two new crossbows, and these they brought with them to show to Ida. She told them about the poor flowers that were dead. They obtained permission to bury the flowers, and both the boys walked in front with the crossbows on their shoulders. Little Ida followed, carrying the dead flowers in the pretty box. In the garden a little grave was dug. Ida kissed the flowers, laid them in the little box, and placed it in the ground; then Adolph and Jonas shot with their crossbows over the grave, for they had neither rifles nor cannon.

THE EMPEROR'S NEW CLOTHES

Many years ago there lived an Emperor who was so inordinately fond of fine new clothes that he paid out all his money for the sole purpose of being particularly well dressed. He cared nothing for his soldiers, he cared not a whit about the theater, or for driving in the park, except alone that he might show off his new clothes. He had a garment for every hour of the day, and just as they usually say of a king, "He is in the council chamber," they always said of this Emperor, "He is in his clothes cabinet."

The great city in which he lived was very gay, and every day visitors came in large numbers. One day two swindlers, who gave themselves out as weavers, arrived, saying that they knew how to weave the loveliest cloth that any one could imagine. Not only were the colors and the pattern something extraordinarily beautiful, but the clothes which were made of the cloth they wove had this wonderful property: they became invisible to every person who was unfit for his office or was too stupid for any use.

"They would certainly be fine clothes to have," thought the Emperor; "by wearing them, I could find out what men in my empire were not fit for the positions they hold; I could tell the wise from the stupid! By all means, that cloth must be woven for me at once." And he gave the two rogues a great deal of ready money with which to begin their work.

They immediately set up two looms and pretended to be working. But they had nothing at all on the frame.

They called continually for the finest silks and the purest
and brightest gold.   This they put into their own pockets
and worked away at the empty looms, even keeping it
up far into the night.

"I should really like to know how they are getting
on with the cloth!" thought the Emperor.   But he had
a slightly uneasy feeling in the region of his heart when
he remembered that any one who was stupid or was ill
suited to his office would not be able to see it.   Of
course he was sure that he needed to have no fears
about himself, but still he wanted to send some one first,
to see how matters stood.

Everybody in the whole city heard of the wonderful
power that lay in the cloth, and everybody was eager to
see how bad or how stupid his neighbor was.

"I will send my honest old minister to the weavers!"
thought the emperor.   "He can best see how the fabric
looks, for he has sense and intelligence, and no one ful-
fills his duties better than he!"

So the good old minister entered the room where the
two rascals sat working at the empty looms.

"Mercy on us!" thought the old minister, opening
his eyes wide, "I can't see a thing!"

But he did n't say it aloud.

Both the rascals begged him to come nearer and asked
if he did n't think the pattern was beautiful and the
colors lovely.   Then they pointed to the empty frame
and the poor old minister stared and stared and opened
his eyes still wider.   But he could see nothing, for there
was nothing.

"Good gracious," he thought, "is it possible that I
am stupid!   I never have thought so, and I am certain

no one else thinks so! Is it possible I am not fit for my office! No, no, it certainly would never do to say I cannot see the cloth."

"Well, sir, you have n't said anything about it!" said the rascal who had continued to weave.

"Oh, it is beautiful! Perfectly lovely!" said the old minister, looking through his spectacles. "What a pattern, and what colors! — yes, yes, I shall tell the Emperor that it pleases me beyond measure!"

"Well, we are glad to hear that!" said both the weavers.

Then they named all the colors, one by one, and described that ghostly pattern. The old minister listened closely, so that he would be able to repeat it exactly when he got back to the Emperor. And repeat it he did.

Now the swindlers demanded more money, and more silk and gold, which they had to use in their work, they said. All of this, too, went into their own pockets. Not a single thread was ever put on the looms, but still they continued to weave, as before, at the empty loom.

The Emperor sent another faithful official to see how the weaving was progressing and if the fabric would soon be finished. With him it fared as it had with the minister. He looked and stared, and looked again, but as there was nothing but the empty loom, he, of course, saw nothing.

"Now is n't that a beautiful piece of cloth?" asked both the rogues, and they pointed out the beauties of the pattern which was not there at all.

"Stupid I am not!" thought the man. "It must be that I am not fit for my good office! It is certainly very queer! But of course I must not give myself away!"

Then he praised the cloth he did not see, and assured the weavers of his delight at the exquisite colors and the artistic pattern.

"It is just too dear for anything," he told the Emperor.

Everybody in town talked about the splendid fabric. And now the Emperor wanted to see it himself while it was still on the loom. So, accompanied by a whole train of chosen men, among whom were the two honest old officials who had been there before, he went to visit the crafty rascals, who were weaving with might and main, without the smallest bit of a thread.

"Isn't it magnificent!" cried the two honest officials. "Just look, your majesty, what a splendid pattern! What wonderful colors!" and they pointed to the empty loom, for they thought the others surely would be able to see the cloth.

"What's this!" thought the emperor. "I don't see anything! This is dreadful! Am I stupid? Am I not fit to be Emperor? This is the most dreadful thing that could happen to me!"

"Oh, it is very beautiful indeed!" said the Emperor aloud. "It has my unqualified approval!"

He nodded his head in a satisfied manner and regarded the empty loom, for never would he say that he could not see anything. The whole retinue that had followed him stared and stared, but with no better results than the others had. Yet, although they saw nothing, they all exclaimed just as the Emperor had done, "Oh, it is very beautiful, indeed!" They advised him urgently to have clothes made of this splendid new cloth, and to wear them for the first time in the great procession which was soon to take place.

"That is magnificent, wonderful, superb!" was the cry that went from mouth to mouth. Everybody was perfectly pleased with the suggestion. Both the rascals were knighted by the Emperor, who gave each of them a cross to wear in his buttonhole and bestowed on them the title of Knight Weavers.

All night before the day the procession was to take place the two rogues sat up at their work. They had more than sixteen candles lighted, and people could see that they must be very busy and hurrying to get the Emperor's new clothes ready for the morrow.

They pretended to take the fabric from the loom; they cut in the empty air with great shears; they stitched away with threadless needles; and finally they said, "At last the clothes are ready!"

The Emperor himself, accompanied by his most distinguished courtiers, now arrived, and each of the rogues lifted one arm in the air as if he were holding up something for inspection.

"See," they said, "here are the trousers! Here is the coat! Here is the mantle!" and so forth and so on. "It is as light as gossamer! A person would think that he had on nothing at all; but that is its greatest merit!"

"Of course!" said all the courtiers. But they could see nothing, for there was nothing to see.

"Will your Imperial Majesty now graciously condescend to take off your clothes?" said the rogues. "Then we shall put on the new ones for you, over here before this big mirror!"

The Emperor took off all his clothes, and the rascals

acted as if they were handing him, piece by piece, the new suit which they pretended to have woven. They reached around his waist and pretended to fasten something. It was the train, they said, and the Emperor turned and twisted in front of the mirror as if to view the effect from all sides.

"My, how becoming they are! How well they fit!" said everybody. "What a pattern! What colors! What splendid garments they are!"

"They are waiting at the door with the canopy which is to be carried over your Majesty in the procession!" said the master-in-chief of ceremonies.

"Well, I am all ready, you see!" said the Emperor. "Don't they hang well?" And he turned around once more before the mirror! For he wanted it to appear as if he were looking closely at all his finery.

The chamberlains who were to carry the train fumbled on the floor with their hands as if they were picking it up. Then they walked along holding their hands high. They did not dare let it be known that they could see nothing.

And so the Emperor marched in the procession under the beautiful canopy and everybody on the street and in the windows cried out: "The Emperor's new clothes are peerless! What a beautiful train! How wonderfully they fit!"

No one would let it be known that he saw nothing, for that would have meant that he was unfit for his office, or else that he was very stupid. No clothes that the Emperor had ever worn had been such a success.

"But he has nothing on!" said a little child.

"Just listen to the innocent!" said the child's father.

But one person whispered to another what the child had said.

"He has nothing on; a little child says he has nothing on!"

"But he really has n't anything on!" at last shouted all the people. The Emperor had a creepy feeling, for it seemed to him that they were right. But then he thought within himself, "I must carry the thing out and go through with the procession."

So he bore himself still more proudly, and the chamberlains walked along behind him carrying the train which was not there at all.

THE SNOW QUEEN

In Seven Stories

THE FIRST STORY

Which Treats of the Mirror and the Fragments

Now then, we are ready to begin. When we have reached the end of the story we shall know more than we do now.

He was an evil goblin. He was one of the very worst, for he was the demon himself.

One day he was in a very good humor, for he had made a mirror that had this peculiarity—everything good and beautiful that was reflected in it shrank to almost nothing, but whatever was worthless and ugly became prominent and looked worse than it really was. The loveliest landscapes, seen in this mirror, looked like boiled spinach, and the best people became hideous, or stood on their heads and had no bodies; their faces were so distorted as to be unrecognizable, and a single freckle appeared to spread out over nose and mouth. That was very amusing, the demon said. When a good, pious thought passed through any person's mind, it was shown in the mirror as a grin, so that the demon had to chuckle at his artful invention.

Those who visited the goblin school—for he kept a goblin school—declared everywhere that a wonder had been wrought. For now, they asserted, one could see, for the first time, how the world and the people in it really looked. They scurried about with the mirror, until there was not a country or a person in the whole world that had not appeared all twisted up in it. Now they wanted to fly up to heaven also, so as to make fun of the angels themselves. The higher they flew with the mirror the more it grinned; they could scarcely hold it. Higher and higher they flew, and then the mirror shook so terribly because of its grinning that it fell out of their hands down to the earth, where it was shattered into a hundred million billion, and still more, fragments.

And now this mirror occasioned much more unhappiness than before, for some of the fragments were scarcely the size of a grain of sand; these flew about in the wide world, and whenever they got into anyone's eye they stuck there, and such persons then saw everything wrongly, or had only eyes for the bad side of things, for every little fragment of the mirror had retained the same power the whole glass had possessed. A few persons even got a fragment of the mirror into their hearts, and that was terrible indeed, for such a heart became a lump of ice. A few fragments of the mirror were so large that they were used as window panes; but it was a bad thing to look at one's friends through these panes. Other pieces were made into spectacles, and when people put on these, for the purpose of seeing aright and being just, things went badly, and the demon laughed till his paunch shook, for it tickled him so.

But some little fragments of this glass still floated about in the air — and now we shall hear

THE SECOND STORY
A Little Boy and a Little Girl

In the great city, where there are so many houses and so many people that there is not room enough for

everyone to have a little garden, and where, consequently, most persons are obliged to be content with a
few flowers in flower pots, were two little children, who
possessed a garden somewhat larger than a flower pot.
They were not brother and sister, but they loved each
other quite as much as if they had been. Their parents
lived opposite each other in two garrets. Just where
the roof of one house met that of the neighboring house,
and where the water-pipe ran along the eaves, two little
windows faced each other. One had only to step across
the pipe to get from one window to the other.

The parents of the children had each a great box in
which grew the kitchen herbs that they used, and a little
rosebush — there was one in each box, and they grew
luxuriantly. Now it occurred to the parents to place
the boxes across the pipe, where they almost reached
from one window to the other, and looked quite like two
embankments of flowers. Pea vines hung down over
the sides of the boxes, and the rosebushes shot forth
long branches, which clustered round the windows and
bent down toward one another; it was almost like a
triumphal arch of flowers and leaves. As the boxes
were very high, and the children knew they must not
crawl up on them, they often had permission to step
out on the roof and sit on their little stools under the
roses; and there they could play capitally together.

In the winter time there was an end to this amusement. The windows were sometimes entirely frosted
over. But then the children warmed copper shillings
on the stove and held the warm coins against the frozen
panes. This made fine peep-holes, as round as round
could be, and through them peeped sweet little eyes,

one at each window; and those eyes belonged to the little boy and the little girl. The boy's name was Kay and the little girl's was Gerda.

In the summer they could get to one another at one bound, but in the winter, while the snowflakes were crowding thick and fast outside, they had to go first down and then up the many stairs.

"Those are the white bees swarming," said the old grandmother, looking out at the flying snowflakes.

"Have they also a queen bee?" asked the little boy. For he knew that there is a queen bee among the real bees.

"Yes, they have," said grandmother. "She always flies where the swarm is thickest. She is the largest of them all, and never remains quiet on the ground; she flies up again into the black cloud. Many a winter's night she flies through the streets of the town, and looks in at the windows, and then the panes freeze in a strange way as if covered with flowers."

"Yes, I've seen that!" cried both the children, and they knew that it was true.

"Can the Snow Queen come in here?" asked the little girl.

"Just let her come," cried the boy; "I'll set her on the warm stove, and then she'll melt."

Grandmother smoothed his hair, and told some other tales.

In the evening, when little Kay was at home and half undressed, he clambered up on the chair by the window, and peeped out through the little hole. A few flakes of snow were falling outside, and one of them, the largest of all, remained lying on the edge of one of the flower boxes. The snowflake grew larger and larger, and at last became a maiden clothed in the finest white gauze, that seemed put together of millions of starry flakes. She was beautiful and delicate, but of ice—of shining, glittering ice. Yes, she was alive; her eyes glittered like two shining stars, but there was no peace or rest in them. She nodded toward the window, and beckoned with her hand. The little boy was frightened, and sprang down from the chair; then it seemed as if a great bird flew by outside, in front of the window.

Next day there was a clear frost; then a thaw set in, and after that came spring. The sun shone, the foliage peeped forth, the swallows built nests, the windows were opened, and the children again sat in their little garden high up on the roof.

How splendidly the roses bloomed that summer! The little girl had learned a psalm. In it something was said about roses, and in singing of roses, she thought of her own. She sang it to the little boy, and he sang with her:

Where roses blow in the flowery vale,
There we the child Jesus shall hail.

And the little ones held each other by the hand, kissed the roses, looked into God's bright sunshine, and spoke to it as if the Christ-child were there. What splendid summer days those were! How beautiful it was out among the fresh rosebushes, which seemed as if they would never stop blooming!

Kay and Gerda sat and looked at the picture book of animals and birds. Just then it was—the clock on the great church tower was striking five—that Kay said, "Ouch! I felt a sharp pain in my heart! And now something flew into my eye!"

The little girl put her arm about his neck; he blinked his eyes. No, there was nothing at all to be seen.

"I think it is gone!" said he; but it was not gone. It was just one of those glass fragments from that magic mirror — the wicked glass in which everything great and good which was mirrored in it seemed small and mean, and everything mean and wicked was reflected in such a way that every fault was noticeable at once. Poor little Kay had also received a splinter in his heart, and that would soon become like a lump of ice. It did not hurt him any longer now, but the splinter was still there.

"Why do you cry?" he asked. "You look ugly like that. There's nothing the matter with me! Oh, fie!" he suddenly exclaimed, "that rose is worm-eaten, and see, this one is quite crooked! After all, they're ugly roses. They're like the box in which they stand!"

And then he kicked the box hard and tore off the two roses.

"Kay, what are you doing!" cried the little girl.

When he saw how he frightened her he tore off another rose, and then sprang in at his own window away from the amiable little Gerda.

When she came later with her picture book, he said it was only fit for nursing babies; and when his grandmother told stories he always interrupted with a "but"; and when he could manage it, he would even walk along behind her, put on a pair of spectacles, and talk just as she did; he could do that very cleverly, and people laughed at him. Soon he could mimic the speech and gait of everybody in the street. Everything that was peculiar or ugly about each one, Kay would imitate, and people said, "That boy must certainly have a remarkable genius!" But it was the glass that had entered his eye and that stuck deep in his heart. That was why he teased even little Gerda, who loved him with all her soul.

His playing now became much different from what it had been; it was very sensible. One winter's day when the snowflakes were flying he came out with a great magnifying glass, held up a corner of his blue coat, and let the snowflakes fall upon it.

"Now look through the glass, Gerda!" he said.

And every flake of snow was magnified and looked like a splendid flower, or a star, with ten points; it was beautiful to look at.

"See how wonderful," said Kay. "They are much more interesting than real flowers! And there's not a single fault in them; they're perfectly regular until they begin to melt."

A little while later Kay came out wearing big gloves, and with his sled on his back. He shouted right into Gerda's ears, "I have permission to go riding in the great square where the other boys play," and away he went.

Yonder in the great square the boldest among the boys often tied their sleds to the country people's wagons, and rode with them a good way. That was capital sport. Now when their fun was at its height, a great sleigh came along. It was painted white, and in it sat a person wrapped in thick white fur and wearing a white fur cap. The sleigh drove twice around the square. Kay quickly got his little sled tied to it, and away he rode. The sleigh went faster and faster, straight into the next street. The person driving turned and nodded in a friendly way to Kay, just as if they knew each other. Each time when Kay wanted to cast loose his little sled, the stranger nodded again, and then Kay remained sitting where he was.   Thus he rode on, right out through the town gate.

Then the snow began to fall so rapidly that the little boy could not see a hand's breadth before him as he rode along.   He hastily dropped the rope, so as to get loose from the great sleigh, but it was of no use.   His little sled was fast bound to the other, and away they went like the wind.   Then he called out very loudly, but nobody heard him; and the snow beat down, and the sleigh sped onward.   Every now and then it gave a leap, and they seemed to be rushing over hedges and ditches.   The boy was quite frightened.   He wanted to repeat "Our Father," but could remember nothing but the multiplication table.

The snowflakes became larger and larger; at last they looked like great white fowls.   All at once they flew aside, the great sleigh stopped, and the person riding in it rose.   It was a lady and Kay saw that her coat and cap were made entirely of snow.   She was tall and slender, and brilliantly white; it was the Snow Queen.

"We have made good headway!" she said.   "But why do you tremble with cold?   Creep into my coat!" And she seated him beside her in the sleigh, and wrapped the white coat round him.   He felt as if he had sunk into a snowdrift.

"Are you still cold?" she asked, and then she kissed him on the forehead.   Oh, that kiss was colder than ice!   It went right through to his heart, half of which was already a lump of ice.   He felt as if he were about to die, but only for a moment.   Then he seemed quite well, and he no longer felt the cold all about him.

"My sled! Don't forget my sled!"

That was the first thing he thought of; and he saw it bound fast to one of the white chickens, which now flew behind him with the sled on its back. The Snow Queen kissed Kay once again, and he forgot little Gerda, and his grandmother, and all the folks at home.

"Now you shall have no more kisses," said she, "for I might kiss you to death!"

Kay looked at her. She was so beautiful, he could not imagine a wiser or lovelier face; she did not appear to him to be made of ice now, as she had when she sat at the window and beckoned him. In his eyes she was perfect; he did not feel at all afraid. He told her that he could do mental arithmetic, with fractions even; that he knew the number of square miles and the number of inhabitants in the country. She always smiled. It seemed to him that what he knew was not enough, and he looked up into the great open sky. She flew with him then high up on the black cloud; and the storm whistled and roared, and it seemed that the wind sang old, old songs. They flew over woods and lakes, over sea and land. Below them roared the cold blast, the wolves howled, the snow glittered, and black, screaming crows flew past; but above, the moon shone big and bright and all through the long winter night Kay gazed up at it. During the day he slept at the Snow Queen's feet.

THE THIRD STORY
THE FLOWER GARDEN OF THE WOMAN WHO COULD WORK ENCHANTMENTS

But how did it fare with little Gerda when Kay did not return? What could have become of him? No one knew, no one could tell anything about it. The boys knew only that they had seen him tie his sled to another very large one which had driven along the street and out through the town gate. Nobody knew what had become of him; many tears were shed, and little Gerda wept long and bitterly. Then they said he was dead, that he had been drowned in the river that flowed close by the town. Oh, those were very long, dark, wintry days!

But now came the spring with warmer sunshine.

"Kay is dead and gone," said little Gerda.

"I don't believe it," said the sunshine.

"He is dead and gone," said she to the sparrows.

"We don't believe it," they replied; and at last little Gerda did not believe it herself.

"I will put on my new red shoes," she said one morning, "those that Kay has never seen; and then I will go down to the river and ask for him."

It was still very early. She kissed the old grandmother, who was still asleep, put on her red shoes, and went, quite alone, out of the town gate toward the river.

"Is it true that you have taken my little playmate from me? I will give you my red shoes if you will give him back to me!"

It seemed to her that the waves nodded strangely. She took her red shoes, her dearest possession, and threw them both into the river; but they fell close to the shore, and the little wavelets brought them back to the land to her. It seemed as if the river would not take from her the things she treasured most, because it had not her little Kay; but she thought she had not thrown the shoes out far enough; so she crept into a boat that lay among the reeds, went to the farthest end, and threw the shoes out into the water. The boat was not tied, and the movement she made caused it to glide away from the shore. She noticed this, and hurried to get back; but before she reached the other end, the boat was a yard from the bank and was drifting fast.

Little Gerda was very much frightened and began to cry; but no one heard her except the sparrows, and they could not carry her to land; but they flew along by the shore, and sang, as if to console her, "Here we are! Here we are!" The boat drifted on with the stream and little Gerda, in her stocking feet, sat quite still. Her little red shoes floated along behind, but they could not come up with the boat, which made more headway.

It was very pretty along both shores. There were beautiful flowers, old trees, and slopes with sheep and cows; but not a human being was to be seen.

"Perhaps the river is carrying me to little Kay," thought Gerda.

She became more cheerful; she stood up in the boat, and for many hours watched the beautiful green shores. She floated down to a great cherry orchard in which stood a little house with strange blue and red windows. It had a straw-thatched roof, and without stood two wooden soldiers, who presented arms to those who sailed past.

Gerda called to them, for she thought they were alive, but of course they did not answer. She passed quite close to them, for the river there carried the boat in toward the shore.

Gerda called still louder, and an old woman leaning on a staff resembling a shepherd's crook came out of the house. She had on a great sunbonnet, on which were painted beautiful flowers.

"You poor little child!" said the old woman. "How did you manage to get out on the great rolling river and be carried so far into the wide world?"

Then the old woman went right into the water and seized the boat with the hook on the end of her staff. She drew it to land and lifted little Gerda out. Gerda was glad to be on dry land again, but she felt a little afraid of the strange old woman.

"Come, tell me who you are, and how you came to be here," said the old lady. Gerda then told her everything, while the old woman shook her head, and said, "Hm! hm!" When Gerda had told all, and asked if the old woman had seen little Kay, she was told that he had not yet come by, but that he surely would. Gerda was not to be sorrowful, but should look at the flowers and taste the cherries, for they were better than those in any picture book, for each one of them could tell a story. Then she took Gerda by the hand and led her into the little house and locked the door.

The windows were very high, and the panes were red, blue, and yellow; inside the daylight shone through these windows in the most wondrous colors. On the table stood the most luscious cherries, and Gerda ate as many of them as she liked, for she had permission to do so. While she was eating, the old lady combed her hair with a golden comb until it clustered in pretty shining, golden curls about her round, friendly little face, which looked as sweet as a rose.

"I have long wished for a dear little girl like you," said the old lady. "Now you shall see how well we can get along together."

And as the old woman combed her hair, Gerda forgot

her adopted brother Kay more and more completely; for this old woman could cast spells. However, she was not a wicked witch. She only practiced a little magic for her own amusement, and now she wanted to keep little Gerda very much. So she went into the garden, stretched out her staff toward all the rosebushes, and, beautiful as they were, they all sank into the earth without leaving a trace to tell where they had stood. The old woman was afraid that when the little girl saw the roses, she would think of her own, and so remember her little playmate and run away.

Now she took Gerda out into the flower garden. My, how fragrant and lovely it was! Every conceivable flower of every season was there and in full bloom; no picture book could have been gayer and prettier. Gerda leaped with joy, and played till the sun went down behind the high cherry trees; then she was put into a soft bed, with red silk featherbeds, stuffed with blue violets, and she slept and dreamed as delightfully as a queen on her wedding day.

The next day she played again in the warm sunshine with the flowers; and thus many days went by. Gerda knew every flower; but, many as there were of them, it still seemed to her as if one were missing, though which one she did not know. One day she sat looking at the old lady's sunbonnet with the painted flowers; the prettiest of them all was a rose. The old lady had forgotten to take it off her bonnet when she had caused the others to disappear into the ground. But so it always is when one does not keep one's wits.

"What, are there no roses here!" cried Gerda, and, running in among the flower beds, she searched and searched; but there was not one to be found.   Then she sat down and wept and her tears fell exactly on a spot where a rosebud lay buried.   When the warm tears moistened the earth, the rose tree at once sprang up, blossoming as when it sank.   Gerda embraced it, and kissed the roses.   She thought of the beautiful roses at home, and also of little Kay.

"Oh, how I have been delayed!" said the little girl. "I was to find little Kay!   Do you not know where he is?" she asked the bees.   "Do you think he is dead and gone?"

"He is not dead," the roses answered.   "You see, we have been in the ground, where all the dead are, but Kay was not there."

"Thank you," said little Gerda, and she went to the other flowers, looked into their chalices, and asked, "Do you know where little Kay is?"

But each little flower stood in the sun, thinking only of her own story.   Gerda listened to many, many of them; but no flower knew anything of Kay.

And what did the Tiger-lily say?

"Do you hear the drum — 'Rub-dub'?   There are only two notes, always 'rub-dub'!   Hear the mourning song of the women; hear the call of the priests.   The Hindoo widow in her long red mantle stands on the funeral pyre; the flames rise around her and her dead husband; but the Hindoo is thinking of the living one there in the circle, of him whose eyes burn hotter than flames, the fire of whose eyes burns into her soul more ardently than the flames which are soon to burn her body to ashes.   Can the heart's flame die in the flames of the funeral pyre?"

"I don't understand that at all!" said little Gerda.

"That's my story," said the Lily.

What says the Convolvulus?

"Over the narrow mountain path hangs an old feudal castle; thickly the ivy grows over the crumbling red walls, leaf on leaf, up over the balcony, where stands a beautiful girl; she bends over the balustrade and gazes down the road. No rose on its branch is fresher than she; no apple blossom borne from the tree by the wind, sways more lightly than she. How her costly silks rustle! 'Why does he not come?'"

"Is it Kay whom you mean?" asked little Gerda.

"I'm speaking only of my story — my dream," replied the Convolvulus.

What does the little Snowdrop say?

"Between the trees hang ropes and a long board; it is a swing. Two pretty little girls, with dresses white as snow, and long green silk ribbons fluttering from their hats, are sitting on it swinging; their brother, who is older than they, stands in the swing with his arm around the rope to hold himself, for in one hand he has a little bowl, and in the other a clay pipe; he is blowing bubbles. The swing flies, and the bubbles rise with beautiful, changing colors; the last still hangs from the pipe bowl and sways in the wind. The swing flies on; the little black dog, light as the bubbles, stands up on his hind legs and wants to be taken upon the swing; the swing flies on, and the dog falls, barks, and grows angry, for he is being teased. The bubbles burst — a swinging board and a bursting bubble — that is my song."

"What you tell may be very pretty, but you tell it so mournfully, and you never mention little Kay!"

What do the Hyacinths say?

"There were three beautiful sisters, transparent and delicate. The dress of the first was red, that of the second blue, and that of the third entirely white; hand in hand they danced by the quiet lake in the bright moonlight. They were not fairies; they were human beings. It was so sweet and fragrant there! The girls disappeared in the forest, and the sweet fragrance became stronger; three coffins, the three beautiful maidens lying in them, glided from the wood away across the lake; fireflies flew about, shining like little hovering lights. Are the dancing girls asleep, or are they dead? The flower scent says they are dead, and the evening bell tolls their knell."

"You make me very sorrowful," said little Gerda. "Your scent is so strong that I cannot help thinking of the dead maidens. Alas! Is little Kay really dead? The Roses have been down in the earth, and they say no."

"Kling! klang!" tolled the Hyacinth Bells. "We are not tolling for little Kay—him we do not know; we merely sing our song, the only one we know."

And Gerda went to the Buttercup, gleaming forth from the shining green leaves.

"You are a little bright sun," said Gerda. "Tell me if you know where I may find my playmate."

The Buttercup shone gayly, and looked up at Gerda. What song could the Buttercup sing? It was not about Kay, either.

"In a little courtyard the clear sun shone warm on the first day of spring. The sunbeams glided down the white wall of the neighboring house; close by grew the first yellow flowers, gleaming like gold in the warm rays of the sun. Old grandmother sat out of doors in her chair; her granddaughter, a poor, pretty maid-servant, came home for a visit; she kissed her grandmother. There was gold, heart's gold, in that blessed kiss — gold on the lips, gold on the ground, and gold in the early morning beams. See, that's my little story," said the Buttercup.

"My poor old grandmother," sighed Gerda. "She is surely longing for me and grieving for me, just as she did for little Kay. But I shall soon go home and take Kay with me. There is no use asking the flowers; they know only their own songs, and give me no information."

Then she tied up her little frock around her, that she might run the faster; but the Jonquil struck against her leg as she sprang over it. So she stopped to look at the tall yellow flower, and said, "Perhaps you know something of little Kay."

She bent down close to the flower, and what did it say?

"I can see myself! I can see myself!" said the Jonquil. "Oh! oh! how fragrant I am! Up in the little attic room stands a little dancing girl; she stands sometimes on one foot, sometimes on both; she seems to tread on all the world. She's nothing but an illusion. She pours water out of a teapot on a bit of cloth—it is her bodice. 'Cleanliness is a fine thing,' she says; her white frock hangs on a hook; it has been washed in the teapot, too, and dried on the roof. She puts it on and ties her saffron handkerchief round her neck, and the dress looks all the whiter. Point your toes! Look how she seems to stand on a single stalk. I can see myself! I can see myself!"

"I don't care at all about that," said Gerda. "You need not tell me that."

And then she ran to the end of the garden. The door was closed, but she pushed against the rusty lock, and it broke off. The door swung open, and little Gerda ran with naked feet out into the wide world. She looked back three times, but no one pursued her. When at last she could run no longer, she seated herself on a great stone. Looking about her she saw that the summer was over—it was late in the autumn; she could not notice it in the beautiful garden, where there was always sunshine, and flowers of every season were always in bloom.

"Alas! how I have loitered!" said little Gerda. "Autumn has come. I must not rest."

She rose to go on. Oh! how sore and tired her little feet were! All around it looked cold and bleak; the long willow leaves were quite yellow, and dripped with water from the dew; one leaf after another dropped; only the sole thorn still bore fruit, but it was sour and set the teeth on edge. Oh! how gray and gloomy the wide world looked!

THE FOURTH STORY
THE PRINCE AND PRINCESS

Gerda was compelled to rest again; then there came hopping across the snow, just opposite the spot where she was sitting, a great Crow. This Crow stopped a long time to look at her, nodding its head. Now it said, "Caw! caw! Good-day! good-day!" It could not pronounce plainly, but it meant well toward the little girl, and asked where she was going all alone in the wide world. The word "alone" Gerda understood very well, and felt how much it expressed; she told the Crow the story of her whole life and fortune, and asked if it had not seen Kay.

And the Crow nodded very gravely, and said:

"That may be! That may be!"

"What? Do you think so?" cried the little girl; and she nearly squeezed the Crow to death and smothered it with kisses.

"Gently, gently!" said the Crow. "I think it may be the little Kay; but he must now certainly have forgotten you for the Princess."

"Does he live with a Princess?" asked Gerda.

"Yes; listen," said the Crow. "But it's so difficult for me to speak your language. If you know the crows' language, I can tell it much better."

"No, that I never learned," said Gerda; "but my grandmother understood it, and could speak it, too. I only wish I had learned it."

"No matter," said the Crow. "I will tell as well as I can, though that will be very badly."

And then the Crow told what it knew.

"In the country in which we now are lives a Princess who is wonderfully clever; you see she has read all the newspapers in the world and has forgotten them again, so clever is she. Not long ago she was sitting on the throne — that's not so pleasant, it is said, as is generally supposed — when she began to sing a song; and these were the words she sang: 'Why should I not marry?'— 'Look here,' she said, 'that's an idea.' And thereupon she wanted to marry. But she wanted a man who could answer when he was spoken to, not one who could only stand around and look handsome, for that is altogether too tiresome. She had all the court ladies summoned. When they heard her intention they were much pleased. 'I like that,' said they; 'I thought about the very same thing not long ago.' You may be sure that every word I am telling you is true," added the Crow. "I have a tame sweetheart who goes about freely in the castle, and she told me everything."

Of course the sweetheart was a crow, for one crow always seeks another, and birds of a feather flock together.

"The newspapers appeared directly," continued the Crow, "with a border of hearts and the Princess' initials. They made the announcement that every young man who was good-looking had permission to come to the castle and speak with the Princess, and he who spoke so that one could hear he was at home there, and who spoke best, the Princess would choose for her husband. Yes, yes," said the Crow, "you may believe me. It's as true as that I am sitting here. Young men came flocking in; there was much crowding, and running to and fro, but no one succeeded the first or second day. They were all able to speak when they were out in the streets; but when they entered at the palace gates and saw the guards standing in their silver lace, and on the staircase the lackeys in their golden liveries, and beheld the great lighted halls, they grew bewildered. Then when they stood before the throne on which the Princess sat, they could no nothing but repeat the last word she had spoken, which, of course, she did not care to hear again. It was just as if they had taken some drug and fallen into a stupor from which they did not recover until they reached the street again. Then they certainly could chatter enough. There was a long row of them stretching from the town gate to the palace. I went there myself to see it," said the Crow. "They were both hungry and thirsty, but from the palace they received not so much as a glass of lukewarm water. A few of the wisest had brought bread and butter with them, but they would not share with their neighbors, for they thought, 'Just let him look hungry, and the Princess won't choose him.'"

"But Kay, little Kay!" asked Gerda. "When did he come? Was he in the crowd?"

"Wait! Give me time! We're right by him. It was on the third day when, without horse or carriage, a little person arrived who walked quite merrily right up to the castle; his eyes sparkled like yours; he had fine, long hair, but his clothes were shabby."

"That was Kay!" cried Gerda, rejoicing. "Oh, then I have found him!" And she clapped her hands.

"He had a little knapsack on his back," observed the Crow.

"No, that must certainly have been his sled," said Gerda, "for he went away with a sled."

"That may well be," said the Crow, "for I did not look at it very closely. But this much I know from my tame sweetheart, that when he entered at the palace gate and saw the guards in silver, and on the staircase the line of lackeys in gold, he was not in the least embarrassed. He nodded and said to them, 'It must be very tedious to stand on the stairs; I'd rather go inside.' The halls blazed with lights; Privy Councilors and Excellencies walked about with bare feet, carrying golden trays; it was enough to make any one feel ceremonious. The stranger's boots creaked noisily, but still he was not embarrassed."

"That is certainly Kay!" cried Gerda. "He had new boots on; I've heard them creak in grandmother's room."

"Yes, they certainly did creak," resumed the Crow. "And he walked boldly, straight to the Princess herself, who was seated on a pearl as big as a spinning-wheel; and all the court ladies with their maids and their maids' maids, and all the cavaliers with their servitors and followers, and their servants' servants, who themselves had a page apiece, were standing round; and the nearer they stood to the door, the prouder they looked. The attendants' attendants' pages, who always went about in slippers, one hardly dared look at, so proudly did they stand in the doorway!"

"That must have been terrible!" faltered little Gerda. "And yet Kay won the Princess?"

"If I had not been a crow I should have married her myself, notwithstanding that I am engaged. They say he spoke as well as I speak when I use the crows' language; I heard that from my tame sweetheart. He was merry and agreeable; he had not come to court her, only to hear the wisdom of the Princess. And he approved of her, and she of him."

"Yes, surely that was Kay!" said Gerda. "He was so clever; he could do mental arithmetic up to fractions. Oh! won't you please lead me to the castle?"

"That's easily said," replied the Crow. "But how are we to manage it? I'll talk it over with my tame sweetheart; she can probably advise us; for this I must tell you—a little girl like yourself will never be admitted."

"Yes, indeed I shall," said Gerda. "When Kay

hears that I'm there he'll come out immediately and take me in."

"Wait for me yonder at the hedge," said the Crow; and it wagged its head and flew away.

It was late in the evening when the Crow came back. "Caw! caw!" it said. "I'm to greet you kindly from my sweetheart, and here's a little loaf of bread for you. She took it from the kitchen. There's plenty of bread there, and you must be hungry. You can't possibly get into the palace, for you are barefooted, and the guards in silver and lackeys in gold would not permit it. But don't cry; you shall go. My sweetheart knows a little back staircase that leads up to the bedroom, and she knows where she can get the key."

They went through the garden into the great avenue of trees where the leaves were falling one after another. And when the lights went out in the palace one by one, the Crow led little Gerda to a back door which stood ajar.

Oh, how Gerda's heart beat with fear and longing! It seemed as if she were about to do something wicked; and yet she only wanted to know if it were little Kay. Yes, it must be he. She fancied she saw his clear eyes and his long hair; she fancied she saw him smile as when they sat among the roses at home. He would certainly be glad to see her; to hear how far she had come for his sake, to know how unhappy they all had been at home when he did not come back. Oh, what a fear and what a joy it was!

Now they were on the staircase. A little lamp was burning on a cupboard, and in the middle of the floor stood the Tame Crow, turning her head in every direction; she looked at Gerda, who courtesied as her grandmother had taught her to do.

"My betrothed has spoken very favorably of you, my little lady," said the Tame Crow. "Your *vita*, as it may be called, is very touching. If you will take the lamp I will precede you. We will go straight ahead and then we shall meet nobody."

"I feel as if someone were coming right behind us," said Gerda, and something went rushing past her. It seemed like shadows on the wall — horses with flying manes and slender legs, hunters, and ladies and gentlemen on horseback.

"They are only dreams!" said the Tame Crow. "They come to carry the noble lords' and ladies' thoughts a-hunting. That's all the better, for you may then look more closely at them in their beds. But I hope when you come into favor and receive honors that you will show a grateful heart."

"That is nothing to talk about!" said the Crow from the wood.

They now entered the first hall. It was hung with rose-colored satin, and artificial flowers were worked on the walls. Here the dreams again came flitting by them, but they moved so quickly that Gerda could not see the highborn lords and ladies. Each hall they entered was more splendid than the last; yes, it was enough to overawe one! Now they were in the bedchamber. Here the ceiling was like a great palm tree with leaves of glass, costly glass, and in the middle of the room hung two beds on a thick stalk of gold, each of them resembling a lily. One was white, and in that lay the Princess; the other was red, and in that Gerda was to seek little Kay.

She bent one of the red leaves aside, and then she saw
a little brown neck. Oh, that was Kay! She called out
his name quite loudly, and held the lamp toward him.
The dreams rushed into the room again on horseback; he
awoke, turned his head, and — it was not little Kay!

It was only the Prince's neck that was like Kay's;
but he was young and good looking. The Princess
peeped out of the white lily-bed and asked who was there.
Then little Gerda wept, and told her whole story, and
all that the Crows had done for her.

"You poor child!" said the Prince and the Princess
together.

They praised the Crows and said that they were not
at all angry with them, but that they should not do such
a thing again. However, they were to be rewarded.

"Should you like to be free?" asked the Princess.
"Or do you wish fixed positions as Court Crows, with the
right to all the leavings in the kitchen?"

And the two Crows bowed, and begged for fixed positions, for they thought of their old age, and said, "It is
so good to have something for the old man, as they say."

And the Prince got out of his bed and let Gerda sleep
in it. More than that he could not do. She folded her
little hands, and thought, "How good men and animals
are!" and then she closed her eyes and went quietly
to sleep. All the dreams came flying in again, looking like angels, and they drew a little sled on which
Kay sat nodding. But all this was only dreaming and
therefore it ended as soon as she awoke.

The next day she was clothed from head to foot in
velvet, and was asked to stay in the castle and have a
good time. But all she asked was a little carriage

with a horse to draw it, and a pair of little boots; then she would ride away into the wide world and find Kay.

They dressed her beautifully and gave her not only boots but a muff; and when she was ready to depart, a coach made of pure gold stood before the door. Upon it shone like a star the coat-of-arms of the Prince and Princess. Coachmen, footmen, and outriders — for there were outriders, too — sat on horseback, with gold crowns on their heads. The Prince and Princess themselves helped her into the carriage and wished her all good fortune.

The forest Crow, who was now married, accompanied her the first three miles. He sat by Gerda's side, for he could not bear to ride backward; the other Crow stood in the doorway and flapped her wings. She did not go with them, because she suffered from headaches that had come on since she had obtained her fixed place at Court and too much to eat. The coach was lined inside with sugar biscuits, and under the seat were gingerbread and fruit.

"Farewell, farewell!" cried the Prince and Princess; and little Gerda wept, and the Crow wept. Thus they traveled the first few miles; then the Crow, too, said good-by, and that was the hardest parting of all. The Crow flew up into a tree, and beat his black wings as long as he could see the coach, which gleamed like the sun.

THE FIFTH STORY
THE LITTLE ROBBER GIRL

They drove on through the thick forest; but the coach shone so like a torch that it dazzled the robbers' eyes.

"Gold! gold!" they cried, and, rushing forward, seized the horses, killed the postilions, the coachman, and the footmen, and then pulled little Gerda out of the carriage.

"She is fat—she is pretty—she has been fattened on nut kernels!" said the old robber woman, who had a very long bristly beard, and eyebrows that hung down over her eyes. "She's as good as a little spring lamb; how I shall relish her!"

And out came her shining knife, glittering in a horrible way.

"Ouch!" screamed the old woman at that moment; her own daughter, wild and unruly, had nipped her ear with her sharp little teeth. "You ugly brat!" she said; and she had not time to harm Gerda.

"She shall play with me!" said the little robber girl. "She shall give me her muff and her pretty dress, and sleep with me in my bed!"

And then the girl gave another bite, so that the woman jumped and danced around. All the robbers laughed, and said:

"Look how she dances with her cub!"

"I want to ride in the carriage," said the little robber girl.

And she would have her way, for she was spoiled and very obstinate; and she and Gerda sat in the carriage, and drove over stumps and stones deep into the forest. The little robber girl was as big as Gerda, but stronger and broader shouldered, and she had brown skin. Her eyes were very black, and they looked almost mournful. She clasped little Gerda round the waist, and said:

"They shall not kill you as long as I am not angry with you. I suppose you are a princess."

"No," replied Gerda.   And then she told all that had happened to her, and how fond she was of little Kay.

The robber girl looked at her seriously, nodded slightly, and said, "They shall not kill you, even if I do get angry with you, for then I will do it myself."

And then she dried Gerda's eyes, and put her two hands into the beautiful muff that was so soft and warm.

Now the coach stopped; they were standing in the middle of the courtyard of a robber castle.   The castle wall was cracked from top to bottom; ravens and crows flew out of the great holes, and great mastiffs—each of which looked as though he could eat up a man— sprang high in the air; but they did not bark, for that was forbidden.

In the huge, smoky, old hall a great fire burned on the stone floor; the smoke rolled along under the ceiling and had to seek an exit for itself wherever it could.   A great cauldron of soup was boiling, and hares and rabbits were roasting on the spit.

"You shall sleep to-night with me and all my little animals," said the robber girl.

They got something to eat and drink, and then went to a corner where straw and carpets were spread out. Above, sitting on sticks and perches, were more than a hundred pigeons.   They all seemed asleep, but turned a little when the two girls came near.

"All these belong to me," said the little robber girl; and suddenly she seized one of the nearest, held it by the feet, and shook it so that it flapped its wings.   "Kiss it!" she cried, and beat it in Gerda's face.   "There sit the wood rascals," she went on, pointing to a number of sticks that had been nailed in front of a hole in the wall.

"Those are wood rascals, those two; they fly away
directly if one does not keep them well locked up. And
here's my old sweetheart 'Baa.'" And she pulled out
by the horn a reindeer that was tied and had a polished
copper ring around its neck. "We're obliged to keep
him tied up, too, or he'd run away from us. Every
evening I tickle his neck with my sharp knife, of which
he's very much afraid."

And the little girl drew a long knife from a cleft in
the wall, and let it slide over the reindeer's neck; the
poor creature kicked out its legs, and the little robber
girl laughed, and drew Gerda into bed with her.

"Do you keep the knife while you're asleep?" asked
Gerda, and looked at it in a rather frightened way.

"I always sleep with my knife," replied the robber
girl. "One does not know what may happen. But tell
me now again what you told me before about little Kay,
and why you came out into the wide world."

And Gerda told her story again from the beginning;
and above them the wood pigeons cooed in their cage,
and the other pigeons slept. The little robber girl put
her arm around Gerda's neck, held her knife in the other
hand, and slept so that one could hear her. But Gerda
could not close her eyes at all she did not know whether
she was to live or die.

The robbers sat round the fire, singing and thinking,
and the old robber woman tumbled about. It was a
terrible sight for a little girl.

Then the Wood Pigeons said, "Coo! coo! We have
seen little Kay. A white hen was carrying his sled, and
Kay was seated in the Snow Queen's carriage, which
rushed by close over the treetops as we lay in our nests

in the wood. She blew upon us young pigeons and all died except us two. Coo! coo!"

"What are you saying up there?" asked Gerda. "Whither was the Snow Queen traveling? Do you know anything about it?"

"She was probably journeying to Lapland, for there is always ice and snow. You might ask the reindeer, there, tied to that cord."

"Ice and snow are there, and there everything is gloriously beautiful," said the Reindeer. "There one may run about in freedom in the great glittering valleys. There the Snow Queen has her summer pavilion; but her great castle home is far up near the North Pole, on one of the Spitzbergen islands."

"Oh, Kay, little Kay!" cried Gerda.

"You must lie still," exclaimed the robber girl, "or I shall tickle you with my knife."

In the morning Gerda told her all that the Wood Pigeons had said. The robber girl looked quite serious, nodded her head, and said, "No matter! No matter!"

"Do you know where Lapland is?" she asked the Reindeer.

"Who should know better than I?" the creature replied, its eyes sparkling brightly. "There I was born and bred, and there I leaped and ran about in the snow fields."

"Listen!" said the robber girl to Gerda. "You see all our men have gone away. Only mother is here and she'll stay; but toward noon she drinks out of the big bottle, and after that she takes a little nap; then I'll do something for you."

Then she sprang out of bed, clasped her mother round the neck, and pulled her beard, crying:

"Good morning, my own sweet old nanny-goat, good morning!" And the mother filliped her daughter's nose till it was red and blue; but it was all done for pure love.

Now when the mother had taken a drink out of her bottle and had fallen asleep, the robber girl went to the Reindeer and said, "I should like very much to tickle you many more times with my knife, for you are so amusing then; but it does n't matter. I'll untie the rope that binds you and help you outside, so that you can run to Lapland; but you must use your legs well, and carry this little girl to the palace of the Snow Queen, where her playmate is, for me. I know you heard what she told me, for she spoke loud enough, and you are an eavesdropper."

The Reindeer leaped with joy. The robber girl lifted little Gerda up on its back and had the forethought to tie her fast, and even to give her a little pillow to sit on.

"There are your fur boots," she said, "for it's growing cold; but I shall keep the muff, for that is so very pretty. Still, you shall not be cold, for here are my mother's big mittens. They'll reach to your elbows. On with them. There now, you look just like my ugly old mother."

And Gerda wept for joy.

"I can't bear to see you whimper," said the little robber girl. "You really ought to look pleased. Here you have two loaves and a ham to keep you from starving."

These were tied on the Reindeer's back. The little robber girl now opened the door, coaxed in all the big dogs, and then cut the rope with her sharp knife.

"Now run," she said to the Reindeer, "but take good care of the little girl."

And Gerda stretched out her hands in the big mittens toward the little robber girl and said good-by.

Away sped the Reindeer over stumps and stones, away through the great forest, over marshes and steppes, as fast as it could go.   The wolves howled and the ravens croaked.

"Choo! choo!" sounded in the air.   It seemed as if the sky were sneezing flashes of red fire.

"Those are my old Northern Lights," said the Reindeer.   "See how they gleam!"   And then it ran on faster than ever, day and night.   The loaves were eaten up, and so was the ham; and then they arrived in Lapland.

THE SIXTH STORY
THE LAPLAND WOMAN AND THE FINLAND WOMAN

They stopped at a little hut.   It was very humble; the roof sloped down to the ground, and the door was so low that the family had to creep on their stomachs when they wanted to go in or out.   No one was at home but an old Lapland woman, who was frying fish over an oil lamp.   The Reindeer told Gerda's whole story, but first it related its own, for that seemed to the Reindeer by far the more important of the two.   Gerda was so overcome by the cold that she could not talk.

"Oh, you poor things," said the Lapland woman, "you still have a long way to run!   You must journey more than a hundred miles to Finland, for there the Snow Queen resides in her country home and burns blue lights every evening.   I'll write a few words on a dried cod, for I have no paper, and I'll give it to you to take to the Finland woman; she can give you better information than I."

So when Gerda had been warmed, and refreshed with food and drink, the Lapland woman wrote a few words on a dried codfish, and, telling Gerda to take good care of it, tied her again on the Reindeer, and away they went. "Choo! choo!" sounded above them in the air; and all night long the beautiful blue Northern Lights kept burning.

And then they came to Finland, and knocked at the chimney of the Finland woman, for she had not even a door.

There was such a heat within that the Finland woman herself went about almost naked. She was very small and dirty. She at once loosened little Gerda's dress and took off the child's mittens and boots, for otherwise the heat would have been too great for her to bear. Then she laid a piece of ice on the Reindeer's head, and read what was written on the codfish. When she had read it three times, she knew it by heart, and then she popped the fish into the kettle, for it was eatable, and she never wasted anything.

Now the Reindeer told first his own story, and then little Gerda's; and the Finland woman blinked with her wise-looking eyes, but said nothing.

"You are very wise," said the Reindeer. "I know you can tie all the winds of the world together with a bit of thread; if the sailor unties one knot, he has a good wind; if he loosens the second, it blows hard; and if he unties the third and fourth, there comes such a tempest that the forests cannot stand against it. Won't you give the little girl a potion, so that she may get twelve men's strength and overcome the Snow Queen?"

"Twelve men's strength!" repeated the Finland woman. "Much good that would be!"

And she went to a cupboard and brought out a great roll of skin, and spread it out. Wonderful characters were written upon it, and the Finland woman read until the perspiration dripped from her forehead.

But the Reindeer again begged so hard for little Gerda, and Gerda looked at the Finland woman with such beseeching, tear-filled eyes that she began to blink again. Then she drew the Reindeer into a corner, and whispered to it, while she laid fresh ice upon its head.

"It is true that little Kay is as the Snow Queen's, and finds everything there to his taste. He thinks it is the best place in the world; but that is because he has a splinter of glass in his heart, and a little fragment in his eye. These must first be removed or he will never be a human being again, and the Snow Queen will keep him in her power."

"But can't you give something to little Gerda, to enable her to have power over it all?"

"I can give her no greater power than she already possesses. Don't you see how great that is? Don't you see how men and animals are obliged to serve her, and how well she gets on in the world, barefooted? She must not be told of her power by us; that power is in her own heart and consists in this, that she is a dear, innocent child. If she herself cannot penetrate to the Snow Queen and remove the glass from little Kay's heart, we can be of no use! Two miles from here the Snow Queen's garden begins; thither you can carry the little girl. Set her down in the snow by the great bush with the red berries, and don't stand gossiping, but make haste to come back here!"

Then the Finland woman lifted little Gerda on to the Reindeer, which ran as fast as it could.

"Oh, I did n't get my boots! I did n't get my mittens!" cried Gerda.

In the piercing cold she soon had noticed their absence; but the Reindeer did not dare stop; it ran till it came to the bush with the red berries; there it set Gerda down, kissed her on the mouth, great shining tears running down over its cheeks; then back again it ran as fast as it could go. Poor Gerda stood where the Reindeer had left her, without shoes, without gloves, in the midst of terrible, icy Finland.

She ran forward as fast as she could and then came a whole regiment of snowflakes. But they did not fall from the sky, for the sky was quite clear and shone with the Northern Lights; the snowflakes ran right along the ground, and the nearer they came the larger they grew. Gerda remembered how large and wonderful the snowflakes had appeared when she had looked at them through the magnifying glass. But here they were larger. Moreover, they were terrible, for they were alive. They were the Snow Queen's outposts, and they had the strangest shapes. Some looked like great ugly porcupines; others like tangled snakes, which stretched their heads toward her; and others, still, like little fat bears, whose hair stood on end. All were brilliantly white; all were living snowflakes.

Then little Gerda said the Lord's Prayer. The cold was so severe that as she spoke the words of the prayer she could see her own breath, which came out of her mouth like smoke. Her breath became thicker and thicker, and the cloud formed itself into little bright angels, which grew and grew when they touched the earth. And all had helmets on their heads and shields and spears in their hands; their number increased, until when Gerda had finished her prayer a whole legion stood about her. They struck with their spears at the terrible snowflakes, shattering them in a thousand pieces; and little Gerda could then go ahead safely and happily. The angels patted her hands and feet, making her feel less cold, and she walked quickly forward toward the Snow Queen's palace.

But now we must see what Kay has been doing. He certainly was not thinking of little Gerda, and least of all that she was standing in front of the palace.

THE SEVENTH STORY

What Took Place in the Snow Queen's Castle, and What Afterwards Happened There

The walls of the palace were formed of the drifting snow, and the windows and doors of the piercing winds. There were more than a hundred halls, all blown together by the snow; the greatest of these extended many miles. The strong Northern Lights illumined them all, and how great and empty, how icily cold and shining they all were! Never was merriment there, not even a little bear's ball, at which the storm could have played the music while the polar bears walked about on their hind legs and displayed their good manners; never any little games of "The biter bit" or "Last tag"; never any whispered gossip over the coffee cups by the young lady white foxes. Empty, vast, and cold were the halls of the Snow Queen. The Northern Lights flamed up with such regularity that one knew exactly when they would be at the highest and when at the lowest. In the midst of this immense empty snow hall was a frozen lake whose surface had cracked in a thousand pieces; but each piece was so like the rest that it formed a perfect pattern. In the middle of the lake, when she was at home, sat the Snow Queen, and she then said that she sat on the Mirror of Reason, and that this was the only one, and the best in the world.

Little Kay was blue with cold — indeed, almost black! but he did not feel it, for, you know, the Snow Queen had kissed away the icy shiverings from him, and his heart was nothing but a lump of ice. He was engaged in dragging about a few sharp, flat pieces of ice, fitting them together in all possible ways, for he wanted to achieve something with them. It was just as when we play with little tablets of wood, and fit them together to form figures — what we call a Chinese puzzle. Kay also made figures, and, very artistic ones, indeed. They formed the icy puzzles of Reason. To him these figures were very remarkable and of the highest importance; that was because of the fragment of the evil glass mirror sticking in his eye. He planned out the figures to form words — but he could never manage to form the word he wished — the word "Eternity." And the Snow Queen had said:

"If you can find out this figure, you shall be your own master, and I will give you the whole world and a new pair of skates."

But he could not.

"Now I'll hasten away to the warm lands," said the Snow Queen. "I want to go and take a look down into the black kettles." These were the volcanoes, Etna and Vesuvius, as they are called. "I shall whiten them a little! That's necessary, it is good for the grapes and olives in the valleys."

And away flew the Snow Queen, leaving Kay sitting quite alone in the vast icy hall, looking at his pieces of ice, and thinking so deeply that something cracked inside of him, and one would have thought to hear it that he was frozen.

It was just then that little Gerda stepped through the great gate into the palace. Piercing winds blew, but she breathed an evening prayer, and the winds lay down as if lulled to sleep.

She stepped into the great cold, empty halls. Then she saw Kay; she ran to him and threw her arms about him and held him tight, crying, "Kay, dear little Kay! At last I have found you!"

But he sat very still, stiff, and cold. Then little Gerda wept hot tears, that fell upon his breast; they penetrated to his heart, thawed the lump of ice, and consumed the little piece of glass in it. He looked at her, and she sang the old song:

Where roses blow in the flowery vale,
There we the child Jesus shall hail.

Then Kay burst into tears; he wept so that the splinter of glass came out of his eye. He recognized Gerda and cried joyously:

"Gerda, dear little Gerda! Where have you been all this time? And where have I been?" He looked all about him. "How cold it is here! How large and empty!"

He clung to Gerda and she laughed and wept for joy. Even the pieces of ice danced round with joy at their happiness; and when they were tired and stopped, they formed themselves into just the letters of the word Kay had been trying to form—the word for which the Snow Queen had promised to make Kay his own master and give him the whole world and a new pair of skates, besides.

Gerda kissed his cheeks, and they became rosy; she kissed his eyes, and they shone like her own; she kissed his hands and feet and he became strong and well. The Snow Queen might now come; his letter of release stood written in shining characters of ice.

They took each other by the hand, and wandered forth from the great palace. They talked about the grandmother and the roses on the roof; wherever they went the winds were stilled and the sun burst forth. And when they came to the bush with the red berries, the Reindeer stood waiting; it had brought another young Reindeer, which gave the children warm milk, and kissed them on the mouth. Then the two carried Kay and Gerda away, first to the Finland woman, where they warmed themselves thoroughly, and received instructions for their journey, and then to the Lapland woman, who had made new clothes for them and had her sled ready to take them home.

Both the Reindeer ran along beside them, accompanying them as far as the boundary of the country. There the first green leaves peeped forth, and there they said good-by to the two Reindeer and the Lapland woman. "Farewell!" they all said.

Now the first little birds began to twitter, the forest was decked with green buds, and out of it, on a beautiful horse (which Gerda knew, for it was the same that had drawn her golden coach), came riding a young girl, with a shining red cap on her head and a pair of pistols in her holsters. This was the little robber girl, who had grown tired of staying at home, and wished to go, first, to the north, and if that did not suit her, to some other region. She knew Gerda at once, and Gerda knew her, too, and it was a joyful meeting.

"You are a fine fellow to gad about!" she said to little Kay. "I should like to know if you deserve to have anyone running to the end of the world for your sake!"

But Gerda patted her cheeks, and asked after the Prince and Princess.

"They've gone to foreign countries," said the robber girl.

"But the Crow?" asked Gerda.

"The Crow is dead," she answered. "The tame sweetheart is now a widow, and goes about with a piece of black woolen thread around her leg. She complains most lamentably, but it's all nonsense. And now tell me how you have fared, and how you got hold of him."

And Gerda and Kay told their story.

"Snipp-snapp-snurre-purre-basellurre!" cried the robber girl. She took them both by the hand, and promised that if she ever came through their town, she would pay them a visit. And then she rode away into the wide world. But Gerda and Kay walked hand in hand, and wherever they went it was beautiful spring with foliage and flowers. The church bells rang, and they recognized the high steeples in the great city where they lived. They entered the city and went to the door of the grandmother's house, up the stairs, and into her room, where everything stood in its usual place. The big clock said "Tick! tack!" and the hands were turning; but as Kay and Gerda entered the room they noticed that they had become grown-up people. The roses out on the roof-gutter were nodding in at the open window, and there stood the children's chairs. Kay and Gerda sat down on their little chairs, and held each other by the hand. The cold, empty splendor at the Snow Queen's had passed from their memory like a bad dream. Grandmother was sitting in God's bright sunshine, and reading aloud out of the Bible, "Except ye become as little children, ye shall not enter into the kingdom of heaven."

Kay and Gerda looked into each other's eyes, and all at once they understood the old song:

> Where roses blow in the flowery vale,
> There we the child Jesus shall hail.

There they sat, both grown up and yet children — children in heart; and it was summer—warm, delightful summer.

THE FLYING TRUNK

There was once a merchant who was so rich that he could pave the whole avenue with silver coins, and then have almost enough left for a little side street. But he did not do that. He knew how to use his money differently. When he spent a penny he got back a dollar; that was the kind of merchant he was.

The merchant died and his son got all his money; and right merrily did he live. He went to mask balls every night, made paper kites out of dollar bills, and played at ducks and drakes on the beach with gold pieces instead of pebbles. In this way the money was quickly spent. At last there was nothing left but four pennies, and no clothes to wear but a pair of slippers and an old dressing gown. The friends of the spendthrift did not care about him any more. Of course they could not be expected to walk on the street with him now. One of them, however, who was good-natured, sent him an old trunk, and told him to "Pack up!" That was all very well, of course, but there was nothing to pack up; and so he seated himself in the trunk.

It was a most peculiar trunk. So soon as any one pressed on the lock, the trunk could fly. That is what it did now and—whisk!—away it flew with him up through the chimney and high over the clouds, far, far away. The bottom of the trunk snapped as if about to break, and he was in great fear lest it go to pieces, for then he would have turned a fine somersault in the air! Goodness me!

But the trunk did not break and he arrived in the

land of the Turks. He hid the trunk in the woods under the withered leaves, and went into the town. He could do that without any trouble, for among the Turks all the people went about dressed, like himself, in dressing-gown and slippers. He met a nurse with a little child.

"Here, Turk nurse," he said, "what great castle is that close by the town, in which the windows are placed so high up?"

"That is where the Sultan's daughter lives," she replied. "A fortune-teller foretold that she would be very unhappy over a lover; and for that reason nobody may visit her, unless the Sultan and Sultana are there too."

"Thank you!" said the merchant's son. Then he went out into the woods, seated himself in his trunk, and flew up on the roof of the castle. Then he crept through the window into the room of the Princess.

She was lying asleep on the sofa and she was so beautiful that the merchant's son had to kiss her. She awoke at once and was very much frightened. But when the stranger told her that he was a Turkish deity who had come down to her through the air, she was very much pleased.

They sat down side by side, and he told her stories about her eyes. He told her they were beautiful, dusky lakes, and that her thoughts were swimming there like mermaids. And he talked to her about her forehead. It was a snowy mountain, he said, with the most splendid halls full of pictures. He told her about the stork that brings the dear little children.

Yes, those were fine stories! Then he asked the Princess if she would marry him, and she said "Yes" immediately.

"But you must come here on Saturday," said she. "On that day the Sultan and the Sultana come to take tea with me. They will be very proud that I am to marry a Turkish deity. But be sure to come with a very pretty fairy tale, for both my parents are very fond, indeed, of stories. My mother likes them high-flown and with a moral, and my father likes funny stories that make him laugh."

"Very well," said he. "I shall bring no other wedding present than a story." Thus they parted. The Princess gave him a scimitar embossed with gold pieces, and things like that were particularly useful to him.

He flew away in his trunk and bought himself a new dressing gown. After that he went into the forest and sat down to make up a story. That was not such an easy matter, for, you remember, it was to be ready by Saturday.

By the time he had finished it, Saturday had come.

When he arrived at the apartment of the Princess, the Sultan and his wife and all the Court were there drinking tea and waiting for him. He was received very graciously.

"Will you tell us a story?" said the Sultana. "One that is deep and instructive."

"Yes, but still one that we can laugh at," said the Sultan.

"Certainly," he replied; and began. And now listen very closely.

"There was once a bundle of Matches. They were extremely proud of their high descent. Their genealogical tree, that is to say, the great fir tree of which each of them was a little splinter, had been a great old tree in the forest. The Matches lay on the shelf between a Tinder Box and an old Iron Pot to whom they were talking about the days of their youth. 'Yes, when we were in the green bough,' they said, 'we really were in very pleasant circumstances. Every morning and evening we had diamond tea—that was the dew. All day we had sunshine—when the sun shone; and all the little birds told us stories. We could plainly perceive that we were rich, too, for the other trees were clothed only in summer, while our family could afford green dresses both summer and winter. But then the woodcutter came, a great revolution took place, and our family was split in pieces. The head of the family got an appointment as mainmast on a magnificent ship, which could sail round the world if it wanted to. The branches went to various places, and now here we are kindling a light for the vulgar masses. That's how we grand people came to be in the kitchen.'

"'My fate was of a different kind,' said the Iron Pot, which stood next the Matches. 'Ever since the moment I came into the world I have been scoured and boiled continually. I attend to the practical side and am really of the first importance here in this house. My only pleasure is to sit on the shelf after dinner, very clean and neat, and carry on a sensible conversation with my comrades. But, except the Water Pail which sometimes is taken down into the courtyard, we all live within doors. Our only newsbearer is the Market Basket; but he speaks in a very disquieting way about the government and the people. Why, the other day an old pot fell down from fright and broke into pieces just listening to his talk. He's a liberal, let me tell you!'

"'Now you're talking too much,' the Tinder Box interrupted, and the steel struck against the flint so that the sparks flew. 'Can we not have a pleasant evening for once?'

"'Yes, let us discuss which one of us is the most distinguished,' said the Matches.

"'No, I don't like to talk about myself," said the Earthen Pot. 'Let us get up an evening entertainment. I will start it. I will relate something that everyone has experienced; then we can easily imagine the situation and take pleasure in it. On the shore of the Baltic near the Danish beach, forests —'

"'That's a fine beginning,' cried each of the Plates. 'That will surely be a story I shall like.'

"'Yes, there I spent my youth with a quiet family, where the furniture was polished, the floors scoured, and clean curtains put up every fortnight.'

"'What an interesting way you have of telling a story!' said the Feather Duster. 'One always knows what to expect when a woman tells a story. Something clean is sure to run through it.'

"'Yes, one feels it!' said the Water Pail, and giving a little gleeful jump it came down with a smack on the floor.

"The Pot went on with her story, and the end was as good as the beginning.

"All the Plates rattled with pleasure and the Feather Duster brought some parsley out of the waste can and put it like a wreath on the Pot, for it knew that that would vex the others. 'Besides,' it thought, 'if I crown her to-day, she will crown me to-morrow.'

"'Now I'm going to dance,' said the Fire Tongs, and it hopped about. Dear me! how that implement could lift its legs in the air! The old Chair Cushion over in the corner burst with looking at it. 'May I be crowned, too?' said the Tongs; and it, too, received a wreath.

"'They're only common people, after all!' thought the Matches.

"Now the Tea-Urn was to sing; but she said she had taken cold, and could not sing unless she was boiling. But that was only affectation. She did not want to sing except when she was on the table in the parlor with the grand people.

"In the window sat an old Quill Pen with which the maid generally wrote; there was nothing remarkable about this pen except that it had been dipped too deep into the ink. But it was proud of that very thing. 'If the Tea-Urn won't sing,' it said, 'she doesn't have to. Outside hangs a nightingale in a cage, and he can sing. He hasn't had any education, but this evening we'll say nothing about that.'

"'I think it entirely out of place,' said the Tea-Kettle, who was the kitchen singer, and half-sister to the Tea-Urn, 'that we should listen to such a foreign bird. Do you call that patriotic? Let the Market Basket decide!'

"'I am vexed,' said the Market Basket. 'No one can imagine how terribly vexed I am. Is this a proper way to spend the evening? Would it not be more fitting to put the house in order, each one to take his proper place? I would arrange the whole affair. That would be the thing.'

"'Yes, let us make a disturbance,' they all cried. Just then the door opened and the maid came in. Then they all stood still and no one made a sound. But there was not one pot among them that did not know how much it could do, and how distinguished it was. 'Yes, if I had liked,' each one thought, 'it might have been a very merry evening.'

"The servant girl took the Matches and struck fire with them. Mercy! how they sputtered and burst into flame! 'Now everyone can certainly see,' thought they, 'that we are first in importance. How we shine! what a light!' And then they burned out."

"That was a capital story," said the Sultana. "I feel myself quite carried away to the kitchen and to the Matches. Yes, now you shall have our daughter."

"Yes, indeed," said the Sultan, "you shall marry our daughter on Monday."

And they treated him as one of the family.

The day of the wedding was fixed and on the evening before, the whole city was illuminated. Biscuits and doughnuts were thrown into the crowds for the people to scramble for; the street boys stood on their toes and shouted "Hurrah!" They whistled on their fingers. It was all very splendid.

"I shall have to do something, too!" thought the merchant's son. So he bought rockets and fire-crackers and every kind of fireworks you could imagine, put them all into his trunk, and flew up into the air.

Whizz! how they sputtered and flared, and how they popped! All the Turks hopped in the air and their slippers flew about their ears; such a sight they had never witnessed before. Now they could see for themselves that it was a real Turkish deity who was to marry the Princess.

As soon as the merchant's son landed in the woods again with his trunk he decided to go into the city to hear what an impression he had made. It was quite natural that he should want to do this.

But what stories people do tell! Everyone whom he asked about it had seen it in a different way; but one and all thought it fine.

"I saw the Turkish deity himself," said one. "He had eyes like glowing stars, and a beard like foaming water."

"He flew in a fiery mantle," said another. "The loveliest little cherubs peeped forth from among the folds."

They were certainly pleasant things that he heard. On the following day he was to be married.

He went back to the forest to seat himself in his trunk. But what had become of it? A spark from the fireworks had set fire to it, and the trunk had burned to ashes. He could not fly any more, and could not go to his bride.

She stood all day on the roof waiting—and she is waiting there still, while he wanders through the world telling fairy tales. But the stories are no longer merry, like the one he told about the Matches.

THE FELLOW TRAVELER

Poor John was heartbroken, for his father was very ill and could not live. Besides these two there was no one in the little room where the father lay. The lamp on the table was almost burned out, and it was very late.

"You have been a good son, John," said the sick man. "I am sure the good Lord will help you on in the world!" Then he gazed at him with calm, gentle eyes, drew a deep breath, and died. It seemed as if he had fallen asleep; but John wept, for now he had no one in the whole world, neither father nor mother, sister nor brother. Poor John! He knelt by the bedside, kissed his dead father's hand, and wept long and bitterly. But at last his eyes closed and he slept, his head against the hard bedpost.

Then he dreamed a strange dream. He saw the sun and moon bow before him, and he saw his father strong and well again. He heard him laugh as he always used to laugh when he was very much pleased. A lovely girl with a golden crown on her long, beautiful hair held out her hand to John, and his father said, "See the bride you have won! She is the most beautiful in the whole wide world." Then John woke up. All the beauty was gone. His father lay dead and cold on the bed. Not a person was there with them. Poor John!

The following week the dead man was buried. John walked close behind the coffin. No more was he to see his good, kind father, who had loved him so much. He heard the earth fall on the coffin. Now he could see only a small corner of it, and with the next shovelful of earth that too was covered. Then it seemed to John as if his heart would burst with sorrow. Those standing around the grave sang a psalm, and it sounded so beautiful that tears filled John's eyes. He wept, and his tears eased his sorrow. The sun shone brightly on the green trees as if to say: "Do not be so sad, John! Can you not see how beautifully blue the sky is? Your father is up yonder, praying to God that you may always prosper!"

"I will always be good," said John; "for then I shall go to heaven to my father. What happiness it will be to see one another again! How much there will be to tell him! And he will show me so many things, and teach me so much of the joy and beauty of heaven, just as he used to teach me here on earth. Oh, what happiness it will be!"

John saw it all so clearly in his thoughts that he smiled, though the tears still ran down his cheeks. The little birds up in the chestnut trees twittered and sang; they were very happy, although they were at a funeral. But they knew that the dead man was now in heaven, and had wings far larger and more beautiful than their own; they knew that he was happy there because he had been good while on earth, and that is why they were glad. John watched them fly away from the green trees far out into the world, and then he too felt a longing to fly far away. But first he made a large wooden cross to put on his father's grave. When he brought it there in the evening he found the grave decorated with sand and flowers. Strangers had done this, for they had all been very fond of the dear, kind father who now was dead.

Early next morning John packed his little bundle and

put his whole inheritance into his belt for safe keeping. There were fifty dollars and a few silver coins, and with these he was about to set out into the world. But first he went to the churchyard to his father's grave, and there he said the Lord's Prayer.

"Farewell, dear father!" he said at last. "I will always be good, and then you may safely pray to God for my welfare!"

Out in the field through which John walked the flowers bloomed fresh and beautiful in the warm sunshine. They nodded in the wind as if to say, "Welcome to the fields and meadows! Is it not delightful here?" But John turned round once more to look at the old church where he as a child had been christened and where he had gone every Sunday with his old father and had sung his psalms. Then, far up in one of the openings in the church tower, he saw the little church-tower elf, standing, with his little red pointed cap on his head, shading his face with his arm to keep the glare of the sun from his eyes.

John nodded good-by to him, and the little elf swung his red cap, laid his hand on his heart, and kissed his fingers many times to show that he wished him happiness and a pleasant journey.

John thought of the many beautiful things he would see in the great splendid world, and walked on and on, farther than he had ever gone before. He did not know the towns through which he passed, or the people whom he met. He was far away, among strangers.

The first night he had to lie down to sleep in a haystack out in the field, for he had no other bed. But it was a very lovely bed, he thought; a king could not have had a nicer. The whole field, the river, the hay-stack, and over all the blue sky, really made a beautiful bedroom. The green grass sprinkled with small red and white flowers was the carpet, and the elders and the wild-rose bushes were bouquets of flowers. John had the whole river to bathe in, with its clear fresh water, where the reeds nodded, bidding him both good evening and good morning. The moon was a great night lamp, hanging high aloft under the blue ceiling; and there was no danger of its setting fire to the curtains. John could sleep quite peacefully, and so he did. He did not awaken until the sun rose. Then all the little birds sang, "Good morning! Good morning! Are you not up yet?"

It was Sunday, and the bells rang for church. People were on their way to listen to the parson's sermon, and John went with them. He sang a psalm and heard a prayer, and felt as if he were in his own church, where he had been christened and had sung psalms with his father.

In the churchyard were many graves, and some of them were overgrown with high grasses. Then as John thought of his father's grave, which might get to look like these now that he was not there to weed it and keep it in order, he set to work pulling up the grasses and raising the wooden crosses that had fallen. The wreaths, which the wind had blown away, he laid back in place on the graves, while he thought, "Perhaps some one will do the same for my father's grave now that I cannot do it!"

Outside the gate of the churchyard stood an old beggar, leaning on a crutch. John gave him the few silver coins he had, and then walked on, happy and contented, into the wide world.

Toward evening a bad storm came up, and John hurried on to find shelter; but darkness soon fell. Then at last he reached a little church standing all alone on top of a hill. Luckily, the door was ajar, and John slipped inside. There he would stay till the storm was over.

"I will sit here somewhere in a corner," he said. "I am very tired and need a little rest." He sat down, folded his hands, and said his evening prayer, and before he knew it he was fast asleep and dreaming, while the lightning flashed and the thunder rolled outside.

When he awoke it was the middle of the night, but the storm had passed and the moon was shining in through the windows. In the center of the floor stood an open coffin in which a dead man lay, waiting for burial. John was not the least bit afraid, for he had a good conscience, and he knew that the dead harm no one; it is the living, evil people who are to be feared. And two such wicked persons whose purpose was to harm the dead man were standing close beside the coffin. They would not let him lie in peace in his coffin, but intended to throw him outside the church door. The poor, dead man!

"Why do you want to do that?" asked John. "It is bad and wicked. In Heaven's name, let him rest!"

"Oh, nonsense!" said the two evil men. "He has cheated us! He owes us money! He could not pay, and now he is dead in the bargain. We shall never get a penny back, so we want revenge. He shall lie like a dog outside the church door!"

"I have only fifty dollars," said John. "That is my whole inheritance, but I will gladly give it to you if you will promise me faithfully to leave this poor dead man in peace. I can manage very well without the money. I am strong and healthy, and our Lord will always help me."

"Very well," said the evil men, "if you will pay his debts like that we certainly will not do him any harm, you may be sure!" Then they took the money that John gave them, laughing loudly at his good nature, and went away. But John laid the body straight again, folded its hands, said good-by, and then went on through the great forest, quite content.

Round about him, wherever the moon could shine through between the trees, he saw the pretty little elves playing merrily. They were not disturbed in their play, for they knew that John was a good, innocent person, and it is only the wicked people who are never allowed to see the elves. Some of them were no taller than a finger. Their long yellow hair was fastened with golden combs, and two by two they rocked on the great dewdrops that lay on the leaves and on the tall grass. Sometimes the dewdrop rolled away, and then the elves fell down between the grass blades; then there was much laughter and merriment among the other little folk. It was great fun! They sang, and John recognized distinctly all the pretty songs he had learned when a little boy. Great colored spiders wearing silver crowns on their heads spun long suspension bridges from bush to bush, and made palaces which looked like shining glass when the dew lay on them in the bright moonlight. Thus the time passed merrily until the sun rose. Then the little elves crept into the flower buds, and the wind seized their bridges and palaces, which floated away in the air as great cobwebs.

John was emerging from the forest when a loud voice

called behind him, "Hello, comrade! Whither away?"

"Out into the wide world, " said John. "I have neither father nor mother. I am a poor lad, but I know the Lord will help me!"

"I am going out into the wide world, too," said the stranger. "Shall we keep each other company?"

"By all means!" said John.

So they walked on together. They soon grew to like each other very much, for they were both good men. But John soon perceived that the stranger was much wiser than he, for he had traveled in almost every part of the world and could talk intelligently about anything, no matter what it might be.

The sun was already high when they sat down together under a large tree to eat their breakfast. Just then an old woman came up, leaning on a crutch. On her back she carried a bundle of sticks that she had gathered in the forest. Her apron was fastened up, and John could see the ends of three large bundles of fern and willow switches that she carried in it. When she was close to John and his companion her foot slipped and she fell with a loud shriek; for the poor old woman had broken her leg.

John would have carried her to her home at once, but the stranger opened his knapsack and took out a jar, saying that it contained an ointment which would make her leg well and strong immediately, so that she would be able to walk home by herself and as firmly and well as if she had never broken her leg. But in return he wanted her to give him the three bundles of switches she had in her apron.

"That would be paying well!" said the old woman,

nodding her head strangely. She did not like to part
with her switches, but neither was it pleasant to lie
there with a broken leg. So she gave him the switches,
and as soon as he had rubbed on the ointment the old
woman got up and walked much better than she had
been able to walk before. And it was all the work of
that ointment. Such ointment was not to be had at
any druggist's!

"What do you want those switches for?" asked John.

"They will make fine brooms," said the stranger;
"and they are just what I like, for I am such a queer
sort of fellow!"

Then they walked on a considerable distance.

"Just look at the storm coming up!" said John,
pointing straight ahead. "Those are terribly heavy
clouds!"

"Oh, no," said the Fellow Traveler, "those are not
clouds. They are mountains, the great beautiful mountains, where you can climb high up above the clouds
into the fresh air! It is certainly glorious to be up
there! To-morrow we shall have gone that far on our
way into the wide world!"

But they were not so near as they had seemed to be.
The companions traveled for a whole day before they
reached the mountains, where the dark forests grew right
up to the sky and where were great bowlders as large as
cities. It was going to be a very difficult matter to reach
the other side, so John and his companion went into an
inn to rest and gather strength for the journey next day.

Many people were gathered in the large taproom at
the inn, for there was a man with a puppet show. He
had just set up his little theater, and the people were

seated before it to see the play. Farthest up toward the stage, in the best seat, sat a fat old butcher. His bulldog sat by his side and, ugh! how ferocious that dog was! It sat staring just as hard as all the others did.

Now the play began. It was really a pretty play, with a king and a queen in it sitting on the most beautiful of thrones and wearing golden crowns and long trains,— for they could well afford it. The prettiest of wooden dolls, with glass eyes and long goatees, stood at the doors, opening and closing them to let fresh air into the room. It was really a very pretty play, and not at all tragic. But just as the queen arose and walked across the floor, then—Heaven knows what the bulldog thought, but as the butcher was not holding him he made one leap right into the theater, seized the queen about the waist, and snap! the doll's head broke off! It was quite terrible!

The poor man who conducted the play was frightened, and very downhearted because of his queen, for she was the very prettiest of his dolls; and now the wicked bulldog had broken her head off.

But when the people had gone away, John's Fellow Traveler said that he could mend her. He brought out his jar, and rubbed the doll with some of the same ointment that had cured the old woman when she had broken her leg. As soon as the doll had been rubbed with the ointment it immediately became whole again; nay, more, it could even move all its limbs by itself, and it was not at all necessary to pull the strings. The doll was like a living person except that it could not talk. The owner of the puppet show was delighted. Now it was not at all necessary to hold this doll, for it could dance by itself. None of the others could do that.

Later on, after nightfall, when all the people at the inn had gone to bed, some one sighed very deeply indeed, and kept it up so long that everybody got up to see who it could be. The showman went over to his little theater, for that was where the sound came from. All the wooden dolls, the king and all his knights, lay in a heap. They were sighing mournfully, and staring out of their big glass eyes. They too wanted to be rubbed with ointment like the queen, for then they also would be able to move by themselves. The queen fell on her knees and held up her beautiful crown, saying, "Take my crown, if you will, but please rub some ointment on my royal husband and my courtiers!"

At that the poor man who owned the theater and the dolls could not keep from crying, for he really felt very sorry for them. He promised the Fellow Traveler that he would give him all the money he should get for the next evening's entertainment if he would rub the ointment on four or five of his nicest dolls. But the stranger said he wanted nothing but the big sword that the showman wore at his side. As soon as it was given to him, he rubbed six of the dolls. They immediately began to dance, and that so prettily that all the girls, the real live girls who saw them, began to dance too.

The coachman danced with the cook, the waiter with the chambermaid, all the guests with each other, and the fire shovel with the fire tongs. But these last two fell over just as they took the first step. That was a merry night, indeed!

Next morning John and his Fellow Traveler left them all, and climbed up the lofty mountains through the great pine forests. They got up so high that the church towers far below them looked like little red berries down among the green. They could see far, far away for many, many miles, to places they had never been. So much of the beauty of the great glorious world John had never before seen at one time. The sun shone warm and bright in the clear blue sky. Far away among the mountains he heard the hunter's horn, and so beautiful did it sound that tears of joy filled his eyes. He could not help exclaiming: "Lord God, I worship Thee for Thy great goodness toward us, and for all the wonderful beauty in the world that Thou hast given us!"

The Fellow Traveler also folded his hands and looked out over the forests and cities in the warm sunlight. At that moment they heard a wonderfully sweet sound over their heads, and looking up they saw a great white swan hovering in the air. It was very beautiful, and it sang as they had never heard any bird sing before. But the song grew fainter and fainter, and the swan sank very slowly to the ground at their feet; and there the beautiful bird lay dead.

"Two such beautiful wings," said the Fellow Traveler, "as this bird has are very valuable. I will take them with me! Do you see now what a good thing it was that I got the sword?"

Then with one blow he struck off both the wings of the dead swan, for he meant to keep them.

They traveled many, many miles over the mountains until at last they arrived before a great city with over a hundred towers, which glittered like silver in the sunlight. In the center of the city was a splendid marble castle, thatched with red gold, and there lived the king.

John and his Fellow Traveler did not want to enter

the town at once. They stayed at an inn outside the walls to dress in their best, for they wished to make a good appearance when they walked through the streets. The innkeeper told them that the king was such a good man he never harmed any one. But his daughter — Heaven preserve us! — was a wicked princess. Of beauty she had enough to be sure; no one could be so beautiful and lovely as she was. But what was the good of that, when she was so evil a witch, and so many fine princes had lost their lives because of her? She had given anybody permission to court her. Anyone could come, were he prince or beggar; that was all the same. He only had to guess three things that she asked him. If he could do that correctly she would marry him and he should be king over all the land when her father died. But if he could not guess the three things she asked, she either had him hanged or had his head cut off. Just so bad and wicked was this beautiful princess! Her father, the old king, was much grieved by all this wickedness, but he could not prevent it, for he had once said that he would never have anything to do with the princess' suitors; she could do as she liked. Every prince who had come to guess the riddles in order to win the princess had failed, and had either been hanged or had his head cut off. But each had been warned in time, and he could have kept himself and his courting away. The old king was so heartbroken by all the sorrow and misery that he and all his soldiers prayed on their knees, for a whole day every year, that the princess might become good. But that she positively would not do. The old women, who drank brandy, dyed it black before they drank it. That was their way of mourning, and more they could not do.

"That wicked princess!" exclaimed John. "She certainly ought to be whipped; that would be the best thing for her. If only I were the old king, I would soon cure her!"

Just then they heard the people outside cheering. The princess was passing by, and she was really so beautiful that all the people forgot how wicked she was, and began to shout and cheer. Twelve beautiful maidens, all clothed in white silk with golden tulips in their hands, rode on coal-black horses behind her. The princess herself rode a snow-white horse, decorated with diamonds and rubies, and her riding habit was of pure gold. The whip which she carried in her hand looked like a beam of sunlight, and the gold crown on her head glittered like the stars of heaven. Her cloak was embroidered with thousands of beautiful butterfly wings. And yet she herself was far more beautiful than all her clothes.

When John beheld her his face grew red as fire, and he could hardly utter a single word, for this princess looked exactly like the lovely girl with the golden crown that he had dreamed about the night his father died. He thought her so beautiful that he could not help loving her very much. It could not be true, he said, that she was such an evil witch, who had people hung or beheaded when they could not guess the riddles she put to them.

"Anybody has permission to court her, even the poorest yokel. I will go to the castle myself, for I cannot do otherwise! I must go!"

They all begged him not to go, for, they said, he would only meet the same fate as all the others. His Fellow Traveler also advised him against it, but John was sure that he would get along all right. So he brushed his clothes and his shoes, washed his face and hands, combed his beautiful yellow hair, and then went quite alone into the city and up to the castle.

"Come in," said the old king when John knocked at the door. John opened it, and the old king, in his dressing gown and embroidered slippers, came to meet him. His golden crown was on his head, his scepter in one hand and his golden ball in the other.

"Wait a moment!" he said, tucking the golden ball under his arm so as to be able to shake hands with John. But when he heard that John was a suitor he began to cry so bitterly that both the ball and the scepter fell to the floor, and he had to dry his eyes with the sleeve of his dressing gown. Poor old king!

"Don't do it!" he said. "You will fail, like all the others. Just look at this!" He took John out into the princess' garden. It was a terrible sight, indeed! In every tree hung three or four princes, who had courted the princess but had not been able to guess the things she asked them. At every breeze the bones rattled so that the little birds had been frightened away and never dared come into the garden. All the flowers were staked up with human bones, and in the flower pots were grinning skulls. That was indeed a nice garden for a princess to have!

"Here you see!" said the old king. "Your fate will be just like that of all the others you see here. So please give up your intention! You will make me very unhappy if you do not, for I take it so much to heart!"

John kissed the good old king's hand, and said he thought he would succeed, for he loved the beautiful princess very much.

At that moment the princess herself came riding into the castle garden with all her ladies. John and the king went up to her and bade her good morning. She acted very pleasantly and shook hands with John, who loved her more than ever. He felt sure she could not possibly be the wicked witch everybody said she was.

They entered the castle hall, where little girls served jam and gingerbread cookies. But the old king was so unhappy that he could not eat a bit; besides, the gingerbread was too hard for his teeth.

It was now decided that John should come to the castle again on the following morning. All the judges and the council would then be assembled to hear him give his answer to the question. If he succeeded he would still have to come twice more. But no one had ever yet succeeded in guessing aright the first time, and so all had lost their lives.

John was not at all worried about himself and his probable fate. Instead, he was in very good spirits and thought only of the lovely princess. He believed sincerely that the good Lord would help him. But in what manner he had not the faintest idea, and moreover refused to think about it. He danced along the highway on his way back to the inn, where his Fellow Traveler was waiting for him.

John could not talk enough about how kind the princess had been toward him, and how beautiful she was. He was already longing for the next day, when he was to go to the castle to try his luck at guessing.

But his companion shook his head and was very sad. "I like you very much," he said. "We might have been together a long time yet, and now I am to lose you!

Poor dear John, I could really cry, but I would not spoil your joy on perhaps the last evening we are together. Let us be merry, very merry. To-morrow, when you are gone, is time enough to weep!"

All the people of the city had heard that a new suitor had come, and there was general mourning. The theater was closed; all the cake women tied black ribbons on their sugar cakes; and the king and the bishops prayed on their knees in the church. So great was the sorrow in the city, for all believed that John would have no better success than all the other suitors before him.

Along in the evening John's companion made a great bowl of punch, saying that they must be right merry and drink to the princess' health. But when John had drunk two glasses he became so sleepy that it was impossible for him to keep his eyes open, and he fell fast asleep. His companion lifted him quietly from his chair and laid him on his bed. Then, at dead of night, he took the two great wings he had struck off the dead swan, and tied them on his shoulders. In his pocket he put the largest of the bundles of switches which had been given him by the old woman who fell and broke her leg. Then he opened the window and flew out over the city, straight to the castle. There he seated himself in a corner under the window of the princess' bedroom.

The whole city was quiet. Then, as the clock struck twelve, the window opened and the princess, in a long white cloak, flew out on great black wings away over the city and out to a great mountain. But the Fellow Traveler made himself invisible and flew behind her, whipping her with his switches so hard that the blood came at every stroke. What a flight that was! The wind caught her cloak and spread it wide like a great sail, and the moon shone through it.

"How it hails! How it hails!" said the princess at every blow of the switches. And it was the best thing for her. At last she reached the mountain and knocked. There was a rumbling like thunder as the mountain opened and the princess entered. The Fellow Traveler followed after her, for no one could see him, as he was quite invisible.

They went through a great, long passage which glittered in a very strange way, for more than a thousand spiders, gleaming like fire, ran up and down the walls, then they entered a great room built of silver and gold. Flowers, red and blue, and as large as sunflowers, shone from the walls. But no one could pick those flowers, for the stems were evil, poisonous snakes, and the flowers were flames coming out of their mouths. The whole ceiling was studded with shining glowworms, and sky-blue bats that flapped their transparent wings. It was a most extraordinary sight. In the middle of the floor was a throne, held up by the skeletons of four horses, with harnesses of red, fiery spiders like those on the walls. The throne itself was of milk-white glass, and the cushions were small black mice holding one another's tails with their teeth. Over the throne was a canopy of rose-colored spiders' webs set with the prettiest little green flies, which glittered like gems. On the throne sat an old ogre, with a crown on his hideous head and a scepter in his hand. He kissed the princess on the forehead, and made her sit beside him on the gorgeous throne. Then the music began. Great black grasshoppers played on jewsharps, and the owl beat time on his stomach,

for he had no drum.   That was a queer concert.   Little
black goblins, each with a firefly on his cap, danced
around in the room.   No one could see the Fellow Traveler.   He had placed himself just behind the throne,
where he could see and hear everything that went on.

The courtiers, who now came in, looked very grand
and distinguished, but any one who had his eyes with
him could see at once how and what they really were.
They were nothing but cabbage heads stuck on the ends
of broomsticks, which the ogre had brought to life by
his witchery and dressed up in embroidered clothes.
But that did not matter, for they were used only for
ornamental purposes.

After the dancing had gone on a little while, the
princess told the ogre that a new suitor had arrived, and
asked what she had better think of for the suitor to guess
the following morning, when he was to come to the castle.

"Listen!" said the ogre.   "I'll tell you what to do!
Choose something very easy, and then he will never
guess what it is.   Think of one of your shoes.   He will
not guess that.   Then have his head chopped off, but do
not forget when you come to-morrow night to bring me
his eyes.   I want to eat them!"

The princess made a deep curtsy and said she would
not forget the eyes.   The ogre then opened the mountain
and the princess flew home again.   But the Fellow
Traveler followed her, beating her very hard with the
switches.   She complained bitterly because of the severe
hailstorm, and hurried as fast as she could through the
window into her bedroom.   But the Fellow Traveler
flew back to the inn where John still slept, took off his
wings, and lay down on the bed, too, for he was very tired.

It was very early in the morning when John awoke. The Fellow Traveler also got up and said that he had dreamed a very strange dream during the night about the princess and her shoe. He asked John, therefore, to be sure to ask whether it could be her shoe that the princess had thought of! For that was what he had heard the ogre say in the mountain. He did not tell John anything about that, however, but only begged him to ask whether she had thought of her shoe.

"I might as well ask about one thing as another," said John. "Perhaps what you dreamed may be true, for I do believe that the Lord will help me! But I will say good-by, for if I guess wrong I shall never see you again!"

So they kissed each other, and John went into the city and up to the castle. The hall was full of people. The judges sat in their armchairs, their heads resting on feather pillows, because they had so much to think about. The old king stood up, drying his eyes with a white handkerchief. Now the princess entered. She was still lovelier than she had been the day before, and greeted everybody graciously. But to John she held out her hand, saying, "Good morning, friend!"

Now the moment came for John to guess what the princess had thought of. She looked at him in a very friendly way, but when she heard him utter the word "shoe," her face turned as white as a sheet, and she trembled all over. But that did not help her any, for he had guessed correctly!

Goodness preserve us, how happy the old king was! He turned one handspring after the other on the palace floor, and everybody clapped his hands for him and for John, who had guessed right the first time.

The Fellow Traveler also was very glad when he found out how happily things had turned out. But John folded his hands and thanked God, who surely would help him the next two times also. The very next day was fixed for his second trial at guessing.

That evening was passed in the same way as the previous evening. While John slept, his companion flew after the princess to the mountain, beating her even more severely than the first time, for this time he had taken two bundles of switches with him.

No one saw him, and he heard everything. The princess was to think of her glove, and this he told to John as if he had dreamed it.

So John guessed correctly again, and there was great joy at the castle. The whole court threw handsprings just as they had seen the king do the first time. But the princess lay upon the sofa, and would not say a single word!

Now everything depended upon whether John could guess correctly the third time. If he did, he would win the princess and inherit the entire kingdom when the old king died; if he guessed wrong, he would lose his life and the ogre would eat his fine blue eyes.

When evening came, John went to bed early, said his prayers, and slept very peacefully and well. But the Fellow Traveler fastened the wings to his back, tied the sword at his side, and, taking all three bundles of switches in his hand, flew away to the castle.

It was pitch dark, and such a storm was raging that the tiles flew off the roofs of the houses, and the trees in the garden where the skeletons hung bent in the wind like reeds. The lightning flashed every moment and the

thunder rolled in one continuous crash that lasted all
night. Now the window opened, and the princess came
flying out.

She was as pale as death, but she laughed at the fearful
storm and thought it was not bad enough. Her white
cloak whirled and flapped in the wind like a great sail,
but the Fellow Traveler whipped her with his switches
till the blood dripped down to the ground and she could
hardly fly any farther. At last, however, she reached
the mountain.

"A storm is raging, and it is hailing," she said.
"Never have I been out in such weather."

"One can get too much of even a good thing!" said
the ogre. Then the princess told him that John had also
guessed aright the second time. If he did the same
to-morrow again, he would have won, and she could never
again come to the mountain and never work enchant-
ments as before. It made her very sad to think
about it.

"He will never guess!" said the ogre. "I will hit on
something he never has thought of! Otherwise he must
be a greater magician than I am. But now let us be
merry!"

He took the princess by both hands and danced
around with all the little goblins and fireflies in the room.
The glowing spiders ran just as merrily up and down the
walls, and it looked as if the fire flowers threw out sparks.
The owl beat his drum, the crickets piped, and the black
grasshoppers played their harps. That was a gay ball!

When they had danced as long as they wanted to it
was time for the princess to go home, for otherwise they
might have missed her at the castle. The ogre said he

would accompany her, so they could be together that much longer.

So away they flew through the storm, the Fellow Traveler beating them on the back with his switches. Never had the ogre been out in such a hailstorm! Outside the castle he said good-by to the princess, and whispered, "Think of my head!" But the Fellow Traveler heard it, and just as the princess slipped through the window into her bedroom, and the ogre turned around to go back, he seized him by his long black beard and chopped off his ugly head with his sword so quickly that the ogre himself did not even see how it happened. The body he threw into the sea to the fishes, but the head he merely dipped into the water, and, tying it up in his silk handkerchief, took it home with him to the inn. Then he went to bed.

Next morning he gave John the handkerchief, but told him not to untie it until the princess asked him what it was she had thought of.

There were so many people in the great hall of the castle that they were packed together like radishes tied in a bunch. The council sat in their chairs with their soft downy pillows, and the old king wore a new suit of clothes. His golden crown and the scepter had been polished, and everything looked splendid! But the princess was very pale, and wore a jet-black dress as though she were going to a funeral.

"What have I thought about?" she asked John. He immediately untied the handkerchief, and was himself very much frightened when he saw the ogre's ugly head. Everybody shuddered, it was such an awful thing to look at; but the princess sat as if turned to stone, and

could not utter a single word. At last she arose and
held out her hand to John, for he had guessed aright the
third time. She would look at no one, but sighed deeply
and said, "You are my master now! To-night our
wedding shall take place!"

"That is just fine!" said the old king. "That's what
I like to hear!" Everybody shouted hurrah, the royal
band played in the streets, the bells rang, and the cake
women removed the black ribbons from their sugar
cakes, for now all was rejoicing. Three oxen, roasted
whole and stuffed with ducks and chickens, were set out
in the public square, and everybody could cut a piece
for himself. The fountains ran with the finest wine
instead of water, and any one who bought a cake at the
baker's got six big buns into the bargain, and stuffed
with raisins, too.

In the evening the whole city was illuminated, the
soldiers fired cannon, and the boys shot off firecrackers
and pinwheels. Up at the castle there was eating and
drinking and toasting and dancing. All the grand
gentlemen and lovely ladies danced together, and their
voices could be heard at a great distance as they sang:

> See the merry maidens fair,
>   Gayly whirling in the dance;
> They love best a merry polka
>   And laugh to see their partners prance.
>   Dancing, prancing,
>   See the slippers fly!

But the princess was still a witch, and did not care
for John at all. The Fellow Traveler remembered this,
and he therefore gave John three feathers from the
swan's wings and a little bottle containing a few drops

of something.   Then he told him that he should have a
large tub of water placed beside the bride's bed, and,
when the princess was climbing into bed he should give
her a little push so that she would fall into the water.
Then he was to dip her under three times, first throwing
in the feathers and the drops out of the bottle.   This
would free her from the magic spell, and she would grow
to love him very much.

John did everything that his companion advised
him to do.   The princess screamed loudly as he ducked
her under the water, and then struggled in his hands in
the form of a great coal-black swan with glittering eyes.
The second time she came up out of the water the swan
had turned white, except for a single black ring around
its neck.   John prayed fervently to God, and let the
water cover the bird a third time.   At that same moment
it changed into the most beautiful princess.   She was
even lovelier than before, and she thanked John, with
tears in her beautiful eyes, for having freed her from the
enchantment.

The next morning the old king came with all his
court, and there were constant congratulations until late
in the day.   Last of all came the Fellow Traveler.   He
had his staff in his hand and his knapsack on his back.
John kissed him many times, and said that he must not
go away; he must stay with him, for he was the cause of
all his good fortune.   But the Fellow Traveler shook his
head and said, quietly and kindly, "No, now my time
is up.   I have merely paid my debt.   Do you remember
the dead man whom the wicked men wanted to mistreat?
You gave all you possessed that he might rest in peace
in his grave.   I am that dead man!"

Saying this, he was gone.

The wedding festivities lasted a whole month. John and the princess loved each other very much, and the old king lived many happy days, trotting his little grand-children on his knee and giving them his scepter to play with.

But John was king over all the land.

THE NIGHTINGALE

In China, as of course you know, the Emperor is a Chinaman, and all those he has about him are Chinamen. The events in this story happened a good many years ago, but that's just why the story should be told before it is forgotten. The Emperor's palace was the most splendid in the world; it was made wholly and entirely of fine porcelain — very costly, and so delicate and brittle that only with the greatest care could one touch it. In the garden were wonderful flowers, and to the most beautiful of these were fastened silver bells, which tinkled continuously so that none could pass by without noticing the flower. Yes, the Emperor's garden was arranged with admirable foresight, and it extended so far that the gardener himself did not know where it ended. If anyone would keep walking in it he would come to a magnificent forest of high trees with deep lakes. On one side the woods extended straight down to the sea, which was blue and deep. Great ships could sail right in under the branches. Here lived a Nightingale, which sang so beautifully that even the poor fisherman, though he had many other things to do, would lie still and listen when he went at night to draw in his nets.

"My, now beautiful that is!" he would say; then, obliged to attend to his work, he would forget the bird. But the next night when it sang again, the fisherman would listen, and once more exclaim, "My, how beautiful that is!"

From all the countries of the world came travelers

to the city of the Emperor. They admired the palace and the garden, but when they heard the Nightingale they said, "That is the best of all!" And, when they went home, the travelers told about, and the learned men wrote many books about, the city, the palace, and the garden. But they did not forget the Nightingale. They praised it above everything else. The poets wrote charming verses about the bird in the forest by the deep sea.

The books went to every part of the world and some of them reached the Emperor. He sat in his golden chair, and read, and read. Every moment he nodded his head up and down, for it pleased him to read the splendid descriptions of the city, the palace, and the garden.

"But the Nightingale is the best of all," were the words he read.

"What!" exclaimed the Emperor. "The Nightingale! Why, I don't know the Nightingale at all! Is there such a bird in my empire — in my own garden even! I've never heard of it! To think that I should have to learn such a thing from a book!"

Thereupon he called his Chamberlain. This Chamberlain was so proud and haughty that if anyone lower in rank than himself dared speak to him or ask him any question, he answered nothing but "P!"—which, of course, meant nothing.

"There is said to be a very remarkable bird here called the Nightingale," said the Emperor. "They say it is the very best thing in all my great empire. Why has nothing ever been said to me about it?"

"I have never before heard it mentioned," replied

the Chamberlain. "It has never been presented at Court."

"I command that it shall appear here this evening and sing for me!" said the Emperor. "The whole world knows what I possess, and I, myself, do not know!"

"I have never before heard it mentioned," repeated the Chamberlain. "I will make search for it. I will find it!"

But where was it to be found? The Chamberlain ran up and down all the stairs, through rooms and halls, but no one among all those he met had ever heard of the Nightingale. The Chamberlain ran back to the Emperor and said that it must be a fable invented by those who wrote books.

"Your Imperial Majesty cannot believe everything that is written. Writing is merely inventing—something that they call the black art!"

"But the book in which I read this," said the Emperor, "is sent to me by the high and mighty Emperor of Japan, and therefore it cannot be false. I will hear the Nightingale! It must be here this evening! It has my imperial favor! And if it does not come, the entire Court shall be thumped on the stomach to-night after it has had supper!"

"Tsing-pe!" said the Chamberlain; and again he ran up and down all the stairs and through all the halls and corridors; half the Court ran with him, for they did not want to be thumped on the stomach.

People far and near were asked concerning the wonderful Nightingale, which, it seemed, was known to all the world, but not to a single person at the Emperor's Court.

At last they came upon a poor little girl in the kitchen,

who said: "The Nightingale? Why yes, I know it
well. My, how gloriously it does sing! Every evening
I am allowed to carry a few scraps from the table to my
poor sick mother, who lives down by the shore. When
I am on my way back and am tired, I rest in the wood,
and then I hear the Nightingale sing! Then the tears
come into my eyes, for it is just as if my mother
kissed me!"

"Little kitchen girl," said the Chamberlain, "I will
get you a permanent place in the kitchen, with permission to see the Emperor dine, if you will but lead us to
the Nightingale, for there is a command that it appear
this evening."

Then they all went out into the wood where the Nightingale was accustomed to sing; half the Court went out.
When they were well on the way a cow began to low.

"Oh!" cried the Courtiers. "There it is! What
wonderful power in so small a creature! I have certainly
heard it before."

"No, those are the cows lowing," said the little kitchen
girl. "We are still a long way from the place."

Now the frogs began to croak in the pond.

"Glorious!" said the Chinese Court Chaplain. "Now
I hear it. The sound is like little church bells."

"No," said the little kitchen maid, "you hear frogs.
But I think we shall soon hear it."

And then the Nightingale began to sing.

"That is it!" said the little girl. "Listen, listen!—
and yonder it sits!" And she pointed to a little gray
bird up among the branches.

"Is it possible?" cried the Chamberlain. "I never
imagined it looked like that! How very simple it looks!

It must certainly have lost its color at seeing so many grand people near it."

"Little Nightingale," cried the kitchen maid quite loudly, "our gracious Emperor wishes so much to have you sing for him."

"With the greatest pleasure!" said the Nightingale, and began to sing gloriously.

"It sounds like crystal bells!" said the Chamberlain. "And look at its little throat, how it's working! It is remarkable that we should never have heard it before. It will be a great success at Court."

"Shall I sing once more for the Emperor?" inquired the Nightingale, thinking that the Emperor was present.

"My excellent little Nightingale," said the Chamberlain, "I have the great pleasure to invite you to a Court festival this evening, where you can charm his Imperial Highness with your lovely song."

"My song sounds best in the green wood," said the Nightingale; still, it went gladly when it heard that such was the Emperor's wish.

The palace was festively adorned. The walls and the floors, which were of porcelain, gleamed in the rays of thousands of golden lamps. The most exquisite flowers — those which tinkled merrily — had been placed in the corridors. There was much running to and fro; and a strong draft which caused the bells to ring so loudly that one could hardly hear one's self talk.

In the midst of the great hall where the Emperor sat, a golden perch had been placed. On this the Nightingale was to stand. The whole Court was there, and the little kitchen maid had permission to stand behind the door, for she had received the title of Court Cook. All

were in full regalia, and everyone looked at the little
gray bird, to which the Emperor nodded.

Then the Nightingale sang, and so enchantingly that
the tears came into the Emperor's eyes and ran down
over his cheeks. The Nightingale sang a second time,
and still more sweetly, and the song went straight to the
heart. The Emperor was so well pleased that he said
the Nightingale should have his golden slipper to wear
around its neck. But the Nightingale thanked him and
said that it had already received sufficient reward.

"I have seen tears in the Emperor's eyes — that is
rich compensation. An Emperor's tears have a peculiar
power. I am rewarded enough!" And again its throat
trembled and there was a glorious burst of song.

"That is the sweetest coquetry I ever saw!" said
the ladies who stood round, and then they held water
in their mouths so as to gurgle when anyone spoke to
them, thinking that by these means they could equal
the Nightingale. The lackeys and ladies-in-waiting
expressed themselves as perfectly satisfied; and that
meant a great deal, for they of all people are the most
difficult to please.

In short, the Nightingale achieved a great success.
It was now to remain at Court, to have its own cage,
with liberty to take a promenade twice a day and once
each night. Twelve servants accompanied the Nightingale when it went out. Each of them had a silken
string, one end of which was fastened to the bird's leg;
to these they held very tight. There was no pleasure
at all in such an outing.

The whole city talked about the wonderful bird, and
whenever two people met, one of them said nothing

but "Nightin —" and the other finished with "gale!"
and then they both sighed, in complete understanding.
Eleven grocers' children were named after the bird,
but not one of them could sing a note.

One day the Emperor received a large parcel, on
which was written, "Nightingale."

"Here we have a new book about our celebrated bird,"
said the Emperor. But it was not a book. It was a
little work of art lying in a rich casket — an artificial
Nightingale. It was intended to resemble the real one;
but it was brilliantly set with diamonds, rubies, and
sapphires. When the artificial bird was wound up, it
could sing one of the songs that the live bird sang, and
could move its tail up and down. It shone with silver
and gold. Round its neck hung a little ribbon, and on
that was written: "The Emperor of Japan's Nightingale is poor compared to that of the Emperor of China."

"That is splendid!" said all, and he who had
brought the artificial bird immediately received the
title, Imperial-Head-Nightingale-Bringer.

"Now they must sing together; what a duet that
will be!"

And so the birds had to sing together; but it did not
sound very well, for the real Nightingale sang in its own
way, and the artificial bird sang in waltz time.

"It is not to blame," said the concert master; "it
sings in perfect time and quite according to my method."

Then the artificial bird had to sing alone and made
just as great a success as the real one. Moreover, it
was much prettier to look at, glittering like bracelets
and breastpins.

Three and thirty times over did it sing the same piece,

and yet was not tired. The people would gladly have
heard it over again from the beginning, but the Emperor
said that he thought the living Nightingale, too, ought
to sing a little. But where was it? No one had noticed
that it had flown away out of the open window, back
to its green, leafy woods.

"But what is the meaning of this?" said the Emperor, and all the Courtiers scolded, and declared that
the Nightingale was a most ungrateful creature.

"Nevertheless," they said, "we still have the better
bird."

And so the artificial bird had to sing again. This
was the thirty-fourth time that they had listened to the
same piece. They did not yet quite know it by heart,
for it was so very difficult. The concert master praised
the bird extravagantly. He declared that it was better
than the real Nightingale, not only in the matter of its
plumage and the many beautiful diamonds, but of the
works as well.

"For you see, ladies and gentlemen, and above all,
your Imperial Majesty, with a real Nightingale one can
never calculate what is coming, but in this artificial bird
everything is certain. One can explain it; one can open
it and make people understand where the waltzes come
from, how they go, and how one note follows another."

"Those are my own ideas, exactly," everyone said.

And the concert master received permission to show
the bird to the people on the next Sunday. They were
also to hear it sing, for so the Emperor had commanded.
And they did hear it, and were as well pleased as if they
had all drunk themselves merry on tea—that is the
Chinese fashion. They all said, "Oh!" and held up

their forefingers and nodded. But the poor fisherman, who had heard the real Nightingale, said:

"It sounds pretty enough, and the melodies resemble each other, but there's something lacking, though I don't know what!"

The real Nightingale was banished from the empire. The artificial bird had its place on a silken cushion close by the Emperor's bed. All the presents it had received— gold and precious stones—were ranged about it, and in title it had advanced to be the High Imperial After-Dinner Singer, and in rank to Number One on the left hand; for the Emperor considered that side the most exalted which was nearest his heart—and the heart is on the left side, even in an Emperor. The concert master wrote a work of five and twenty volumes about the artificial bird. It was very learned and full of the most difficult Chinese words. Therefore, all the people declared that they had read it and understood it. Otherwise they would have been considered stupid, and would have been thumped on the stomach.

A whole year went by. The Emperor, the Court, and all the other Chinese knew every little twitter in the artificial bird's song by heart. But just for that reason it pleased them most, for they could join in the song with it; and this they always did. The street boys sang, "Tsi-tsi-tsi-glug-glug-glug!" and the Emperor himself sang it! Yes, that was certainly splendid.

But one evening when the artificial bird was singing its best, and the Emperor lay in bed listening to it, something inside the bird said, "Zip!" Something snapped. "Whirr-r!" All the wheels ran round, and then the music stopped.

The Emperor immediately sprang out of bed and sent for his body physician; but what could the doctor do? Then they sent for the watchmaker, and after much talking and investigation, he got the bird put into something like order; but he said that it must be carefully treated, and used as little as possible, for the works were worn, and it would be impossible to put in new ones in such a manner that the music would be correct. There was great lamentation! Only once a year was the bird to be permitted to sing, and even that was almost too much! But then the concert master made a little speech, full of difficult words, and said that it was just as good as before, and then, of course, it was as good as before.

Five years went by, and then a great grief came to the whole nation. The Chinese were really fond of their Emperor, and now he was ill and could not, it was said, live much longer. Already a new Emperor had been chosen. The people stood in the street outside the palace and asked the Chamberlain how their Emperor was getting on.

"P!" said he, and shook his head.

Cold and pale lay the Emperor in his great, magnificent bed; the whole Court thought him dead, and every one of them ran to pay homage to the new Emperor. The pages ran out to talk it over, and the ladies' maids had a great coffee party. Everywhere, in all the rooms and corridors, cloth had been laid down so that no footstep should be heard; and so it was very, very quiet there.

But the Emperor was not yet dead. Stiff and pale he lay on the gorgeous bed with the long velvet curtains and the heavy gold tassels; high up a window stood open, and the moon shone in upon the Emperor and the artificial Nightingale.

The poor Emperor could scarcely breathe; it was just as if something weighed heavily upon his chest. He opened his eyes, and then he saw that it was Death that sat on his breast. He had put on the Emperor's golden crown, and in one hand he held the Emperor's sword, and in the other, his beautiful banner. All around, from among the folds of the splendid velvet curtains, strange heads peered, some evil and repulsive, others beautiful and kindly. These were all the Emperor's bad and good deeds, that stood before him now when Death sat upon his breast.

"Do you remember this?" whispered one. "Do you remember that?" said another, and they told him of so many things that the perspiration stood out on his forehead.

"I never knew that!" said the Emperor. "Give me music! music! Sound the great Chinese drums," he cried, "so that I may not hear all that they are saying!"

But they continued speaking, and Death nodded like a Chinaman to all that was said.

"Music! music!" cried the Emperor. "You little precious golden bird, sing, sing! I have given you gold and costly presents; I have even hung my golden slipper round your neck. Oh, sing now, sing!"

But the bird remained silent; no one was there to wind it up, and so it could not sing. But Death continued to stare at the Emperor with his great empty eye sockets, and it was fearfully quiet.

Then there suddenly sounded, close by the window,

a lovely song. Outside on a branch sat the little live Nightingale. It had heard of the Emperor's plight and had come to sing to him of comfort and hope. As it sang the specters grew paler and paler and the blood ran quicker and quicker through the Emperor's weak body. Death himself listened, and said:

"Keep on, little Nightingale, keep on!"

"Then will you give me the splendid golden sword? Will you give me the rich banner? Will you give me the Emperor's crown?"

And Death gave up all these treasures for song. The Nightingale sang on and on; it sang of the quiet churchyard where the white roses grow, where the elder blossoms fill the air with fragrance, and the fresh grass is watered by the tears of those whom the dead leave behind. Then Death felt a longing to return to his quiet garden, and like a cold white mist floated out at the window.

"Thanks! thanks!" said the Emperor. "You heavenly little bird; I know you well! I banished you from my empire, and yet you have come back and with your song driven away the evil visions from my bed, and drawn Death from my heart! How can I reward you?"

"You have rewarded me!" replied the Nightingale. "Tears came to your eyes when I sang to you for the first time — I shall never forget. Such are the jewels that delight a singer's heart. But sleep now, and rest. You will be strong again. I shall sing to you."

It sang, and the Emperor fell into a peaceful sleep. Ah! how invigorating that sleep was! The sun shone upon him through the windows when he awoke, refreshed and restored; not one of his servants had yet returned, for they all thought he was dead. But the Nightingale still sat beside him, singing.

"You must stay with me always," said the Emperor. "You shall sing only when you please and I'll break the artificial bird into a thousand pieces."

"Do not do that," replied the Nightingale. "It did as well as it could; keep it as you have always done. I cannot build my nest in the palace or dwell in it. But let me come when I please; and in the evening I will sit on the bough yonder by the window, and sing for you; then you will be both glad and thoughtful. I will sing of those who are happy and of those who suffer. I will sing of the good and the evil that lie hidden round about you. The little songbird flies far, to the poor fisherman, to the peasant's roof, to all who dwell far away from you and from your Court. I love your heart more than your crown, and yet there is an air of sanctity about the crown, too. I will come and I will sing to you — but one thing you must promise me."

"Everything!" said the Emperor; and he stood there in his imperial robes, which he had himself put on, and held to his heart the sword which was heavy with gold.

"One thing I ask of you. Never say that you have a little bird that tells you everything. It will be better so."

And the Nightingale flew away.

Then the servants came in to see their dead Emperor, and — there they remained standing.

"Good morning," said the Emperor.

THE BEETLE

The emperor's horse was being shod with golden shoes — a gold shoe on each foot.

Why was he to have golden shoes?

He was the loveliest creature, with fine slender legs, intelligent eyes, and a mane which hung like a veil of silk down over his neck. He had carried his master amid the smoke of gunpowder and hail of lead, and had heard the whining song of bullets. He had taken part in the struggle against the foe. He had used his teeth, biting about him savagely, and had kicked out in every direction. With his emperor he had made a leap over the prostrate horse of the enemy, and so had saved his emperor's red-gold crown. Moreover, he had saved his emperor's life, and that was worth more than gold.

That is why the emperor's horse was now being shod with golden shoes — a golden shoe on each foot.

Now the Beetle crept forth.

"First the great, then the small," it said, "though it is not always the size that does it." And it stretched out its thin legs toward the smith.

"What do you want?" asked the blacksmith.

"Gold shoes!" said the Beetle. "Am I not just as good as that big beast yonder, that is waited upon, curried, tended, and given food and drink? Do I not belong to the imperial stable, too?"

"But why does the horse get gold shoes?" asked the smith. "Can you not grasp that?"

"Grasp? I grasp that it is a mark of small respect toward me," said the Beetle. "It is an injury, an insult, and so now I am going away into the wide world."

"Get along with you!" said the smith.

"Ruffian!" said the Beetle. Then he went outside a little way and thus came into a beautiful little flower garden, fragrant with roses and lavender.

"How lovely it is here!" said one of the little lady-birds which flew about with black dots on their strong red shields. "How sweet it smells and how pretty it is here!"

"I am used to better things," said the Beetle. "Do you call this place pretty? Why, there is not even a dungheap."

And then he continued on his way, into the shade of a large gillyflower on the stalk of which crawled a caterpillar.

"Oh, how lovely the world is!" said the caterpillar. "The sun is so nice and warm! Everything is so enjoyable! And finally I shall fall asleep and die, as they call it; then I shall wake up as a butterfly!"

"What notions you have!" said the Beetle. "Flutter about like a butterfly, indeed! I come from the emperor's stable, but no one there, not even the emperor's favorite horse who wears my cast-off gold shoes has such crazy notions. Get wings! Fly! Indeed! Yes, now let us fly!"

And then away flew the Beetle. "I do not want to feel vexed, but still, I am vexed."

Then it came down with a thump on a large patch of grass. Here it lay a little while and then fell asleep.

Gracious, what a shower poured down! The Beetle was awakened by the splash, and immediately tried to get down into the ground, but could not. It tumbled over and over, swam on its stomach, and then on its

back. Flying was out of the question. It was doubtful
if it could get away from that spot alive. There it lay
and there it remained lying.

When the rain had moderated a little and the Beetle
had blinked the water out of its eyes, it perceived something white. It was linen that had been placed on the
grass to bleach. The Beetle managed to reach the cloth
and crawl into one of the wet folds. This was certainly
not like lying in the dungheap in the warm stable. But
there was nothing better to be had, and so it stayed there
a whole day and a whole night; and the rainy weather
stayed, too. In the early morning the Beetle came out.
He was terribly vexed at the climate.

On the linen sat two frogs. Their bright eyes shone
with enjoyment. "It is blessed weather!" said one of
them. "How refreshing it is! And the linen gathers
the water so nicely! I feel a sensation in my hind legs
as if I just had to swim."

"I should like to know," said the other, "whether
the swallow which flies so far and wide has ever found
on its many journeys to foreign lands a better climate
than ours. Such a drizzle and such wetness! It is just
like lying in a wet ditch! Anyone who is not glad and
happy because of it certainly does not love his native
country."

"You have never been in the emperor's stable, have
you?" asked the Beetle. "There the wetness is both
warm and spicy! That is what I am accustomed to.
That is my climate, but of course a person cannot take
it with him when he goes traveling. Is there not a hotbed
here in the garden where a person of distinction like
myself can take up quarters and feel at home?"

But the frogs did not, or would not, understand him.

"I never ask a question twice," said the Beetle, when it had asked three times without getting a reply.

Then it walked away a short distance. There lay a fragment of an earthen jar which should not have been there. It lay in such a way as to provide a shelter, and beneath it lived several earwig families. They did not require much house room—just sociability. The females are particularly gifted with mother love, and for that reason each one thought her child the most beautiful and the most intelligent.

"Our son is engaged to be married," said one mother, "the sweet innocent! His highest aim is at some time to be able to crawl into someone's ear. He is so dear and childlike, and his engagement keeps him steady. That is such a joy for a mother."

"Our son," said another mother, "got right out of the egg and was immediately out to see what he could stir up; he is so bursting with life and spirit. He will surely run his horns off. What an enormous happiness for a mother! Isn't that true, Mr. Beetle?" They recognized the stranger by the sheath he wore.

"You are both right," said the Beetle; and then he was invited into the room—as far as he could get under the broken fragment.

"Now you must see my little earwigs, too," said a third mother, and a fourth. "They are the dearest children and so funny! They are never naughty except when they have a stomach ache, and at their age that is very easy to have."

And then each mother talked about her children; and the young ones talked with them and, with the little fork on the end of their tails, pulled the Beetle's whiskers.

"They are always finding all kinds of things to do, the little rogues!" said the mothers, almost bursting with mother love. But it bored the Beetle and he asked if it was far from there to the hotbed.

"That is far out in the world, on the other side of the ditch," said the earwig, "so far as that I hope none of my children will ever go, for then I should certainly die."

"Still, I am going to try to go that far," said the Beetle; and away he went without saying good-by. That is the most fashionable way to do.

By the side of the ditch he met others of his own kind —all beetles.

"We live here," they said. "It is warm and comfortable! Will you accept an invitation to step down here an enjoy the fat of the land? You must be weary after your journey."

"That I am," said the Beetle. "I have had to lie on linen in the rain, and cleanliness is very trying to me. I have also taken rheumatism in my wing joint from standing in the draft under a fragment of earthen jar. It certainly is refreshing to meet one's own kind again."

"You have come, perhaps, from the hotbed?" asked the eldest of the beetles.

"Higher up," said the Beetle. "I come from the emperor's stable where I was born with golden shoes. I am traveling on a secret mission about which you must not bother me with questions for I will not say what it is."

And then the Beetle stepped down into the soft, rich mud. There sat three young lady beetles. They giggled because they did not know what they should say.

"They are not engaged," said the mother. And then they giggled again, but this time from bashfulness.

"I have seen none more beautiful in the emperor's stable," said the traveler Beetle.

"Don't spoil my girls for me and do not speak to them unless you have serious intentions. But I know you have and I give you my blessing."

"Hurrah!" said all the others, and with that the Beetle was engaged.

First engagement, then marriage. There was no reason to wait, you see.

The next day passed very pleasantly, the second tolerably well, but on the third day one must begin to think of providing for the wife and perhaps the little ones.

"I have permitted myself to be taken by surprise," said the Beetle, "the only thing to do is to surprise them in return."

And surprise them he did. He was gone, gone all day and gone all night; and the wife was a widow. The other Beetles said that they had taken a vagabond into the family. The wife was now a burden on their hands.

"Then she shall take her maiden name again," said the mother, "and come back as my child. What a shameful good-for-nothing, to forsake her."

He, meanwhile, was well on his way. He had sailed across the ditch on a cabbage leaf. Along in the morning, two people came by, saw the Beetle, picked him up and turned him over and over. They were very learned, especially one, a boy.

"Allah sees the black beetle in the black stone in the

black mountain side! Is it not written thus in the Koran?" he asked. Then he translated the Beetle's name into Latin, and explained its nature and species. The elder scholar voted against taking it home with them for they had specimens that were just as good, he said.

"That was very uncivilly spoken," thought the Beetle and so it flew out of the scholar's hand. It flew a considerable distance, for its wings had now become quite dry. Then it reached the hotbed, where, with the greatest ease, for one of the windows was open, it was able to slip in and dig down into the fresh rich soil.

"How delicious," it said.

It soon fell asleep and dreamed that the emperor's horse had fallen, and that Mr. Beetle had received his gold shoes and a promise of two more. That was all very nice, and when the Beetle awoke he crawled out and looked about. What splendor in that hothouse! Great palm leaves spread high in the air. The sun made them transparent, and beneath them sprang forth a wealth of green growing things. All about glowed flowers, red as fire, yellow as amber, and white as new-fallen snow.

"This is a matchless splendor of foliage! How good it will taste when it decays!" said the Beetle. "This is a fine larder! There must be some of my relatives here. I will start a search and try to find someone with whom I feel that I can associate. I am proud, and that is what I am proud of!" Then he started out and thought of his dream about the dead horse and the gold shoes he had gained.

All at once a hand seized the Beetle, squeezing it and turning it over and around.

The gardener's little son and a playmate had entered the hothouse, had seen the Beetle, and were about to have a little fun with it. It was wrapped in a grape-vine leaf and then put down into a warm trousers' pocket. It wriggled and wiggled about and then got a squeeze from the hand of the boy who hurried off to the large pond at the end of the garden. There the Beetle was put into an old cracked wooden shoe. A stick was fastened to it to serve as a mast and to this the Beetle was tied, at the end of a woolen thread. Now it was a skipper and was to go sailing.

It was not a very large pond, but the Beetle believed it to be a vast ocean and was so astonished and alarmed that it fell over on its back and kicked and wriggled its legs.

The wooden shoe sailed along nicely, for there was a current in the water. But when the boat got a little too far out one of the boys rolled up his trousers, waded out, and brought it back. When it started to drift out again someone called the boys in a peremptory way they had to obey. So they hurried off, leaving the wooden shoe on the water.

It drifted farther and farther from the shore. The Beetle was terribly frightened. Fly it could not, for it was tied to the mast.

A fly paid a visit.

"Lovely weather we are having," said the fly. "Here I can rest! Here I can sit and bask in the sunshine. You have a very nice and agreeable time of it here!"

"You talk according to the amount of sense you have!" said the Beetle. "Do you not see that I am tied?"

"I am not tied," said the fly, and flew away.

"Now I know the world," said the Beetle; "and it is a low-down world! I am the only worthy person in it! First I am denied golden shoes, then I have to lie on wet linen and stand in a draft, and then they foist a wife on me. Then when I make a quick step out into the world to see how a person can live there and how I ought to live, along comes a human whelp and sets me on the raging ocean, tied to a mast. And meanwhile the emperor's horse is wearing gold shoes! That is what is most exasperating. But one cannot expect sympathy in this world! My career has been very interesting, but what is the good of that when nobody knows it! The world does n't deserve to know it, else it would have given me golden shoes in the emperor's stable, when the favorite horse was holding up its feet to be shod. Had they given me golden shoes, I should then have become an honor to the stable. Now it has lost me, the world has lost me. All is over!"

But all was not yet over. A boat came by in which were several young girls.

"There sails a wooden shoe," said one of them.

"There is a little bug tied fast in it," said another.

When they were close beside the wooden shoe they lifted it out of the water. One of the girls then brought out a little pair of scissors and cut the woollen thread without harming the Beetle, and when they reached the shore she set it down on the grass.

"Creep, creep! Fly, fly! if you can!" she said. "Freedom is a splendid thing."

Right through the open window of a large building the Beetle flew and there sank down wearily on the fine, soft, long mane of the emperor's favorite horse, which stood in the stable where it and the Beetle had their home. It clung fast to the mane and sat a little while resting.

"Here I sit on the emperor's favorite horse! Here I sit as the rider himself! What am I saying! Why, now I see it all! That is a good idea and a correct one. Why was the horse given golden shoes? That was just what he asked me, too, that blacksmith fellow. Now I see into it! The horse was shod with golden shoes on my account."

And then the Beetle recovered his good humor.

"Traveling makes a person clear headed," said he.

The sun shone in upon it, shone very beautifully, indeed.

"The world is not so bad after all," said the Beetle. "A person must just know how to take it!"

The world was lovely, for the emperor's favorite horse had been shod with golden shoes because the Beetle was to be its rider.

"Now I will go down to the other Beetles and tell how much has been done for me. I will tell about all the pleasant things I enjoyed in my foreign travels, and I will say that I shall remain at home now until the horse has worn out his golden shoes."

WHATEVER THE OLD MAN DOES IS ALWAYS RIGHT

Now I will tell you a story I heard once when I was small. Every time I think of it, it becomes more and more charming. For it is with stories as it is with many people, they grow nicer and nicer with age; and that is really delightful!

You have been in the country, have you not? You have seen a real old farmhouse with a straw-thatched roof? Moss and vegetables grow wild on the roof, and on the gable is a stork's nest, for we could not do without the stork. The walls are crooked, the windows low; and there is but a single one of them that can be opened. The oven sticks out of the wall just like a little fat stomach, and the elderbush leans over the fence where there is a little pool of water with a duck or a few ducklings, right under the gnarled willow. And there is the watch-dog barking at each and all.

There was just such a farmhouse in the country, and in it lived a couple, a peasant and his wife. Albeit they had little, there was one thing more they could do without, and that was the horse, which lived on the grass in the ditch by the side of the road. Father rode it to town, he lent it to the neighbors, and he got favors in return. But it would be more profitable to sell the horse or exchange it for something or other which would be of still more benefit.

But what should that something be!

"That, old man, you will know best!" said the wife. "There is a market fair in town just now. Ride in to the fair, get money for the horse, or make a good trade. Whatever you do is always right.   So ride to the fair!"

Then she tied his neck cloth for him, for that at least she understood better than he. She tied it in a double bow, for it looked smart that way; then she smoothed his hat with the palm of her hand and kissed him on his mouth. Then away he rode on the horse which he was to sell or trade away. Yes, indeed, the old man knew what he was doing!

The sun was hot; there was not a cloud in the sky; and the road was dusty. There were many people bound for the market, in wagons and on horseback and on their own legs. The heat of the sun was intense and there was not a spot of shade anywhere on the road.

Among the rest walked a man driving a cow which was as fine and good-looking as any cow can be.

"I am sure she gives nice milk!" thought the peasant. "It would be a very good exchange to get her. "Look here, you with the cow!" he said, "let us have a little talk. Now you see, a horse, I believe, costs more than a cow. But that is all the same to me. I would have more benefit from a cow· Shall we trade?"

"To be sure!" said the man with the cow. And so the exchange was made.

That settled, the peasant could have turned about and gone home, for he had done what he had set out to do. But as he had once made up his mind to go to the fair, he was going to the fair, if just to have a look at it. So on he went with his cow. He walked fast and the cow walked fast, and they soon were walking right beside a man who was leading a sheep. It was a good sheep, well fatted and with a quantity of fleece.

"I should like to own that sheep," thought the peasant. "It would have plenty of grass to eat on the edge of our ditch, and in winter we could take it into the house with us. It would really be better for us to keep a sheep than to keep a cow. Shall we exchange?" he said to the owner of the sheep.

The other was willing, and so the trade was made. The peasant continued on his way along the road with his sheep. By the stile at the roadside he saw a man with a big goose under his arm.

"That is a fine fellow you have there!" he said to the man. "It has plenty of feathers and plenty of fat, too! It would look fine tied up by the side of our pond! Mother would have something to save peelings for. She has often said, 'If we only had a goose!' Now she can have one and she shall have it! Will you trade? I will give you the sheep for the goose, and thanks besides!"

The man had no objection at all and so they traded. The peasant got the goose. He had now come close to the town, and the crowd on the road increased. Men and beasts swarmed thick. They walked on the road and in the ditch, right up along the edge of the toll collector's potato patch, where a hen stood tied with a string lest it stray away in fright and get lost. It had short tail feathers, blinked with one eye, and looked very desirable. "Cluck, cluck!" it said. What it was thinking when it said this I cannot say, but the peasant thought when he saw her: "She's the finest hen I have ever seen; she is better than the parson's brooder. I certainly wish I owned her! A hen always finds something to eat, it can almost provide for itself! I think it will be a good exchange if I trade the goose for her."

"Shall we trade?" he asked.

"Trade!" said the hen's owner. "Why, that would not be so bad!" and so they traded. The toll collector got the goose and the peasant got the hen.

He had now accomplished a good deal on that journey to town. He was hot and tired. He felt that he needed a bit of brandy and a bite to eat. He had reached the tavern and there he wanted to enter. But the hostler at that moment was going out and so they met right in the doorway. The hostler was swinging a bag filled with something.

"What have you got there?" asked the peasant.

"Rotten apples," replied the hostler; "a whole sackful for the hogs."

"My, but that is an awful lot! I wish mother could see this. Last year we had one single apple on the old tree by the wood shed. That apple had to be kept, and it stood on the cupboard till it split open. 'It is a bit of a luxury,' said mother. Well here she could get to see what luxury and abundance is! I wish she could see those apples!"

"Well, what will you give me?" asked the hostler.

"Give? I'll give my hen in exchange." Then he handed over the hen and received the apples in return. He entered the inn, going straight to the room where drinks were served, and set his sack of apples against the stove. There was a fire in the stove but that he did n't know or think about. There were many strangers in the room,—horse-dealers, cattle-dealers, and two Englishmen. And they were so rich their pockets bulged with gold coins. They made wagers—and now listen!

"Hiss! hiss!" What was that sound from the stove? The apples were beginning to roast.

"What is that?" they all asked.

They soon heard the whole story about the horse that was traded away for a cow and right through to the rotten apples.

"Well, you will get it good from the old woman when you get home!" said the Englishmen. "There will be an awful racket!"

"I will get kisses and not scoldings," said the peasant. "The old woman will say: 'What the old man does is always right!'"

"Shall we wager?" they said. "A barrel of gold coin, a hundred pounds to a hundred weight!"

"A bushel full is enough!" said the peasant. "I can only fill the bushel with apples and throw in myself and the old woman. But that is piling up the measure!"

"Done! Taken!" they cried; and thus the wager was made.

The innkeeper's carriage came up, the peasant and the strangers got in, and the rotten apples were lifted up, too; and then they journeyed to the peasant's house.

"Good evening, old woman!"

"Thank you, old man!"

"I have made the trade!"

"Yes, you know how!" said the woman, and then she put her arms round him and forgot both the sack and the strangers.

"I traded the horse for a cow!"

"Thank heaven!" she said. "We shall have plenty of milk and butter and cheese on the table. That was a fine trade!"

"But I traded the cow away again for a sheep!"

"Why, that really is still better!" said the wife. "You are always prudent and thoughtful. We have all the pasture necessary for a sheep. Now we can have sheep's milk and cheese, and woolen stockings, yes, and woolen night shirts! We couldn't get that from a cow! She sheds her hair! You are a wonderfully thoughtful man."

"But I exchanged the sheep for a goose!"

"Are we really to have roast goose this year, my dear old man? You always think of something to give me pleasure! That was lovely of you! We can keep the goose tied and so get her still fatter before we roast her!"

"But I traded away the goose for a hen!" said the man.

"A hen! that was a fine trade," said the woman. "The hen lays eggs, it hatches them; we shall have little chickens and soon we shall have a whole hen yard. That is just what I have been wishing for so much!"

"Yes, but I traded the hen for a sack of rotten apples!"

"Now I positively must kiss you!" said the woman. "Thank you, my own dear husband! Now I will tell you something. When you were gone I thought of making a real good meal for you; egg pancake with onions. I had the eggs. But I had no onions. Then I went over to the schoolmaster's. There they have leek in their garden, I know. But the wife is so stingy! I asked if I could borrow an onion. 'Borrow?' she said. 'Nothing grows in our garden, not even a rotten apple, and you cannot lend to me even that!' Now I can lend her ten, yes, even a whole sackful! That's a fine joke, old man!" and she kissed him right on the mouth.

"I like that!" said the Englishman. "Always down-hill and yet always contented! It's worth the money!" And they paid a bushel of gold coins to the peasant who had not been scolded, but kissed.

It certainly always pays when the wife sees and declares that her old man is wise and always does the right thing.

There is the story! I heard it as a child and now you, too, have heard it, and know that whatever the old man does is always the right thing to do.

THE DARNING NEEDLE

There was once a Darning Needle, who believed herself to be as fine and polished as a sewing needle.

"Pay careful attention there to what you are holding!" said the Darning Needle to the Fingers that picked her up. "Do not drop me! If I should fall on the floor I might never be found again, I am so very fine!"

"There is a limit!" said the Fingers, and then they squeezed her round the waist.

"See, I am accompanied by a retinue!" said the Darning Needle, drawing a long thread after her. There was no knot in the thread, however.

The Fingers directed the needle straight against the cook's slipper at a place where the upper leather had cracked. The crack was now to be sewed up, you see.

"This is mean work!" said the Darning Needle. "I shall never get through this! I am breaking! I am breaking!" And then she broke.

"Did I not say so?" asked the Darning Needle. "I am too fine!"

"She is good for nothing now," was the opinion of the Fingers. But the cook dripped lacquer on the end from which the eye of the Darning Needle had been broken and then stuck the pin in her scarf.

"See, now I am a breast-pin!" said the Darning Needle. "I knew well enough that I should come to honor. When one is something, one always gets to be something!"

Then she laughed inwardly — one can never see a Darning Needle laugh outwardly. There she sat as proudly as if she were riding in a coach and looking round her on all sides.

"May I have the honor to ask if you are made of gold?" she asked of the pin who was her neighbor. "You have a lovely appearance and quite a head of your own, though it is very small! You must take pains to make it grow, for we cannot all be lacquered on the end!" With that the Darning Needle drew herself up so proudly that she came out of the scarf and fell down into the sink, just as the cook was rinsing the clothes.

"Now we are off on a journey!" said the Darning Needle. "If only I don't get lost!"

Now, that is just what happened.

"I am too fine for this world!" she said, as she sat in the gutter. "But I am aware of what I am, and that is always a little satisfaction!"

So the Darning Needle held herself upright and did not lose her good humor.

All kinds of things sailed by above it, sticks, straws, and bits of newspapers.

"See how they sail along!" said the Darning Needle. "They don't know what is sticking below them! I am sticking! Here I sit! See, there goes a stick. He thinks of nothing in the world but 'Stick,' and that is what he is himself. There floats a straw. See how it turns, see how it whirls! Do not think so much of yourself, you might bump yourself against the paving stones! There floats a newspaper! What is in it is all forgotten, and yet see how it spreads itself! I sit patient and quiet! I know what I am, and that I shall continue to be!"

One day something glittered very brightly close by and the Darning Needle immediately thought it was a diamond. It was, however, a bit of a broken bottle, and as it glittered, the Darning Needle spoke to it and introduced herself as a breast-pin!

"You are a diamond, are you not?"

"Yes, I am something of the sort."

And then each thought the other must be something very precious indeed. Then they talked to each other about how arrogant and conceited the world was.

"Yes, I used to live in a box in a young lady's room," said the Darning Needle, "and the young lady was a cook. She had five fingers on each hand, and anything so conceited as those five fingers I have never known. And yet the only reason for their existence was to hold me, to take me out of my box, and to lay me back in my box!"

"Did they shine in any way?" asked the bit of Broken Bottle.

"Shine!" said the Darning Needle. "No, they were very dull, and so conceited! They were five brothers, all born 'Fingers.' They held themselves upright, one against the other, though they were of different lengths. The outside one, Thumbkin, was short and fat. He marched out of line, and besides, he had but one joint in his back. He could bow only once, but he said that if he were chopped off a person, the entire man would be ruined for military service. Pointer, the second finger, also known as 'Lick Dish,' got into the sweet and the sour, pointed at the sun and the moon, and was the one that pressed down on the pen when the Fingers wrote. Longman looked over the heads of all the others. Ringman went about with a gold ring about his stomach, and Little Man did nothing at all, and that was what he was proud of. Bragging and boasting it was, and nothing but bragging and boasting; and then I went into the wash!"

"And now here we sit and glitter!" said the glass fragment. At that moment more water poured into the gutter. It overflowed in every direction and carried the broken glass away with it.

"See, now, he has had a promotion!" said the Darning Needle. "I remain sitting. I am too fine, but that is my pride, and my pride is worthy of respect!" And then she sat up proudly, and many thoughts came to her.

"I could almost believe that I am born of a sunbeam, so fine am I! Have I not noticed that the sun always seems to seek me under the water? Alas, I am so fine that my mother cannot find me. If I had my old eye which broke, I believe I could cry, though of course that wouldn't do; it is not refined to cry!"

One day two street boys came grubbing and digging in the gutter. There they found old nails, pennies, and other things of that sort. It was very dirty play, but they took great delight in it.

"Ouch!" said one of them. He had pricked himself on the Darning Needle. "What kind of a fellow is that!"

"I am no fellow, I am a young lady!" said the Darning Needle. But no one heard it. It had lost its lacquer and had become black. But black gives a more slender appearance, and thereupon it believed that it was finer than ever.

"There comes an eggshell, sailing!" said the boys. Then they stuck the Darning Needle into the shell.

"White walls and black myself!" said the Darning

Needle. "That is becoming! Now I can be seen! I hope I won't get seasick, for then I should be all broken up!" But it did not get seasick, and it was not broken up.

"It is a good preventive for seasickness to have a steel stomach, and then to remember always that one is a little more than a human being! Now my seasickness is gone! The finer one is the more one can bear."

"Crunch!" went the eggshell, as a loaded wagon rolled over it.

"Oh, how it squeezes!" said the Darning Needle. "Now I shall be seasick! I shall break! I shall break!"

But it did not break, though a whole wagon load went over it, for it lay lengthwise. And there let it lie!

FORTUNE'S OVERSHOES

I. A BEGINNING

At a reception in one of the houses in a certain street in Copenhagen not far from King's Newmarket, was once gathered a very large company. (A person must have a house full of company once in a while; for then it is over with, and one can expect invitations in return.)

Half the company were already seated at the card tables. The other half waited for what should be the result of the hostess' announcement: "Now we must think up something to do!"

Thus far had things progressed. The conversation moved as it does when there is no settled topic. Among other things the talk turned upon the period of the Middle Ages. A few considered that period far better than our own, and one of the guests—Councilor Knap—defended this view so vigorously that the hostess immediately sided with him. Both argued very strongly against an author who had just written a treatise comparing ancient and modern times. The writer thought our age preferable. The Councilor believed the times of King Hans to be the best and happiest of all.

While this talk is going on pro and con—with nothing to interrupt it but the arrival of the newspaper, which had nothing in it worth reading—we shall see what was happening in the ante-room, where the guests' coats, canes, umbrellas, and overshoes had been left.

In the ante-room sat two maids, one young and the other old. At first glance they seemed to be servants waiting to attend their masters and mistresses on the way home after the reception. But, on close scrutiny, it was clear that they were not ordinary servant girls. Their hands were too fine, their attitude and movements too graceful. Moreover, their clothes had a decidedly individual cut.

They were fairies. The younger, though of course not Fortune herself, was one of her lady's maid's chambermaids, they who bring around the lesser gifts of Fortune. The older fairy looked so extremely serious that one recognized her at once as Sorrow. She always goes on her errands herself, for then she knows they will be well performed.

They were telling each other where they had been that day. She was who chambermaid to Fortune's lady's maid, had, so far, performed only a few unimportant errands. She had saved a new hat from being ruined in a sudden shower, had secured a passing recognition on the street for an honest man from a distinguished nobody—and other little things like that. But what she still had left to do was something quite out of the ordinary.

"I must inform you," she said, "that it is my birthday to-day, and in honor of this a pair of overshoes has been intrusted to me to bring to human beings. These overshoes have this peculiar property! Everyone who puts them on finds himself instantly in the time or place where he wishes most to be. Every wish with regard to time and place is immediately fulfilled and thus at last can man be happy here below!"

"Believe that if you will!" said Sorrow. "He will become very unhappy, indeed, and will bless the moment he gets rid of the overshoes!"

"You are all wrong!" said the other. "I am going to set them right here by the door. Someone will take them by mistake and become the fortunate one!"

Now you know what conversation went on in the ante-chamber.

II. WHAT HAPPENED TO THE COUNCILOR

It was late. Councilor Knap, his thoughts deep in King Hans' time, wanted to go home. Now fate had willed it that he should get Fortune's Overshoes instead of his own, and out he stepped into the street with them. But by the magic power of the overshoes he had been put back to the time of King Hans, and for that reason he now set his foot into the mud and mire of an unpaved street, for in those days paving was still unknown.

"Why, how terribly muddy and dirty it is here!" said the Councilor. "The whole walk is gone and all the street lamps are out!"

The moon was not yet high enough in the sky to give much light. The air was rather thick besides, and the surroundings were swallowed up in the darkness. At the nearest corner a lamp hung before an image of the Madonna, but the light might almost as well not have been there at all for all the illumination it gave. The Councilor noticed it only when he was standing directly beneath it. His eyes fell on the painted image of the Mother and Child.

"This must be an art shop," he thought, "where they have forgotten to take down the sign for the night."

A few people passed by him, dressed in the costume of times gone by.

"What a strange appearance they have! They

must have come from a masquerade ball!" said the Councilor to himself.

Suddenly there was a sound of fife and drum, and bright lights appeared. The Councilor stood still and watched a strange procession go by. First of all marched a whole troop of drummers, who handled their drumsticks with much dexterity. After them came men-at-arms, bearing long-bows and harquebuses. The most distinguished man in the procession seemed to be of clerical rank. Astonished, the Councilor asked the meaning of such a procession, and who the man might be.

"That is the Bishop of Zealand," was the answer.

"What in the world is the Bishop thinking of?" sighed the Councilor. He shook his head, refusing to believe that it could possibly be the Bishop. Pondering deeply what he had seen, and looking neither to right nor left, the Councilor walked through East Street and over Highbridge Square. The bridge leading to the palace square was not to be found. He could make out a swampy beach and at last stumbled upon two men, who had a boat tied up at the shore.

"Does the gentleman wish to be taken over to the Bottoms?" they asked.

"Over to the Bottoms?" said the Councilor, who, you see, did not know that he was living in a by-gone period. "I want to go to Christianshaven to Little Turf Street!"

The fellows looked at him.

"Will you just tell me where that bridge is?" he said. "It is shameful that no lamps are lighted, and it is as muddy and dirty as if a person were walking in a marsh!"

The longer he talked with the boatmen, the less could he understand their speech.

"I don't understand your Bornholm[1] dialect," he said, finally angry, and turning his back he walked off.

But he could not find the bridge, and there was neither river wall nor fence! "It is scandalous how things look!" he said. Never had he thought his own times so miserable as on that evening.

"I believe I will take a cab!" he thought. But where were the cabs? None were to be seen.

"I will have to go back to King's Newmarket, where some must surely be standing, or else I will never get to Christianshaven."

He went back to East Street and was almost through it when the clouds parted and the moon shone brightly.

"Good gracious, what in the world have they been putting up here!" he said as he perceived the East gate which in those days stood at the end of East Street.

He finally found a little passage-way, and through this he came out on what is now Newmarket but which was then a great meadow. A few bushes stuck out here and there from the level of the meadow, and straight across it flowed a broad canal or stream of some kind. Some miserable wooden sheds for the Dutch skippers lay on the opposite shore.

"Either I am seeing a mirage, or else I am drunk!" groaned the Justice. "What can this be! What in the world is this?"

He turned back in the firm belief that he was ill. When he was again in the street he looked a little closer at the houses, and discovered that most of them were built of laths and that many had only thatched roofs.

[1] An island possession to the east of Denmark where the language spoken is a peculiar dialect very unlike the Danish language.

"No, I am not at all well!" he sighed. "And yet I
drank just one glass of punch! It was very wrong to
give us punch and warm salmon! I cannot stand it!
I shall certainly tell our hostess about it! Ought I go
back and let them know how I feel? But that would be
embarrassing! Besides, I wonder if they are still up!"

He looked for the place, but it was not to be found.

"This is terrible! I don't recognize East Street!
There is not a single store! Old, miserable shacks are
all I see, as if I were in Roskilde or Ringsted! Oh, I am
ill! This is not a time to hold back for manners' sake!
But where in the world is the agent's house? It does n't
look like the same place! But there are people up there
anyway; oh! I am surely ill!"

He now came to a half-open door, where the light
shone through the opening. It was one of the inns of
that time, a kind of alehouse. The room had the appearance of a Dutch tavern! A number of people, including
sailors, citizens, and a couple of scholars, sat in lively
discussion over their mugs. They paid little attention
to the stranger as he stepped in.

"Beg pardon," said the Councilor to the proprie-
tress, who came toward him, "I feel very ill! Will you
call a cab to take me to Christianshaven?"

The woman looked at him and shook her head.
Then she addressed him in German. The Councilor
then supposed that she could not speak Danish and so
repeated his request in German. This, and his dress,
convinced the woman that he was a foreigner. That
he felt ill, she soon understood and so she gave him a
mug of water. It certainly tasted brackish. It had
been brought from the well outside.

The Councilor leaned his head on his hand, drew a deep breath, and wondered at all the strange things about him.

"Is that this evening's issue of 'The Day'?" he asked, just for the sake of saying something, as he saw the woman take up a large sheet of paper.

She did not understand what he meant, but she handed the paper to him. There was a wood cut showing a strange appearance in the sky observed from the city of Cologne. "That is very old!" said the Councilor, and he was much surprised and delighted at discovering such an old thing. "Where in the world did you run on to that rare paper? It is very interesting, although the whole thing is imagination! Such appearances in the sky are explained as the Northern Lights. It is quite probable that they are caused by electricity!" Those who sat nearest and heard what he said looked at him wonderingly, and one of them stood up, took off his hat respectfully, and said with the most serious expression: "Sir, you must certainly be a very learned man."

"Oh, no!" answered the Councilor. "I can talk about this and that, things that everybody must and ought to know."

"*Modestia* is a beautiful virtue to possess," said the man. "Moreover, I must say to your words, '*mihi secus videtur.*' Yet here I will gladly suspend my *judicium!*"

"May I ask with whom I have the pleasure of speaking?" asked the Councilor.

"I am Baccalaureate in the Holy Writ!" answered the man.

This reply was enough for the Councilor. The title corresponded with the costume. "This must certainly

be an old country schoolmaster," he thought, "a queer
fellow, such as one still finds up in Jutland."

"This is not a *locus docendi*," began the man, "but
I pray you to take the trouble to speak! You are doubtless widely read in the ancients!"

"Oh, yes, indeed!" answered the Councilor. "I am
fond of reading old, useful writings. But I also like the
newer ones, excepting only the 'Every-Day Stories';
we have enough of them in reality!"

"Every-Day Stories?" asked the Baccalaureate.

"Yes, I mean the new novels."

"Oh," said the man with a smile; "still they are
rather clever and they are much read at Court. The
King likes them, especially the tale about Iffven and
Gaudian which deals with King Arthur and his Knights
of the Round Table. He has jested about it with his
noble lords!"

"That is one I have not read!" said the Councilor.
"It must be a very new one published by Heiberg!"

"No," answered the man. "It is not by Heiberg, but
by Godfrey von Gehmen!"

"Indeed! Is he the author?" asked the Councilor.
"That is a very old name! Why, that is the first printer
who appeared in Denmark."

"Yes, he is our first printer," replied the man.

Thus the talk progressed smoothly enough. One
of the good burghers now spoke about the pestilence
that had raged a few years past, meaning the one in
1484. The Councilor supposed that he was talking
about the recent cholera epidemic, and thus the discussion
went on nicely. The Freebooters' War in 1490 was so
recent that it could not escape mention. The English

freebooter had taken ships at the very wharves, they said. And the Councilor who had investigated and who knew intimately the events of 1801, took part strongly in the talk against the English.

The rest of the conversation, on the other hand, did not run so smoothly. Every moment there was a contradiction. To the Councilor the good Baccalaureate seemed altogether too ignorant of things, and to the Baccalaureate, the Councilor's simplest statements sounded altogether too unreasonable and fantastic. They looked at each other, and when it got too bad, the Baccalaureate spoke in Latin, in the belief that he would be better understood. But it was of no use.

"How are you feeling now?" asked the hostess, pulling at his coat sleeve to attract his attention. Then his recollection came back, for while he talked he had forgotten completely all that had happened beforehand.

"Where am I?" he asked, and his head felt dizzy when he thought of it.

"We'll drink claret! Mead and Bremen beer!" cried one of the guests, "and you shall drink with us!"

Two girls then came in. One of them wore a cap of two colors. They filled the glasses and curtsied to the guests. An icy shiver ran down the Councilor's back.

"What in the world is this! What is this!" he cried. But he had to drink with them. They took entire possession of the good man. He was in complete despair, and when one of them said he was drunk, he had not the least doubt that the fellow was right. All he asked was that they would get him a droshky[1]; and then they thought he was talking Russian.

[1] The Russian word *drozhki* is commonly used in Denmark for cab or carriage.

Never had he been in such rough and vulgar company. One would think the country had returned to heathendom, was his silent comment. Just then the idea came to him to get under the table, crawl to the door, and then wait for a chance to slip out. But when he reached the exit, the others discovered his intention, seized him by the legs, and then, to his great good fortune, the Overshoes came off — and with them, the whole enchantment.

The Councilor saw quite plainly in front of him a bright lamp burning, and behind it was a large residence. He recognized it, as well as the neighboring residences. It was East Street as we all know it. He lay with his feet toward a gate, and directly opposite sat the night watchman, asleep.

"Good Heavens, have I been lying here in the street dreaming!" he said. "Yes, this is East Street! How splendidly lighted it is and cheerful! It is terrible how that glass of punch must have affected me!"

Two minutes later he sat in a cab which took him to Christianshaven! He thought of the anxiety and despair he had experienced, and praised from the bottom of his heart his own time, which with all the shortcomings was nevertheless far better than that from which he had just come. And that was quite sensible of the Councilor.

III. THE WATCHMAN'S ADVENTURES

"Why, there is a pair of overshoes," said the Watchman. "They must belong to the Lieutenant, who lives up yonder. They are standing right at the door!"

The honest man would gladly have rung the bell and

delivered them, for lights were burning upstairs; but he did not like to wake the other people in the house.

"It must be pleasant to have on a pair of such warm things," he said; "the leather is so soft and nice." He put them on his feet and they fitted very well.

"What a queer world this is!" he reflected. "Now there is the Lieutenant; he might go to bed and be comfortable; but does he do it? No; up and down the floor he trips! He is a lucky man! He has neither wife nor little ones! Every evening he is at a party. I wish I were in his place, then I certainly should be a happy man!"

The moment he uttered the wish the Overshoes did their work, and the Watchman was in the Lieutenant's place, mind and body. There he stood upstairs in the Lieutenant's room, his fingers holding a little pink sheet of paper, upon which was a poem — a poem by Mr. Lieutenant himself. For what man has not once in his life had a poetic moment, when just to write down one's thoughts brings the verses!

People write such verses when they are in love, but a prudent man does not have them printed. Lieutenant, love, and necessity, that is a triangle, or, as good—the half of Fortune's broken die. The Lieutenant felt this way about it, too, and he laid his head on the window sill and sighed very deeply.

"The poor Watchman out on the street is far happier than I! He does not know what I call longing! He has a home, a wife and children, who weep when he grieves, and rejoice when he rejoices! Oh, I should be happier than I am, could I change into him completely, for he is happier than I!"

At that moment the Watchman was again the Watch-man, for it was because of the Overshoes that he had become Lieutenant. But, as we have seen, he then felt still less satisfied and would, nevertheless rather be what he really was.

So the Watchman was again watchman.

"That was an ugly dream!" he said, "but rather funny, anyhow. I thought I was the Lieutenant up yonder and that it wasn't anything pleasant by any means. I missed mother and the little ones, who are ready to stifle me with kisses."

He began to nod again. He kept thinking of the dream, and still wore the Overshoes. A shooting star gleamed across the sky.

"There, that's gone!" he said. "There are enough, anyway. I certainly should like to see those things a little closer, especially the moon, for that wouldn't slip away between one's fingers. When we die, says the student for whom my wife does the washing, we fly from one star to another. That is a lie, but it would be a nice thing if it were true. I wish I could make a little jump up yonder; then my body could lie here on the stair for all I care!"

You see there are certain things in this world which one must be very cautious about uttering, but still more cautious ought one to be when wearing Fortune's Over-shoes. Now listen to what happened to the Watchman.

As far as we human beings are concerned, we nearly all know the speed of travel by steam. We have tried it either on the railroad or on a ship on the ocean. But that speed is just like the movements of a snail compared with the speed with which light travels. It travels nineteen million times faster than the best runner can go; and yet electricity is still faster. Death is an electric shock we receive in our hearts. On the wings of electricity the liberated soul flies away. The light of the sun requires eight minutes and some seconds for a journey of over twenty million miles. By electricity's fast mail the soul needs still fewer minutes to make the same flight. The space between the heavenly bodies is no larger for it than the space between our friend's houses in the same city is for us, even though these may live close together. However, to travel so fast we must leave our bodies forever here below, unless, like the Watchman, we could have Fortune's Overshoes on our feet.

In a few seconds the Watchman traveled two hundred and forty thousand miles to the moon, which, as we know, consists of a much lighter material than our earth, and is what we should consider soft as new-fallen snow. He found himself on one of the numberless mountains with which we are acquainted from Dr. Mädler's great map of the moon. For that you know, of course? Within, the sides of the ring mountain went straight down into a hollow to a depth of several miles. Down there lay a town that had the appearance of the white of an egg in a glass of water; just as soft, and similar in appearance, with towers and cupolas and balconies, transparent and swaying in the thin air. Our earth hung in the air over the Watchman's head like a great, fiery-red ball.

There were a great many creatures, and all of them what we should certainly call human beings; but their appearance was very different from ours. They had a language, too; but no one would have expected that the Watchman's soul could understand it. Nevertheless, it could.

The Watchman's soul understood the language of the moon's inhabitants very well. They disputed about our earth and doubted if it could be inhabited. The air must be too thick for any sensible creature to live in. They believed that only the moon had living beings upon it. It was the original sphere where the real sphere people dwelt.

But let us go down again to East Street and see how the Watchman's body is faring.

Lifeless, it sat on the stair. The star-tipped staff had fallen out of its hand and the eyes stared up at the moon after the honest soul which was wandering about there.

"What time is it, Watchman?" asked a passerby. But the Watchman answered nothing.

Then the passerby tweaked the Watchman's nose very gently, and in so doing made him lose his balance. There the body lay at full length. Why, the man was dead! And the passerby who had tweaked the Watchman's nose was terribly frightened.

The Watchman was dead, and dead he was declared. It was reported and discussed, and in the morning the body was carried to the hospital.

It might have been a nice joke on the soul if it had returned to seek the body in East Street and had not found it! In all probability it would first of all hurry to the police station, later to the lost and found office to examine the list of unclaimed goods, and finally to the hospital. But we may take comfort in the knowledge that the soul is at its best when it acts alone; it is the body that makes it stupid.

As we have said, the body of the Watchman was taken to the hospital, where it was brought into the cleaning and disinfecting room. Naturally, the first thing they did there was to take off the Overshoes, and then the soul had to come back. It took its way straight to the body, and in a flash the man was alive. He declared it had been the most terrible night of his life. Not for two twenty-five cent pieces would he have such sensations again. But now it was over and done with.

He was allowed to leave the same day, but the Overshoes remained at the hospital.

IV. A VERY UNUSUAL JOURNEY

Every citizen of Copenhagen knows what the entrance to Frederick's Hospital looks like. But since a few who are not citizens of Copenhagen will probably read this story, we must give a short description of it.

The hospital is separated from the street by a tall fence, whose thick iron bars are so far apart that many thin students are said to have squeezed themselves through and in this way paid their little visits outside. The part of the body, which was most difficult to work through the bars was the head. Here then, as is often the case in this world, the small heads were the most fortunate. That will be sufficient as an introduction.

One of the young volunteer assistants, of whom it could be said only in a physical sense that his head was thick, had the watch that evening. The rain was pouring down. But in spite of such hindrances, the young man was determined to get out. He would be gone only a quarter of an hour; and that was not worth mentioning to the gatekeeper, he thought, when a man could so easily slip out between the iron bars. Near by lay the overshoes that the Watchman had forgotten to take with him.

The thought did not for an instant occur to the Assistant that they were Fortune's Overshoes. However, they would be very nice to wear in rainy weather; so he put them on.

Now the question was, whether he could squeeze through the bars of the gate. He had never tried it before. He reached the fence and stood there.

"How I wish I had my head outside!" he said to himself; and immediately, although his head was very large and thick, it slipped through easily and without mishap. Just depend upon the Overshoes! But now he had to get the rest of his body out, and there he stood.

"I'm too fat!" he said. "I thought the head would have been the hardest to get through! I see I am not going to get out."

Then he wanted to pull his head back quickly, but he could not. He could move his neck without discomfort, but that was all. At first he felt angry; then his spirits sank into his boots.

Fortune's Overshoes had brought him into the most awful situation, and, unfortunately, it did not occur to him to wish himself free.

He kept trying, but could not stir from the spot. The rain poured down; not a person was to be seen on the street. The gate bell was too far away to reach. How in the world was he to get loose? He feared that he might have to stand there till morning, when they would send for a blacksmith to file through the iron bars. But it would not all be done so quickly. The whole boys' school opposite would be on its legs watching him; the entire neighborhood would come to see him stand in the pillory. There would be a crowd, indeed.

"Whew! the blood is rising to my head, and I shall go mad! Yes, I *am* going mad! Oh, if only I were loose again, it might pass over!"

That, you see, is just what he should have said a little while sooner; for, as soon as he uttered the thought, his head was free. He rushed inside, quite dazed with the fright Fortune's Overshoes had caused him.

But you must not think for a moment that the whole thing was over with this incident. Something still worse was coming.

The night passed and also the following day, and no inquiry was made for the Overshoes.

In the evening an entertainment was to take place in the little theater on a distant street. The theater was filled completely. Among the recitations was a new poem called "Grandmother's Spectacles." When looking through these spectacles people appeared like playing cards and by looking at them one could tell fortunes, and prophesy future events.

The poem was splendidly recited, and received much applause. Among the spectators was the Assistant from the hospital, who seemed to have forgotten his adventure of the preceding evening. He was wearing the Overshoes, for they had not been sent for, and as the streets were wet and muddy they came in very handy.

He liked the poem very much. He kept turning the idea over in his mind, thinking that it would be quite nice to have such spectacles. Perhaps, if one used them right, he could look straight into other people's hearts. That would be more interesting, he thought, than to foresee what was to happen in the coming year; for the future one would come to know anyway in time, but the other, never.

"Now, for instance, those ladies and gentlemen in the first row there; could one but look into their breasts he would surely see in each a sort of shop! In that lady's there I should certainly find a great fashion shop. That store over there would be found empty, but a good cleaning would not hurt it. Good reliable shops there must be also. Ah, yes!" the young man sighed, "I know of one. There everything is in fine shape; but a store clerk has already found a place there, and he is the most worthless thing in the shop! From some of the stores would come the invitation to 'Step inside!' I wish I *could* step inside, and like a little thought go through their hearts!"

That was enough for the Overshoes! The hospital Assistant became a thought; and then began a very unusual journey right through the hearts of the first row of spectators. The first heart he passed through was a lady's. But he immediately thought he was in the Orthopaedic Institute, where the doctors straighten out deformities. He was in the room where plaster casts of the deformed limbs hang on the walls. The difference was that at the Institute the casts are made when the patient comes in, but here in this lady's heart they were taken and preserved when the good persons were away. They were casts of the faults and defects of lady friends that were here preserved.

Quickly he passed into another lady's heart, but this appeared to him like a great holy church. The white dove of innocence fluttered over the altar. How gladly he would have knelt there, but away he had to go, into the next heart. He could still hear the tones of the organ, however, and he felt that he had become a new

and better man, and not unworthy to enter the next sanc-
tuary.   This was a poor attic room in which lay a sick
mother.   Through the open window came God's warm
sunshine; lovely roses nodded from the little wooden
box on the roof, and two sky-blue birds sang joyously,
while the sick mother prayed for blessings on her daughter.

Now he crept on hands and feet through an overfilled
butcher's shop.   Meat, and only meat, could he see.   It
was the heart of a respectable rich man whose name is
certainly to be found in the directory.

Now he found himself in the heart of this man's wife.
It was an old, dilapidated dove-cote.   The man's picture
was used as a weathervane; it connected with the doors,
which by its means opened and shut as the husband
turned.

Next he entered a cabinet of mirrors, like the one
at Rosenborg Castle.   These mirrors magnified everything.   In the middle of the floor sat, like a Grand Lama,
the insignificant owner of the cabinet, taking delight in
his own greatness.

Then he entered what seemed to be a narrow needle
case, full of sharp needles.   He thought this must certainly be the heart of an old maid.   But it was not.
It was that of a young military officer wearing several
orders — one of those persons that people speak of as a
man of heart and spirit.

Quite confused, the poor Assistant emerged from the
last heart in the row.   He could not collect his thoughts.
He believed that his overstrong imagination had run
away with him.

"Gracious!" he sighed.   "I certainly have tendencies
toward insanity!   Moreover, it is extremely hot here!"

Then he remembered the event of the preceding evening, how his head had stuck fast between the bars at the hospital.

"That is where I got it!" he thought. "I must attend to this thing in time. A Russian bath would be good. I wish I was lying on the topmost shelf!"

And there he lay on the topmost shelf in the vapor bath, but with all his clothes on, and both shoes and overshoes. The hot water dripped on his face from the ceiling.

"Whew!" he cried and rushed down to take a plunge bath. The attendant uttered a loud cry at seeing a person fully dressed in the room!

The hospital Assistant had, meanwhile, so much presence of mind that he whispered to him, "It is a wager!"

But the first thing he did when he got to his own room was to put a big porous plaster on his neck and one down his back to draw out his madness.

Next morning he had a very sore back. That was what he got out of Fortune's Overshoes.

V. THE COPYING CLERK'S TRANSFORMATION

Meanwhile, the Watchman, whom we, of course, have not forgotten, happened to be reminded of the overshoes which he had found and taken with him to the hospital. He went to the hospital and brought them away with him, but as neither the Lieutenant nor any one else in the street would claim them, they were sent to the police station.

"They look just like my overshoes!" said one of the copying clerks, as he looked at the unclaimed goloshes and placed them side by side with his own. "It would take a shoemaker's eye to tell them apart!"

"Mr. Copying Clerk!" said an officer who had stepped in with some papers.

The Copying Clerk turned, talked with the man, and when he again looked at the overshoes he was in great doubt as to whether it was the pair to the left or the pair to the right that belonged to him.

"It must be the ones that are wet!" he thought. But he was wrong there, for those were Fortune's. But why should not the police sometimes make mistakes!

He put on the Overshoes and stuck some papers, to be read through and copied at home, in his pocket and under his arm. It happened to be forenoon of a Sunday, and fine weather. He thought a trip to Fredericksberg would be great fun. And to Fredericksberg he went.

No one could have been a quieter, more industrious man than this young Copying Clerk, and we would not for the world deprive him of that little pleasure trip. It would certainly do him a great deal of good after so much sitting. At first he walked along without thinking of anything in particular, and for that reason Fortune's Overshoes had no opportunity to show their magic power.

In the avenue he met an acquaintance, a young poet, who told him that he was going to start next day on his summer outing.

"What! Are you off again!" said the Copying Clerk. "You certainly are a free and happy man. You can fly wherever you please, while the rest of us are chained by the leg!"

"But the chain is fastened to the bread tree!" laughed

the Poet. "You do not need to think of to-morrow; and when you get old you get a pension!"

"But you are better off, anyway!" said the Copying Clerk; "it must be a pleasure to sit and write poetry! All the world tells you nice agreeable things, and, moreover, you are your own master! You ought to try sitting in the courtroom and working with the trivial matters that come up there!"

The Poet shook his head, and the Copying Clerk shook his head. Each stuck to his opinion, and so they parted.

"They are a race by themselves, those poets!" said the Copying Clerk. "I should like to try to be a poet, myself. I am sure that I would not write such mournful verses as the others do! It is just the right kind of a spring day for a poet! The air is so unusually clear, the clouds so beautiful, and there is such a fragrance from leaves and grass! Yes, for many years I have not felt as I do at this moment."

We already perceive that he had become a poet. Of course the change was not particularly apparent to the sight, for it is a foolish notion to think that a poet must look different from other people. Among the latter there are natures far more poetic than many a famous poet's. The poet has a better spiritual memory; that is the only difference. He can remember the idea and the feeling clearly and plainly until they have been put into words; this the others cannot do. To change from a commonplace being to a gifted one is certainly a transformation. But that was what the Copying Clerk had done.

"That delightful fragrance!" he said. "How it

reminds me of the violets at Aunt Lona's, when I was a little boy! Oh, how often I have thought of it! The good, old girl! She lived there back of the Exchange. She always had a twig or a couple of green shoots in water, no matter how severe the winter. The violets gave out their fragrance while I put hot copper coins on the frozen window pane and made peep-holes. Through the holes I could see outside, in the canal, ships frozen fast, deserted by the entire crew. A screaming crow was the only living creature aboard. Then spring breezes came, and there was a busy time. Amid singing and loud hurrahs the ice was sawed away. The ships were tarred and rigged, and then—away they sailed to foreign lands. Meanwhile, I remain here, in the office of the police station; and here I must always stay, and see the others take passports to travel abroad. That is my lot! Oh, yes!" he sighed deeply. Then he suddenly stood still.

"Good heavens, what is the matter with me! I have never felt this way before, or had such thoughts! It must be the spring air! It is both disquieting and pleasant!"

He put his hand in his pocket for his papers. "These will give me other things to think about!" he said, letting his eyes travel over the first sheet.

"Lady Sigbrith, Original Tragedy in Five Acts," was what he read. "What is this! and it is in my own handwriting. Have I written a tragedy? 'The Intrigue on the Promenade; or The Day of Penance, a Farce,'" he read. "But where did I get that? Some one must have put it into my pocket. Here is a letter."

The letter was from the theatrical manager. The

plays were rejected, and the letter itself was not at all politely worded.

"Hm! hm!" said the Copying Clerk, seating himself on a bench. His thoughts were vivid, his heart so impressionable. Without thinking, he seized one of the flowers nearest him. It was a simple little daisy. It told him all about itself in a moment—more than a botanist could tell in many lectures. It told the myth about its birth; it told about the power of the sun, which made it spread out its delicate petals, causing them to yield their fragrance. This set him thinking of life's struggles, which in the same way awaken feelings in our breasts. Air and Light were the flower's suitors, but Light was the favored one. The flower bent itself toward the Light, and when the Light disappeared, it rolled up its delicate leaves and slept in the Air's embrace.

"It is the light that perfects me!" said the flower.

"But it is the air that you breathe!" whispered the voice of the poet.

Close by stood a boy, striking with a stick at the mud in a ditch. The drops of water spurted up among the green branches, and the Copying Clerk thought of the millions of invisible creatures which were cast in the air to a height that, according to their size, was to them as it would be for us to be whirled high up over the clouds.

As the Copying Clerk thought of these things and of all the changes that had come over him, he smiled. "I am asleep and dreaming! How remarkable it really is! How realistically one may dream and still know that it is only a dream. If only I could remember it to-morrow when I awake! I seem to be unusually fit just now! I have a clear perception of everything, I feel so wide

awake; but I am sure tnat wnen, to-morrow, I recall
any part of it, it will seem nothing but nonsense. I have
tried it before. All the wise and splendid things we hear
and say in our dreams are like the gold of the elves.
When we get it, it is rich and beautiful, but seen by daylight, it is nothing but stones and withered leaves.

"Ah, me!" he sighed, very sorrowfully, as he looked
at the songbirds hopping contentedly from bough to
bough, "they are much better off than I! To fly—that
is a delightful art. Happy the one who is born with it!
If I could change to something, it certainly would be to
a little lark like that!"

At that moment coat tails and sleeves grew together
into wings; clothes turned to feathers; and Overshoes
became claws. The Copying Clerk felt it very plainly
and laughed.

"There now, I can clearly see that I am dreaming!
But so foolishly I have never dreamed before!" And
up he flew among the green branches and sang. But
there was no poetry in the song, for the poet nature was
gone. The Overshoes, like those who do anything well,
could do only one thing at a time. The Copying Clerk
had wanted to be a poet, and he had become a poet.
Just now he had wanted to be a little bird, and he had
been changed into a little bird, but, in becoming a bird,
his poetic nature disappeared.

"This is very good," he said. "During the day I
sit at the police office, busy with the most weighty
transactions, and at night I dream that I am flying about
like a lark in the Fredericksberg Gardens. A regular
popular comedy could be written about it!"

Then he flew down on the grass, turned his head on

all sides, and pecked with his bill at the bending blades
of grass, which, in comparison with his present size,
seemed as large as a branch of the palm trees of Northern
Africa.

The next moment all became black as night around
him. Something which seemed to him of enormous
size had been thrown down over him. It was a large
cap, which a boy from the sailors' quarters had dropped
over the bird. A hand came in and seized the Copying
Clerk around his back and wings so hard that he squeaked.

In his first fright he shouted loudly, "You impudent
whelp! I am the Copying Clerk at the police head-
quarters!" But it sounded to the boy like "Peep, peep,
peep!" He tapped the bird's beak and walked away
with him.

In the avenue he met two schoolboys of the upper
class, that is, regarded in a social sense, for in mind they
ranked among the lowest in the school. They bought
the bird for eight pennies, and thus the Copying Clerk
got into the home of a family on a fashionable street in
Copenhagen.

"It is a good thing I am dreaming!" said the Copying
Clerk, "otherwise I should certainly be very angry!
First a poet, now a lark! It must have been the poet
nature that got me over into this little creature! This
is miserable, especially when one falls into the clutches
of a couple of boys. I should like to know how this
thing is going to turn out!"

The boys carried him into a very elegantly furnished
room. A fat, smiling woman received them, but she
was not at all pleased that the common field bird, as she
called the lark, should come in, too, though she would

permit it for that day. They would have to put it into
the empty cage that stood by the window!

"Perhaps Polly will be pleased," she added, and
smiled at a large green parrot swinging proudly in his
ring in a splendid brass cage.

"It is Polly's birthday," she said in her simple
foolishness, "and so the little field bird wants to
congratulate!"

Polly answered not a word, but kept swinging grandly,
back and forth. But a pretty canary bird that had
been brought from its fragrant native land the preceding
summer, began to sing loudly.

"Screamer!" said the woman, throwing a white
handkerchief over the cage.

"Peep! peep!" sighed the Canary, "that was a terrible
snowstorm!" and with that sigh remained silent.

The Copying Clerk or, as the woman said, the field
bird, was put into a little cage close by the canary and
not far from the parrot. The only human utterance
Polly could stutter forth, one which often sounded very
comical, was, "Come, now, let us be human!" Everything else it screamed out was just as unintelligible as the
canary's twittering; but the Copying Clerk, who was now
a bird himself, understood his comrades perfectly.

"I flew about under the green palm branches and the
blossoming almond tree!" sang the Canary. "I flew
with my brothers and sisters over the glorious flowers
and over the crystal sea where plants nodded in the
depths. I saw many beautiful parrots, too, who told
the funniest stories, many of them, and very long ones."

"They were wild birds," replied the Parrot. "They
had no raising. Come, now, let us be human! Why do

you not laugh? If the lady and all the visitors can laugh at it, you can, too. It is a great deficiency to be without a sense of humor. Come, now, let us be human!"

"Oh, do you remember the beautiful girls that danced in the pavilion near the blossoming trees? Do you remember the sweet fruits, and the cooling juices in the wild herbs?"

"Oh, yes!" said the Parrot; "but here I am much better off! I get good food and am treated as one of the family; I know I am considered a smart fellow, and more I do not ask. Come, now let us be human! You are a poet-bird, as they call it. I have substantial talents and wit. You have a certain genius, but no prudence; you lose yourself in those high notes and then they cover you up. They don't treat me that way, for I have cost them more! I can make an impression with my beak and say bright and witty things! Come, now, let us be human!"

"Oh, my warm, flowering, native land!" said the Canary. "I will sing of your dark green trees, of the silent inlets of the sea where the branches kiss the clear surface of the water. I will sing of the joy of my dear brothers and sisters flashing to and fro among the flowers of the desert!"

"Pray leave off those mournful tunes!" complained the Parrot. "Say something a person can laugh at! Laughter is the mark of the highest intellect! Can a dog or a horse laugh! No, they can weep, but not laugh; that is vouchsafed to human beings alone. Ho, ho, ho!" laughed Polly boy, and added his witty "Come, now, let us be human!"

"Little gray bird," said the Canary, "you have also

been made a prisoner! It must be cold in your northern forests, but then, freedom is there. Fly out! They have forgotten to close the door of your cage. The upper window is open. Fly, fly away!"

In a twinkling the Copying Clerk was out of the cage. At that moment the half-open door leading to the next room creaked on its hinges, and the house cat, lithe, with green, shining eyes, stole into the room and made chase after him. The canary fluttered in the cage, the parrot beat with his wings and cried, "Come, now, let us be human!"

The Copying Clerk was in mortal terror and flew away through the window, over the houses and streets. At last he had to rest a little.

The house opposite had something homelike about it. A window stood open and he flew in. It was his own room. He perched on the table.

"Come, now, let us be human!" he said, without himself thinking what he was saying. He had involuntarily imitated the parrot, and at that same moment he was the Copying Clerk. But he was sitting on the table.

"Good heavens!" he said. "How did I get up here and fall asleep like this? That was a restless dream I had, too. The whole thing was fearful bosh!"

VI. WHAT THE OVERSHOES BROUGHT ABOUT
THAT WAS GOOD

The day after, in the early morning, while the Copying Clerk was still lying in bed, someone knocked at his door. It was his neighbor on the same floor, a student who was studying to be a preacher.

"Lend me your overshoes," he said; "the grass is wet

in the garden, but the sun is shining beautifully and I should like to smoke my pipe down there."

He put on the Overshoes and was soon in the garden. Here stood a plum tree and a pear tree. Even such a little garden as that is considered a great luxury in a large city.

The student walked up and down the path. It was only six o'clock, and from the street outside sounded the horn of the mail coach.

"Oh, travel! travel!" he burst out. "That is the greatest happiness in the world! That is the best thing I could wish for! Then this restlessness I feel would be quieted. But I should want to travel very far away! I should like to see Switzerland, travel in Italy, and —"

Well, it was a good thing that the power of Overshoes worked immediately, otherwise he would have had to go through altogether too much—both for himself and for us. He traveled. He was in the middle of Switzerland, but packed inside of a carriage where there were eight others. He had a headache, a tired feeling in the back of his neck, and his blood had gone to his feet, which were swollen and squeezed by his shoes. He swayed between a half-waking and a half-dozing condition. In his pocket on the right side he carried his letters of credit, in his left-hand pocket his passport, and sewed tight in a little leather purse in his breast pocket were a number of *louis d'or*. In every dream one or the other of these precious possessions was lost. Then he would start up feverishly and the first movement of his hand would be to describe a triangle, from right to left and up to his breast, to feel whether he had them or not.

In the net above him swung umbrellas, canes, and

hats, almost completely obscuring the impressive view.
He looked through the window out of the corner of his
eye, though with difficulty, while his heart sang what
at least one poet in Switzerland has sung but has not
printed.

Great, grave, and dark was all nature round about
him. The pine forests looked like shrubs on those lofty
cliffs, whose summits were hidden in mist. Now it
began to snow, and the wind blew cold.

"Huh!" he sighed, "if we were only on the other side
of the Alps, then it would be summer and then I would
have drawn some money on my letter of credit. The
worry over that prevents me from enjoying Switzerland.
Oh, how I wish I were on the other side!"

And there he was on the other side, far on his way
into Italy, between Florence and Rome. Lake Trasi-
menes lay in the evening glow like flaming gold between
the dark blue mountains. There, where Hannibal de-
feated Flaminius, the grape vines clung peacefully to
one another with twining fingers. Pretty, half-naked
children guarded a herd of coal-black swine beneath a
group of fragrant laurels by the wayside. Could we
describe this picture accurately, all would delightedly
cry, "Lovely Italy!" But that is not what the student of theology said, nor a single one of his traveling
companions inside the Italian cabman's vehicle.

Poisonous flies and gnats flew in on them by the
thousands. In vain they beat about them with myrtle
branches. The flies bit them just the same. There
was not a person in the carriage whose face was not
swollen and discolored from bites and stings. The flies
piled on the poor horses in heaps. The poor beasts

looked like carcasses. It helped only for a moment
when the driver got down and scraped them clean. The
sun sank. A momentary chill went through all nature
like a gust. It was not pleasant at all. But round
about, the mountains and the clouds took on the most
beautiful tints of green, oh, so very clear, so very shining.
Oh, you must go yourself and see! That is better than
reading a description! It was glorious! The travelers
thought so, too; but their stomachs were empty, their
bodies tired, and the one desire was to reach quarters
for the night — how would the lodgings turn out? All
were far more eager for a first sight of the stopping place
than for a look at the beautiful scenery.

The road led through an olive wood. It was just
like driving at home between rows of gnarled willows.
In the wood stood the solitary inn. Half a score of
begging cripples had camped outside. The healthiest
among them looked like "Hunger's eldest son, who had
come of age." The others were blind, had withered
legs and crawled on their hands, or withered arms with
fingerless hands. It was misery itself, stripped of its
rags. "Eccellenza, miserabili!" they whined, stretching
out their diseased limbs. The hostess herself, with
bare feet and uncombed hair, and dressed only in a
dirty blouse, received the guests. The doors were tied
together with twine. The floor was a pavement of
bricks that had been half grubbed up. Bats flew about
under the ceiling — and the smell within! —

"If she would only lay the table down in the stable!"
said one of the travelers. "There at least one knows
what one is breathing!"

The windows were opened, to let in a little fresh

air, and in came withered arms and the eternal wail, "Miserabili, Eccellenza!" On the walls were many inscriptions; half of them were of *la bella Italia.*

The food was brought in. There was a soup of water, seasoned with pepper and rancid oil. The same kind of oil was on the lettuce. Spoiled eggs and roasted cocks' combs were the main courses. Even the wine had an "off" taste. It was a regular poison dose.

The trunks were piled up against the door for the night. One of the travelers kept watch while the others slept. The student of theology had the watch. Oh, how close it was in the room! The heat oppressed him, the gnats buzzed and stung, the *miserabili* outside moaned in their sleep.

"Traveling would be nice enough," sighed the student, "if a person had no body. If that could only rest and the spirit fly! Wherever I go, there is something lacking, and that makes my heart heavy. What I want is not something that gives me momentary pleasure. I want something better. But where is it? What is it? I really do not know what I want. I want, finally, to reach a happy stopping-place, the happiest possible!"

And as he uttered the words, he was at home. The long white curtains hung down over the window and in the middle of the floor stood a black coffin, and in it he lay in his quiet sleep of death. His wish was fulfilled. The body rested and the spirit was free to travel unencumbered.

"Consider no one happy before he is in his grave," were Solon's words. Here they were proved anew.

Every dead body is a riddle of the hereafter. Nor would this sphinx-like body here in the black coffin have answered for us what the living man had written two days before:

> Thou strong, stern Death, thy silence waketh fear,
> The churchyard graves, thy footsteps' only trace.
> The Jacob's ladder which our minds uprear,—
> Shall it be broken?   Shall our rising be in grass?

> The world oft little knows our deepest woe!
> And thou whose life was lonely to the end,
> Much more the heart oppresses here below,
> Than the hard earth encompassing thy tomb.

Two forms moved about in the room. We know them both: they were the fairies, Sorrow and the messenger of Fortune. They were bending over the dead.

"Do you see," asked Sorrow, "what happiness your Overshoes have brought to mankind?"

"They brought at least to him who is sleeping here a lasting good!" answered Happiness.

"Oh, no!" Sorrow replied. "He went away of himself, he was not called! His spirit was not strong enough to lift the treasures which he felt he must lift! I will do him a favor!"

She took the Overshoes from his feet. Then the sleep of Death was ended, and the awakened man arose.

Sorrow disappeared, and with her the Overshoes. She must have considered them her own property.

THE BRONZE BOAR

In the city of Florence, not far from the Piazza del Granduca, runs a little side street; I think it is called Porta Rossa. On that street, in front of a market called the Mercato Nuevo, where vegetables are sold, is a well-modeled bronze boar. Fresh, clear water pours out of the mouth of the animal, which has become greenish black with age. Only the snout shines as if it were brightly polished, and, indeed, that it really is by the many hundred children and *lazzaroni* who take hold of it with their hands, and put their mouths to the animal's snout to drink. It is a perfect picture to see the well-shaped creature, embraced by a handsome, half-naked boy who puts his fresh young lips to its mouth.

Everyone who comes to Florence may find the place. He need only ask the first beggar he sees about the Bronze Boar, and he will find it.

It was late one evening in winter. The mountains were covered with snow; but the moon was shining, and moonlight in Italy gives as much illumination as there is on a dark winter's day in the North; yes, even more, for the air itself shines; the air is uplifting, while in the North the cold, gray, leaden day presses us down to the ground, the cold, wet ground that some day is to press round our coffins.

Over in the Grand Duke's palace garden, under the pent-house roof where thousands of roses bloom in winter, a little ragged boy had been sitting all day long—a boy who might be the very picture of Italy, so pretty, so laughing, and yet so full of suffering. He was hungry and thirsty. No one gave him a single penny, and when it grew dark and the garden was to be closed, the gate-keeper drove him away. He stood a long time on the bridge over the Arno, dreaming and looking at the stars, which gleamed in the water between him and the splendid marble bridge called della Trinità.

Then he set out on the way to the Bronze Boar. There he half knelt down, threw his arms about the animal's neck, put his little mouth to its shining snout, and drank the fresh water in long, deep draughts. Close by lay some lettuce leaves and a few chestnuts, and these were his supper. There was not another soul on the street. The boy was alone. He seated himself on the Bronze Boar's back, leaned forward, until his little curly head rested on the head of the animal, and, before he himself knew it, was sound asleep.

It was midnight. The Bronze Boar moved and the child heard it say distinctly: "Little boy, hold tight, for now I am going to run!" And away it ran with him. It was a wonderful ride. First they came to the Piazza del Granduca, and there the metal horse which bears the statue of the Grand Duke neighed aloud. The many-colored coats-of-arms on the old council house shone like transparent pictures, and Michelangelo's "David" swung his sling. It was a strange life that stirred about them. The bronze groups, "Perseus" and the "Rape of the Sabines," stood all too lifelike, and from this last group came a death shriek that rang over the beautiful, lonely square.

At the Palazzo degli Uffizi, in the Arcade, where the nobility gathers during Lent for the joys of the Carnival, the Bronze Boar stopped running.

"Hold tight," said the Boar, "hold tight, for now we are going up the stairs!"   The little boy had not yet uttered a word; he was half trembling, half delighted.

They stepped into a long gallery, which the boy knew well, for he had been there before.   The walls were bright with pictures; here and there stood statues and busts, all in the loveliest light, as if it were day.   But most splendid of all was when the door of one of the side rooms opened.   The boy knew the great splendor that was there, but that night everything was at the very height of loveliness.

Here stood a beautiful, unclothed woman, possessing beauty such as only nature and the greatest masters of marble could produce.   She moved her beautiful limbs; at her feet dolphins leaped; immortality shone out of her eyes.   The world calls her the Venus de Medici.   On both sides of her were marble statues, whom the breath of life had entered.   They were beautiful, unclothed men.   One of them was sharpening a sword — The Grinder he is called.   The Wrestling Gladiators formed the other group.   While the sword was being sharpened, the gladiators contended for the Goddess of Beauty.

The boy was dazzled by the splendor.   The walls shone with color, and everything was full of life and movement.   The picture of Venus appeared double; it was the earthly Venus, glowing with life and passion, whom Titian had held to his heart — two beautiful women, their lovely, unveiled limbs extended on soft cushions, their breasts heaving, their heads moving, their long, thick locks falling on their round white shoulders, the dark eyes telling the impetuous thoughts within.   But none of the figures dared step out of the frame entirely. The Goddess of Beauty, the Gladiators, and the Grinder remained in their places, for the glory which shone from the Madonna, Jesus, and John held them immovable. The holy pictures were no longer pictures; they were the holy ones themselves.

What grandeur and what beauty in every room! And the little boy saw everything, for the Bronze Boar went step by step through all the splendor in that palace of delight. Each sight was so wonderful it made one forget all the others, and just one picture fixed itself firmly in the boy's mind, and that one chiefly because of the joyful, happy children that were in it. The little boy had once nodded to them by daylight.

Many people pass quickly by this picture; and yet it has in it much poetry. Jesus is seen descending into the Underworld; but it is not tortured souls we see about him. The heathen are there. The Florentine, Angelo Bronzino, painted the picture. Particularly wonderful is the expression of the children in their certainty that they will go to heaven. Two little ones already embrace each other; one child stretches his hand to another below him and points to himself as if saying: "I am going to heaven!" All the older persons stand uncertain, hoping, or bow themselves humbly before the Saviour in prayer.

At that picture the boy looked longer than at any other. The Bronze Boar rested quietly before it. A soft sigh was heard. Did it come from the picture or from the Bronze Boar's breast? The boy lifted his hand toward the smiling children; then the animal hurried away with him out through the open vestibule.

"Thanks, and blessings upon you, dear creature!" said the little boy and patted the Bronze Boar, which with a bump, bump, sprang down the stairs with him.

"Thanks, and blessings upon you," said the Bronze Boar. "I have helped you, and you have helped me, for only with an innocent child on my back have I the power to run. Yes, I dare even go under the rays of the lamp in front of the Madonna picture. I can carry you everywhere, except into the church! but from without, when you are with me, I may look in at the open door! Do not get off my back. If you do I shall be dead just as you see me in the daytime in Porta Rossa!"

"I will stay with you, you good, kind animal!" said the little one. And then away they went, whizzing through the streets of Florence, out to the square before the church of Santa Croce!

The great folding doors flew open, the lights upon the altar shone through the church and out upon the lonely square.

An unearthly light streamed from the tomb monument in the left aisle; thousands of moving stars seemed to form a halo about it. A coat-of-arms gleamed on the tomb—a red ladder on a blue ground. It seemed to glow like fire. The tomb was Galileo's. The monument is a simple one, but the red ladder on the blue ground is a significant device. It is as if it were the device of art itself, for the path of Art is up a burning ladder, but it leads to heaven. All the prophets of the spirit go to heaven, as did the prophet Elias of old.

In the aisles to the right, every sculptured figure on the rich sarcophagi seemed warm with life. Here stood Michelangelo, there Dante — with the laurel wreath round his brow — Alfieri, and Machiavelli. Here these great men rest side by side — the pride of Italy. It is a splendid church, and though not so large as the marble Cathedral of Florence, far more beautiful

It seemed as if the marble garments moved; as if the great statues raised their heads higher, and amid singing and organ music looked up toward the radiant, colored altar where white-clad boys swung golden censers. A strong odor of incense floated from the church out into the open square.

The boy stretched his hand toward the glow of light, and in the same instant the Bronze Boar rushed away. He had to cling tightly to it, and the wind whistled about his ears. He heard the church doors creak on their hinges as they closed, but at that moment his consciousness seemed to leave him; he felt icy cold, and opened his eyes.

It was morning. He sat halfway slipped from the back of the Boar, which stood where it had always stood in the Porta Rossa.

Fear and anxiety filled the boy's mind at thought of his mother, who had sent him out yesterday and told him to get money. He had none. He was hungry and thirsty! Once again he put his arm around the Bronze Boar's neck, kissed its snout, and nodded to it. Then he wandered off into one of the narrowest streets, which is just wide enough for a heavily-laden donkey to pass. A large iron-studded door stood half open. Through this he went, and up a stone stairway, with dirty walls and a smooth rope for a balustrade, until he came to an open gallery hung with rags. A stair led from this place to the yard in which there was a well. Large iron cables stretched from the well to every story of the house, and water buckets dangled side by side. When the roller creaked and the buckets danced in the air the water splashed out. Another tumbled-down brick stairway led farther up. Down this stair two Russian sailors came running, and almost knocked the poor boy down. They came from their nightly carousal. A large woman, no longer young, with thick black hair, followed after them.

"What have you brought home?" she asked the boy.

"Don't be angry," he pleaded. "I have nothing, nothing at all!" and he seized his mother's dress as if he would have kissed it.

Then they went inside. In the room they entered stood a jar with handles, filled with live coals; *marito*, it is called. This the mother took on her arm and warmed her fingers. Then she pushed the boy with her elbow. "Of course you've got money!" she said.

The child wept. She struck him with her foot. Then he cried out loudly.

"Will you be quiet, or must I break your screaming head to pieces!" and she swung the brazier that she held in her hand. The child crouched on the floor with a scream. Just then a neighbor woman stepped in at the door. She, too, had her *marito* on her arm.

"Felicita! What are you doing with the child!"

"The child is mine!" answered Felicita. "I can kill it if I want to and you too, Giannina," and she swung her brazier again. The other raised hers in defense and the two pots clashed together so hard that fire and ashes flew about the room.

But the boy was out at the door in that instant, across the courtyard, and out of the house. The poor child ran till he was completely out of breath. He stopped at the Santa Croce Church, the church whose great doors had opened to him the night before, and went in. Everything was radiant. He moved to the right and knelt at the first tomb. It was Michelangelo's, and soon he was sobbing aloud. People came and went, mass was said, but no one paid any attention to the boy. Only one elderly citizen stopped and looked at him— and then went on as the others had done.

The child was so hungry and thirsty he could hardly walk. He felt very weak and sick. He crept into a corner between the wall and the tomb and fell asleep. Toward evening he was awakened by some one shaking him. He started up and before him he beheld the same elderly citizen who had stopped to look at him earlier in the day.

"Are you ill? Where do you live? Have you been here all day?" were a few of the many questions the old man asked him. He answered them, and the old man took him to a little house close by in one of the side streets. It was a glove-maker's shop they entered. A woman sat working busily as they came in. A little white dog, with hair clipped so close that his pink skin was visible, jumped up on the table and leaped about playfully before the little boy.

"Innocent souls recognize one another," said the woman and patted both the dog and the boy. The good people gave the hungry child food and drink, and said he should be permitted to stay there for the night. The next day Father Giuseppe—that was the glove-maker—would speak to his mother about him. They gave him a poor, tiny bed, but to one who often had slept on the hard stones, as he had, it seemed a royal

couch.   He slept well and dreamed about the wonderful
pictures and the Bronze Boar.

Next morning Father Giuseppe set out, and the poor
child was very unhappy, for he knew that this departure
was to bring him to his mother.   He cried and kissed the
playful little dog, and the woman nodded approvingly
at them both.

And what did Father Giuseppe find out?   He talked
a long time with his wife, and she nodded and caressed
the boy.   "He is a lovely child!" she said.   "What a
handsome glove-maker he can grow to be — just like
you!   And his fingers are so fine and limber.   The
Madonna has intended him for a glove-maker!"

So the boy remained at the house, and the wife herself
taught him to sew.   He ate well and slept well, and he
grew merry.   One day he teased Bellissima — that was
the dog's name — and the woman was angry — shook
her finger at him, and scolded.   The rebuke went to the
boy's heart, and he sat thoughtfully in his little room,
which had windows on the street.   In that room the
glove-skins were dried.   There were thick iron bars over
the windows.   The boy tried to go to sleep but could not.
He was thinking of the Bronze Boar, and suddenly he
heard a sound outside, "Pit-a-pat!"   Why, that must
be it!   He ran to the window, but there was nothing
to be seen, and the noise had ceased.

"Help the gentleman carry his box of colors!" said
the woman to the boy next morning, as a young artist,
their neighbor, went by carrying his box and a large roll
of canvas.

The child took the box and followed the painter.
They walked toward the Gallery, and went up the stair

he knew so well — the stair up which he rode one night on the Bronze Boar's back. He recognized the statues, and the pictures, the beautiful marble Venus, and the figures that lived in colors. He saw again the Saviour's mother, and Jesus and John.

Now the two halted before the picture by Bronzino, representing Jesus descending to the Underworld with children about him, smiling in the sweet certainty of heaven. The poor child smiled, too, for there he was in a heaven of his own.

"Go home, now!" said the painter, when the boy remained until he had raised his easel.

"May I watch you paint?" said the boy. "May I see how you put a picture on that white canvas?"

"I am not painting yet!" answered the man. He took his crayon. His hand moved quickly; he measured the great picture with his eye, and though it was just a thin line that appeared, there stood the Christ as in the colored picture.

"But now you must go!" said the painter. The boy walked slowly homeward, seated himself on the table, and — learned to sew gloves.

But all day his thoughts were in the picture gallery, and consequently he pricked his fingers and was awkward with his work; but he did not tease Bellissima. When evening came, the street door being open, he slipped outside. It was chilly, but the sky was bright with beautiful gleaming stars. He wandered through the streets, which were now quiet and deserted, and soon he was standing before the Bronze Boar. He leaned over it and kissed its shining snout. Then he seated himself on its back.

"You good creature," he said, "how I have longed for you! We must go riding to-night!"

The Bronze Boar remained motionless and the fresh water ran sparkling from its mouth. The little boy sat like a rider. Then something tugged at his clothes. He looked down, and there beside him stood Bellissima— the little close-clipped Bellissima. The dog had slipped out of the house and had followed the child without his noticing it. He barked as if to say, "See, here I am with you. Why do you sit there?" No fiery dragon could have frightened the boy more than the little dog in that place. Bellissima — on the street, and without being dressed, as the old wife called it! What would happen! The dog was never allowed to go out in winter unless dressed in a little sheepskin coat, cut out and sewed especially for it. The skin could be tied with a red ribbon around the neck. There were bows and bells on it, and it was also tied fast under the animal. The dog looked almost like a little kid, when in winter, dressed in that garb, it was allowed to take a walk with the Signora. Bellissima was out with him now with nothing on! What would come of it? All his fancies took flight, but he kissed the Bronze Boar and picked up Bellissima in his arms. The animal was shaking with cold, and therefore the boy ran as fast as he could.

"What are you running with there?" shouted two policemen he met. Bellissima barked.

"Where did you steal that fine dog?" they asked, taking it away from him.

"Oh, give it back!" wailed the boy.

"If you have n't stolen it, you can say at home that the dog can be sent for at the station!" They told him where it was and away they went with Bellissima.

It was a moment of despair and lamentation. He did not know whether to jump into the Arno or to go home and confess everything.

"They will surely kill me," he thought. "But I will gladly be killed; then I will go to Jesus and the Madonna!" So he went home, chiefly for the purpose of being killed.

The door was locked. He could not reach the knocker, and there was no one in the street. But a loosened stone lay there, and with this he hammered on the door.

"Who is it?" they shouted within.

"It is I!" he said. "Bellissima is gone! Open the door and kill me!"

There was a panic of fright and anxiety, especially on the part of the wife, for the poor Bellissima! She looked instantly over to the wall where the dog's dress usually hung. The little lambskin was there.

"Bellissima at the station!" she cried loudly. "You wicked child! How did you get him out! He will freeze to death. That fine, delicate creature among the rough soldiers!"

The old man had to start out at once! The woman wailed and the boy wept! All the people in the house came in, the painter among them. He took the boy between his knees and asked him all about it. He heard the whole story, though broken and disconnected, about the Bronze Boar and the Gallery. It wasn't easy to understand. The painter consoled the little boy, and talked soothingly to the old woman. But she kept on lamenting until the old man returned with Bellissima, who had been among the soldiers. Then there was great rejoicing. The painter patted the little boy's head, and gave him a handful of pictures.

Oh, they were so splendid — such comical heads! But best of all, there was one of the Bronze Boar itself, lifelike and beautiful! Could anything be more glorious! There it was in just a few lines, drawn on the paper; and even the house behind it was sketched in.

Oh, if one could only draw and paint he could get the whole world for himself!

The next day, the first moment he found himself with nothing to do, the little boy seized a pencil and on the back of one of the pictures tried to copy the drawing of the Bronze Boar; the drawing was a little crooked; one leg was thick and the other thin. But still it could be recognized, and he himself rejoiced over it! He noticed, however, that the pencil did not want to go as straight as it should. But the next day another Bronze Boar stood beside the first, and this was a hundred times better. The third was so good that any one could recognize it.

But the glove-making went badly, and errands to town were not quickly performed. For the Bronze Boar had taught him that all pictures could be transferred to paper; and the city of Florence is a complete picture book if one will just turn the pages to see. On the Piazza della Trinità is a slender column, and on the top of it stands the Goddess of Justice with blind-folded eyes and scales in her hands.

The goddess soon appeared on paper, and it was the glove-maker's little boy who had put her there. The collection of pictures grew larger, but everything in it was still of lifeless objects. Then one day as the boy sketched, Bellissima ran, playing, in front of him.

"Stand still!" he said. "Then you shall become beautiful and be one of my pictures!" But Bellissima would not stand still and so he had to be tied, head and tail. The dog barked and tried to jump and the rope had to be tightened. Just then the Signora appeared.

"You wicked, wicked boy! The poor creature!" was all she could say. She thrust the boy aside, kicked him, and drove him out of the house, calling him an ungrateful good-for-nothing and a wicked child! And weeping, ske kissed her little half-strangled Bellissima.

Just then the painter came up the stairs and—here is the turning-point in the story.

There was an exhibition in the Art Academy of Florence in the year of 1834. Two paintings placed side by side drew a large number of spectators. In the smallest picture a merry little boy sat drawing. The model was a little white, close-clipped dog. The dog would not stand still, so he had been tied by the head and the tail. There was truth and life in this picture which could not but attract and interest everyone. The painter, it was said, was a young Florentine who had been found on the street when a little child. He had been brought up by an old glove-maker and had taught himself how to draw. A painter, now become famous, had discovered his talent when the boy had been driven out into the street because he had tied the Signora's little pet dog to use as a model.

The young glove-maker had become a great painter! This picture proved it, and still better, a larger picture which hung beside this one. In it there was just a single figure, a ragged but beautiful boy, who sat sleeping on the street. He leaned against the Bronze Boar in the Porta Rossa. All the spectators recognized the place. The child's arms rested on the Boar's head. The little one slept soundly, and the lamps by the Madonna picture cast a strong light on his pale, beautiful face. It was a splendid painting. A great gilded frame was round it, and in the corner of the frame was a laurel wreath. But among the green leaves was wound a black ribbon, and crêpe hung down from it.

The artist was lying, during those days, cold in death!

THE HAPPY FAMILY

Of all green leaves that grow in our country, the largest is certainly the burdock leaf. It is so very large that if you hold it in front of you, around your little waist, it is just like an apron; lay it on your head in rainy weather, and it is almost as good as an umbrella.

A burdock never grows singly. Wherever one grows, many others are growing. It is really splendid—and all its splendor is food for snails.

In olden days the grand, rich folk had the large white snails cooked and made into fricassee, and when they ate of it they said, "Mm! how good that tastes!" for they really thought it was very delicious. These white snails lived on burdock leaves, and that is why the burdocks were planted.

Now there was an old estate where snails were no longer eaten. The snails had died out almost entirely. But not the burdocks; they grew and grew, so luxuriantly that they filled all the walks and all the flower beds.

It was impossible to keep them down, and a whole forest of burdocks covered the garden. Here and there stood an apple or a plum tree. Except for these one would never have believed that the place was a garden. Everything was burdocks—and there lived the two very last of the snails, two very, very old ones.

They did not know how old they were, but they could remember distinctly that there had once been many more of their kind, that they were the descendants of a family from foreign lands, and that the whole forest had been planted for them and theirs. They had never been outside, but they knew that there was something in the world which was called the manor house, and that there snails were cooked, that they turned black, and that then they were laid on a silver platter. But what happened afterwards they did not know.

Moreover, just how it felt to be cooked and to lie on a silver platter they could not imagine. But it was said to be very pleasant, and particularly grand. Neither the beetle, nor the toad, nor the earthworm could give any information when they were asked about it. None of them had been cooked or laid on a silver platter.

The old white snails were the most distinguished and the grandest persons in the world, that they knew; the forest existed on their account, and the manor house existed in order that they might be cooked and laid on a silver platter.

They lived a very lonely, though happy, life. As they had no children, they had taken an ordinary little snail to raise, and had brought it up as their very own. But the little one did not grow, for he was one of the common kind. The old snails, however, and especially the mother snail, thought she could see now fast he was growing. If Father Snail could not see it, she would ask him to feel the little snail's shell, and then he had to acknowledge that Mother Snail was right.

One day it rained very hard.

"Listen to the drumming, rub-a-dub-dub, on the burdocks!" said Father Snail.

"Yes, and see the raindrops!" said Mother Snail. "The water is running right down the stalk! Things are going to be very damp here! I am glad that we have such good houses, and the little one also has his. More has certainly been done for us than for all other creatures. It is plain to see that we are the grand folk of the world! We have a house from the moment we are born, and the burdock forest was planted for our sake! I wish I knew how far it extends, and what lies beyond!"

"There is nothing beyond," said Father Snail. "No place can be better than ours here at home, and I have nothing to wish for."

"But I have," said Mother Snail; "I wish I could be taken up to the manor house, and cooked, and laid on a silver platter. That is what has been done to all our forefathers, and you may be sure there is something very distinguished about it!"

"The manor house is very probably in ruins," said Father Snail, "or the burdock forest may have grown over it so that the people cannot get out. But there is no need to be in such a hurry. You are always hurrying so, and the little one is beginning to be the same way. Has he not been crawling up that stalk for the last three days? It gives me a headache when I look up at him!"

"Don't scold," said Mother Snail. "He crawls very slowly and carefully. He will be a great joy to us, and we old people have nothing else to live for! But have you ever given this any thought: where we shall get a wife for him? Don't you think that somewhere within this burdock forest there may still be some of our kind?"

"There are some black snails, I am sure," said the old snail, "black snails without houses, but they are so common and so conceited! We might turn the matter over to the ants. They are always running about as if they had something to do. They must know of a wife for our little snail!"

"We certainly do know the very loveliest of brides!" said the ants. "But we fear she would not do, for she is a queen."

"That does not matter," said the old snail. "Has she a house?"

"She has a castle," said the ants, "the finest of ant castles, with seven hundred passages!"

"No, thank you!" said Mother Snail. "Our son shall not have to live in an ant hill! If you cannot suggest anything better, we will turn the matter over to the white gnats. They fly about in sunshine or rain, and they know the burdock forest inside and out."

"We have a wife for him!" said the gnats. "A hundred man steps from here, on a gooseberry bush, sits a little snail with a house. She is quite alone, and old enough to be married. It is only a hundred man steps from here!"

"Yes, she will do; but she will have to come to him," said the old snails. "He has a burdock forest, while she has only a bush!"

So they sent for the little maiden snail. It was eight days before she arrived; but that was the nice thing about it, for by that one could see that she was truly one of the race.

Then the wedding was celebrated. Six glowworms gleamed as brightly as they knew how. Otherwise things went very quietly, for the old snail folk could not stand dissipation and merry-making! But Mother Snail made a capital speech, for Father Snail was so agitated he could not talk. Then they gave the young couple the whole burdock forest for an inheritance, saying, as they had always said, that it was the best place in the world, and if they lived an orderly and quiet life, and increased and multiplied, they and their children would some day be taken up to the manor house, boiled black, and laid on a silver platter.

After that speech was finished the old snails crept into their houses and never came out again; for they slept. The young snail couple ruled in the forest, and had numerous descendants. But they were never boiled, and never put on a silver platter. From this they concluded that the manor had fallen into ruins, and that all people in the world were dead; and since no one contradicted them, they must have been right. The rain beat on the burdock leaves, just to make drum music for them, and the sun shone in order to fill the burdock forest with a glow of color for them, and they were very, very happy. The whole family was really very happy!

THE BELL

Often in the evening, just as the sun was setting and the clouds were gleaming like gold up between the tall chimneys, a curious sound like the ringing of a distant church bell could be heard in the narrow streets of the great city. Sometimes this person would hear it, sometimes that; but only for a moment, there was such a rumbling of wagons and such a disturbing clamor of voices.

"That is the evening bell," people would say. "The sun is just setting."

Those who went outside the city where the houses stood farther apart, and where there were gardens and little fields, saw a still more splendid sunset glow in the evening sky and heard far more clearly the ringing of the bell. The sound seemed to come from a church far within the silent, fragrant forest. And people would look in that direction, and feel quite solemn.

A long time passed, and people began to say one to the other: "I wonder if there is a church out yonder in the forest? That bell has such a strange, beautiful sound. We ought to take a trip out there and get a closer look at it."

So the rich people drove out and the poor people walked out. But the road seemed strangely long, and when the people reached a large grove of willows growing at the edge of the forest, they sat down and looked up among the long swaying branches, believing themselves really in the heart of the great wood.

A confectioner came out from town and put up a

tent here; then came another confectioner, and this one hung a bell over his tent, a bell that was covered with a coat of tar so as to stand the rain, and without a clapper. When people returned to town they said that it had been so romantic, meaning something quite beyond a mere cup of tea. Three people declared that they had made their way into the forest right to its farthest edge, and that they had heard the strange bell all the time; but it seemed to them as if the sound had come from the city. One of them wrote a long poem about it in which he said that the bell sounded like the voice of a mother to a beloved child. No melody was sweeter than the sound of that bell.

The emperor also heard of it, and promised that whoever could discover just where the sound came from should receive the title of the "World's Bell-Ringer," even if there were no bell at all.

A great many people now went to the woods for the sake of the high honor that had been offered, but there was only one who returned home with anything like an explanation. None of them had penetrated far enough into the forest, and neither had he. But he nevertheless said that the bell-like sound came from a very large owl in a hollow tree. It was a wise owl, which beat its head constantly against the tree, but whether the sound came from its head or from the hollow tree he could not as yet say with any certainty. Thereupon he was appointed World's Bell-Ringer, and every year he wrote a little treatise about the owl. But nobody was any the wiser.

Now, on a certain confirmation day, the minister had made a very beautiful and touching sermon. The young people who were to be confirmed had been deeply

moved. It was an important day for them, for all at
once from children they were to become grown people.
The child soul was, as it were, to fly over into a more
responsible person. It was the brightest of sunny days,
and after confirmation the young people walked out from
the city. From the forest came the sound, wonderfully
clear, of the great unknown bell.

Immediately they all felt a strong desire to go there;
all except three. One of these had to go home to try
on her ball dress, for it was really because of that dress
and that ball that she had been confirmed now; otherwise
she would not have been permitted to go! The second
was a poor boy who had borrowed his confirmation clothes
and shoes from the landlord's son, and had to return
them at a certain hour. The third said that he never
went to any strange place without his parents, that he had
always been a good child, and would continue to be so
now even after he had been confirmed.

So these three did not go. The others trudged off.
The sun shone and the birds sang, and the young people
took each other by the hand and sang with them; for
you see they had not yet received any offices, and were
all young people on this day of their confirmation.

Soon two of the youngest became tired and turned
back to the city. Two little girls sat down by the way
and made wreaths. They too were left behind. When
the others reached the willow grove where the con-
fectioners lived they said: "Well, here we are! The
bell, of course, really does not exist; it is only something
people imagine!"

Just at that moment, from somewhere deep in the
forest, the bell sounded so sweetly and solemnly that

four, five even, decided to go a little farther into the forest. The forest was dense and the undergrowth so thick that it was hard to make any progress. The anemones and the hyacinths grew rank, and the flowering convolvulus and the vines hung in long garlands from tree to tree. There the nightingale sang and the sunbeams played. Oh, it was very delightful! But it was no place for girls to go walking; their clothes would have been torn to shreds. Great bowlders lay scattered about, overgrown with moss of all colors. Springs of fresh water gurgled forth with a curious sound like "kluk, kluk!"

"Can that be the bell!" said one of the young people, lying down to listen. "This must be thoroughly looked into!" So he stayed and let the others go on.

They came to a little hut built of bark and branches. A large crab-apple tree leaned over it as if about to shake its load of apples on the roof, which was covered with roses. The long branches lay right along the gable, on which there hung a little bell. Could this be the bell they had heard? All agreed that it was, all except one, and he said that the bell was too small and delicate to be heard so far away as they had heard it, and that the tones which moved the hearts of men were quite different from the tones of this bell. The one who spoke thus was a king's son, and the others said, "A fellow like him always wants to be a little wiser than the rest." So they let him go on alone.

As the king's son walked, the forest filled his breast with its deep solitude. But he still could hear the little bell with which the others were so pleased, and at times, when the wind came from the direction of the confectioner's tent, he could also hear the call to tea. But the deep tones of the bell were stronger than these sounds, and it seemed as if an organ were playing with it. The sound came from the left, from the side where the heart is placed.

There was a rustling in the bushes, and a little boy stood before the king's son — a boy wearing wooden shoes, and a jacket so short that his wrists stuck far out of the sleeves. They knew each other, for the little boy was one of the three who had not started out with the others, the poor boy who had to go home to return the coat and shoes to the landlord's son. He had done this, and then, wearing wooden shoes and shabby clothes, he had started out alone; for the deep, strong notes of the bell drew him on.

"Then we can go together!" said the king's son. But the poor boy in the wooden shoes was too bashful. He pulled at his short coat sleeves, and said that he was afraid he could not walk fast enough. Besides, he believed that the bell was to be found to the right, for all things great and splendid had a place to the right.

"Well, then, we will not meet at all," said the king's son, nodding to the poor boy, who walked away into the darkest and densest part of the forest, where the thorns tore his shabby clothes to tatters and scratched his face and hands and feet till they bled. The king's son also got some deep scratches, although the sun shone along his pathway. He was a bright little chap, and he is the one we will accompany.

"I will and must find the bell," he said, "even if I have to go to the end of the world for it!"

The ugly monkeys sat in the treetops, grinning and showing all their teeth.

"Let us pelt him!" they cried. "Let us pelt him! He is the king's son!"

But he went blithely on, deeper and deeper into the forest, where grew the most extraordinary flowers. There were white star-like lilies with blood-red streamers, sky-blue tulips, which glittered as they swayed in the wind; apple trees where hung apples that looked exactly like great shining soap bubbles. Just think how those trees must have glistened in the sunshine!

Around the edges of beautiful green meadows, where stags and hinds gamboled in the grass, grew great, splendid oaks and beech trees. Wherever the bark was broken and cracked, long grasses and vines grew. There were also great forest glades and quiet little lakes where white swans swam about and stretched their great white wings. The king's son often stopped and listened. Often he thought that the sound of the bell came up to him from one of these deep lakes. But then when he listened again he was quite sure that it was not there, but farther still within the forest.

Now the sun was sinking, the sky gleamed red as fire, and a deep, deep stillness came over the forest. The king's son sank to his knees, sang his evening psalm, and said: "Never will I find what I am seeking! The sun is setting; the dark night is coming on. But perhaps I can once more see the round red sun, before it sinks below the earth. I will climb up those rocky heights yonder. They rise as high as the highest of the trees!"

He seized the vines and roots and clambered up the wet stones, where the water snakes wriggled and the toads seemed to bark at him. But he reached the top before the sun had set entirely. Seen from that height, oh, what splendor met his gaze! The sea, the vast, wonderful sea, stretched before him, its long waves tumbling against the shore. The sun stood like a great shining altar far away where sea and sky met. Everything melted together in a bright glow of color; the forest sang, and the ocean sang, and he sang with them. All nature was a great holy temple, in which the trees and the swaying clouds were the pillars, flowers and grass a woven tapestry of velvet, and the sky itself the great dome. Far on high the red colors vanished as the sun went down, but millions of stars gleamed out like millions of diamond lamps, and the king's son stretched his arms toward the sky, toward the sea and the forest,—and at that moment, from the right, came the poor boy with the wooden shoes and the short sleeves. He had reached the same place by his road. They ran to meet each other, and held each other's hands in the great temple of nature and poetry. And over them sounded the invisible holy bell. Glorious spirits swayed about it, singing a joyous Hallelujah!